APACHE STRIKE

The army scout was quick. He grabbed the jug of pulque before it could slide off the table and tried to smash it into the Apache hunter's skull. The Apache hunter sprawled backward, the wind knocked out of him. Sucking air into his anguished lungs, he saw that Horn had brandished a knife and was moving in; the six-shooter was still at his hip. The Apache hunter lashed out with a kick, knocking Horn's legs out from under him. Horn fell clumsily.

Still heaving for air, the Apache hunter stood there for a moment, staring down at the unconscious man. Belatedly he remembered the bartender and turned to see what the Mexican was doing. He found himself face-to-face with a short, stocky man with broad, coarse Indian features. He also caught a glimpse of the pistol in the man's hand, just as it came down on his head.

His world went black.

APACHE
STRIKE

❖ ❖ ❖ ❖ ❖

Jason Manning

A SIGNET BOOK

SIGNET
Published by New American Library, a division of
Penguin Group (USA) Inc., 375 Hudson Street,
New York, New York 10014, USA
Penguin Group (Canada), 90 Eglinton Avenue East, Suite 700, Toronto,
Ontario M4P 2Y3, Canada (a division of Pearson Penguin Canada Inc.)
Penguin Books Ltd., 80 Strand, London WC2R 0RL, England
Penguin Ireland, 25 St. Stephen's Green, Dublin 2,
Ireland (a division of Penguin Books Ltd.)
Penguin Group (Australia), 250 Camberwell Road, Camberwell, Victoria 3124,
Australia (a division of Pearson Australia Group Pty. Ltd.)
Penguin Books India Pvt. Ltd., 11 Community Centre, Panchsheel Park,
New Delhi - 110 017, India
Penguin Group (NZ), cnr Airborne and Rosedale Roads, Albany,
Auckland 1310, New Zealand (a division of Pearson New Zealand Ltd.)
Penguin Books (South Africa) (Pty.) Ltd., 24 Sturdee Avenue,
Rosebank, Johannesburg 2196, South Africa

Penguin Books Ltd., Registered Offices:
80 Strand, London WC2R 0RL, England

First published by Signet, an imprint of New American Library,
a division of Penguin Group (USA) Inc.

First Printing, January 2006
10 9 8 7 6 5 4 3 2 1

Copyright © Jason Manning, 2006
All rights reserved

 REGISTERED TRADEMARK—MARCA REGISTRADA

Printed in the United States of America

PUBLISHER'S NOTE
This is a work of fiction. Names, characters, places, and incidents either are
the product of the author's imagination or are used fictitiously, and any resemblance to actual persons, living or dead, business establishments, events, or
locales is entirely coincidental.

The publisher does not have any control over and does not assume any
responsibility for author or third-party Web sites or their content.

Chapter 1

As usual, there were two soldiers standing guard at the gate of the army outpost on the outskirts of Dolorosa. One of them was a gray, grizzled veteran of twenty years service. The other was a wet-behind-the-ears new recruit. The older sentry—whose name was Delgado—knew that this was not by accident. It was the way of Captain Menendez to pair, whenever possible, a veteran with one of the new recruits. Mendoza thought this would help the recruits learn those survival skills so crucial to a soldier in the Mexican army posted on the northern frontier. In Delgado's opinion, it *was* helpful. Sometimes. Although the Apache threat was much less than had been the case just a few years before, there were still plenty of perils awaiting the inexperienced soldier in the deserts of Sonora. Chief among them were the bandoleros—the gangs of gunmen and outcasts who roamed the border territory. Many of these had honed their killing skills in the war against Maximilian and the French. But now Maximillian was dead and the French interlopers were gone and these bandoleros had nothing to do save make trouble.

Delgado was leaning against the peeling adobe of

the perimeter wall just to one side of the gate, and now he shifted two feet to his left. The day was waning, and as the sun sank in the western sky, it was casting long, moving shadows. The old soldier tried to stay in the shade, for even at this late hour, the sun's heat was a merciless hammer. He glanced across at the recruit, who was leaning against the wall on the other side of the gate. The young man was dozing, his chin resting on his chest. Delgado shook his head. The greenhorn was always sleeping. He could sleep anywhere, at any hour of the day. He was very accomplished at sleeping while on his feet. Delgado envied him that. To be able to get some rest when and where you could was a very useful ability for a soldier to have. But after a few weeks of observation he had concluded that the boy had few other useful abilities. He doubted that his protégé would long survive.

At least they no longer had to worry about the Apaches. Delgado's eyes narrowed as he gazed westward, into the setting sun, at the jagged line of blue mountains that lay across the horizon. Those were the Sierra Madre, for generations the stronghold of the fierce Apache. For centuries they had come down out of those mountains to attack Mexican villages just like this one. Delgado knew that Dolorosa had been attacked many times by the Enemy—the name by which Mexicans knew the Apache Indian. And, once, the people of Dolorosa had participated with the Mexican army in arranging an ambush of the Apaches, luring the Indians into the village with promises of food and friendship. Delgado was of the opinion that this had been a very ill-advised course of action for the citizens of Dolorosa to take. For nearly two decades following the massacre, the village had been a favorite target of vengeful Apache raiders. Perhaps no village had suffered more from the Apache scourge than Dolorosa. Eventually the army had agreed to build an outpost here to protect the surviving citizens. For a time the Apaches, undeterred by the presence of Mexican soldiers, had persisted, and several fierce actions had ensued. Delgado had participated in a couple of these.

But all that had happened years ago. Now most of the Apaches lived on reservations in the United States. There were still a handful of renegades in the Sierra Madre, but not enough to pose a serious threat. In the old days, a Mexican ventured into the mountains only if he cared nothing about his life. These days, mining and lumber concerns were beginning to prosper in the high country. When he contemplated how much things had changed with respect to the Apaches, Delgado just had to shake his head. As a child growing up in Sonora he'd come to view the Apaches as devils incarnate, a menace that would always exist in the desert—like *alacrun*, the scorpion, or the rattlesnake. He had certainly not expected to survive what seemed to be a perpetual war against the Enemy. Yet here he was, still alive, though much scarred, both on the outside and within, by the ordeal. He had witnessed many terrible things. He prayed he could live the rest of his days in peace, just like all old soldiers everywhere. His young protégé wanted war, to prove himself on the field of battle. But he didn't know any better.

Delgado looked away from the distant

mountains—and then his narrowed gaze swung back in the direction. There was something. . . . Yes, there—a black speck moving through the shimmer of heat haze that made the Sierra Madre seem to float in midair. Just a speck of black, moving first a little to the left, then to the right, and then back again. Delgado knew immediately, even at a distance of well over a half mile, that the speck represented a horseman. Or maybe more than one. Coming from the direction of the Sierra Madre. Despite everything he knew—that the Apaches were gone, that times were not nearly as dangerous as once they had been—the old soldier still felt a cold shiver run down his spine. Too often in his life he had seen men riding out of the heat haze—and later wished they had not come his way.

"Hey," he said, trying to rouse the young soldier, but the young man did not move. "Hey, you jackass, wake up," growled Delgado.

Still the young man slept on. Exasperated, Delgado raised his rifle and jabbed the butt of the weapon, harder than was necessary, into the young man's shoulder. The blow was enough to throw him off balance. He came awake with a start, stumbling, barely able to regain his balance. He gave a shout of startled outrage.

"What did you do that for, you old fool?"

"Next time I will leave you here so that the Apaches can capture you and peel the skin from your body or hang you by your feet over a slow fire."

"Apaches? There are no more Apaches."

Delgado didn't say anything. On occasion he enjoyed telling his protégé stories of Apache battle and torture. Stories that were often unbelievable, but never embellished. He didn't bother correcting the young man, either. There were still a *few* Apaches out there. But let the boy stew in his own ignorance for a while.

The grizzled veteran merely pointed with his chin. The young soldier looked west—and saw the black speck in the heat shimmer. He stepped forward, and then took another step—as if by moving a few feet closer he might have a better chance of identifying that speck when, in fact, ten more minutes would have to pass before they'd have any realistic hope of accomplishing as much. The young soldier stared for a moment, then looked slowly at Delgado, eyes wide.

"Is it . . . ?"

Delgado might have told him that you usually didn't see Apaches until they were close enough to kill you. Instead, he said, "Go tell the lieutenant."

The young soldier did not hesitate. He slipped through the narrow door set into the heavy wooden gate. Delgado kept an eye on the approaching horseman, and as the rider drew closer, the old soldier concluded that he was alone. A moment later he spotted the second horse, trailing along behind the first. The second *caballo*, however, was riderless. Delgado was well on in years, but his eyesight was still keen. Even at this great distance he could see that the second horse was carrying a load, he assumed that this consisted of provisions.

A moment later the officer of the day, Lieutenant Moreno, emerged through the door in the gate, followed by the new recruit. Moreno had a spyglass; he brought it to his right eye and peered through it for a moment, studying the approaching rider.

"He is alone, Lieutenant," said Delgado. "Except for the dog."

Moreno lowered the spyglass slightly, squinted in the direction of the horseman, then looked with surprise at the veteran. "You can see the dog from here, Delgado?"

"Yes, sir."

Moreno resumed his spyglass-assisted scrutiny. "I cannot make out anything about him. He rides with the sun at his back."

"He must be an Indian," said the new recruit, eager to demonstrate that he knew something of the way of things out here on the malpais. "No gringo— and no bandolero—would travel with a dog."

"He is not Indian," said Delgado confidently.

"How do you know?" asked the lieutenant.

"The way he rides. He comes straight on. No Indian does that. The Indian, he rides this way, and he rides that way, but almost never does he go straight at where he wants to be. It is as though he does not know where he wants to go. But he knows. He just doesn't want anyone else to know."

Moreno grunted and resumed his study of the horseman. He envied Delgado's vast knowledge and experience. Yet he was sometimes perturbed by it; after all, Delgado was a lowly private, while he was an officer. And officers were supposed to know more than lowly privates.

"Should I go tell the captain, sir?" asked Delgado.

It was, mused Moreno sourly, Delgado's tactful way of suggesting just such a course.

"No. Why bother him about this? It is but one man."

Delgado shrugged. Just as long as the lieutenant was here to take responsibility for whatever happened, the old soldier was satisfied with standing back and letting events unfold. His gut instinct, though, was that the lone rider brought danger with him. He could not have explained to Moreno why he felt this way, so he made no mention of the feeling. But he had not survived this long without heeding his instincts.

A few moments later the horseman was near enough to the outpost for Delgado to see that he was not an Indian, and that the packhorse was not laden with provisions, after all, but rather with a body, wrapped in a blanket and draped belly down over the animal in what was called the "dead man's ride." Close enough too to see that the dog loping alongside the rider looked very much like a black wolf, so much so that Delgado experienced a chill of primeval fear running down his spine.

Delgado was so preoccupied with the corpse and the wolflike dog that he did not pay the rider much attention until the latter was approaching the gate. The horseman wore a sombrero pulled low over his face. His frame was obscured by a ragged gray serape. The old soldier noticed that the man's left boot was worn at the heel and cracked across the middle of the sole. Conchos studded his trousers. He dressed, then, very much like a bandolero. And he had that aura about him—the aura that made wise men adopt an extra measure of caution. But there was something familiar about this man; Delgado had the feeling they had met before. The veteran tried to see the rider's face as the latter checked his dust-caked horse. But the long shadows of the waning afternoon, and the pulled-low brim of the battered sombrero, stymied him.

Lieutenant Moreno stepped up to the rider's left side, his right hand resting on the flap of a pistol-laden holster on his right hip. If this was meant to intimidate the horseman, Delgado decided that it would not work. Clearly, the horseman was a man who had survived so many perils that a federale officer and two gate guards were not going to alarm him.

"Identify yourself, senor," said Moreno. "What are you doing here? And what is *that*?" As he spoke, he looked at the dead man draped over the second horse.

"Netdahe," said the rider gruffly.

"*Madre de Dios*," murmured Delgado.

Everyone—the lieutenant, the new recruit, the rider, even the wolf-dog—looked at him, and only then did Delgado realize that he had spoken out loud. He hadn't meant to do so. But now, at last, he knew the identity of the horseman.

"He is the Apache hunter," he told Moreno. "He was here eight, ten months ago. I remember now. . . ."

Moreno looked at Delgado, then at the horseman—and took a step backward. He did this instinctively, and when he realized what he had done, and what it looked like, he tried to recover by moving toward the corpse-laden horse. He took two steps, then froze in his tracks, because the wolf-dog, which had been quartering through the dust picking up various scents, suddenly came around the back of the second horse and stood in the lieutenant's path. The beast's tail was lowered, and so were his ears, and his black lips curled slowly back away from fangs that were nearly two inches long. Delgado realized only then just how large the animal was.

"Better back away," advised the rider, though his tone of voice made abundantly clear that Moreno's fate was of little consequence to him. "He can smell fear."

The lieutenant, of course, resented the implication, but he was wise enough to comply.

"There are no Netdahe left alive," he said gruffly.

The horseman dismounted, slowly, stiffly. Here was a man, mused Delgado, who had spent too many years in the saddle, and whose bones complained as a consequence. He watched as the Apache hunter walked to the second horse and began to untie the rope that lashed the blanket to the corpse.

"The dog's kind of protective of this one," he said conversationally as his gloved fingers plucked at the hard knots. "It was the dog, you see, who finished him off. I only nicked him, and he got off into the brasada, and was coming around behind me when the dog got to him."

As he came to the conclusion of this laconic narrative, he unwrapped an edge of the blanket and showed the soldiers the corpse's throat—or rather, what was left of the throat. It was a ragged black hole of dried blood and torn flesh, and despite the protection of the blanket, the flies had managed to lay their eggs in the wounds, and maggots had begun to crawl through the rotting flesh. The new recruit, the son of a clerk, had never seen anything so grotesque in his life. His stomach did a slow roll, his bile rose, and he whirled quickly and whiplashed forward to puke up his breakfast.

Moreno, somewhat more pale than was usually the case, swallowed the lump in his throat and said, "Clearly it is an Indian. But there are no more Net-dahe left in the mountains. The government has said so."

"Governments say lots of things that aren't so," observed the Apache hunter. He motioned for Mor-eno to follow him and went around to the other side of the horse. Once again he worked the lashings loose and pulled back the edge of the blanket, this time exposing the dead man's legs.

Though his stomach was still doing slow rolls, the new recruit let his curiosity get the better of him, and he moved to a spot from which he could see what the Apache hunter was showing the lieutenant.

"See here," said the Apache hunter, pointing to long scars running laterally across the calves of the dead man, just above the n'deh b'keh—the desert moccasins favored by Indians of the desert South-west. "Only the Netdahe do this to themselves."

The recruit saw the scars and, puzzled, glanced at Delgado. He assumed the old soldier had the answer to his question. Delgado knew just about everything worth knowing.

"Is that true?" he asked. "Is that a Netdahe?"

Delgado nodded. "As far as I know, he's right. The Netdahe cut themselves. It isn't easy to explain the Apache way of thinking, but since they are outcasts among their own people, the Netdahe brand themselves as such. The scars are, in a way, badges of honor among their kind. But sometimes I wonder if maybe they scar themselves because they hate what they have become. They will cut their arms, their legs, their bellies. Sometimes even their faces."

"There is no longer a bounty for Apache scalps," Moreno told the Apache hunter.

"I'm not a scalphunter."

"Then why do you bring him here?"

The Apache hunter looked suddenly exasperated. He brushed by Moreno on his way around to the lee side of his horse. "Let me in," he told Delgado. "I want to see the captain."

Delgado looked to Moreno for permission to open the gate. The lieutenant was perturbed. He felt as though he'd been summarily dismissed by the Apache hunter, who obviously was not inclined to have any further business with him. But Moreno had no legitimate reason for preventing the stranger from passing through the outpost's gate. He hesitated, then gave a curt nod. Delgado was relieved. By this time, the Apache hunter was back in the saddle. He was sitting there on his dust-caked mustang, waiting to pass through the gate, fully expecting to do so, and Delgado didn't think he would meekly accept being denied access.

Delgado went through the door cut into the gate,

and opened the portal from the inside. Moreno ordered him to escort the Apache hunter to the commandant's office.

"I've been here before," said the Apache hunter. "I know the way."

"A simple courtesy, senor," replied Moreno, with an oily and insincere smile.

Of course it was not a courtesy. Delgado knew this, and he assumed that the Apache hunter, who was no fool, knew it too. This was Moreno's way of saying that he thought the Apache hunter was an untrustworthy sort who could not be allowed to roam freely inside the stockade. If the Apache hunter took offense, he didn't show it. With just the trace of a sardonic smile at the corner of his mouth, he nodded to Moreno, and heel-tapped the horse through the gate, towing the corpse-laden pony along behind. The wolf-dog loped alongside.

Life in a frontier outpost was 99 percent unadulterated boredom, so any new arrival was bound to elicit a great deal of interest from the post denizens. The Apache hunter drew more than his share, primarily since it was evident that the second horse was carrying a dead man. Yet it was the Apache hunter who caused even the most curious to keep a respectful distance.

For his part, Delgado tried to keep a respectful distance from the wolf-dog. That was easier said than done; at one point the beast dropped back and fell in just inches from the old soldier's heels. Delgado might have rounded on most dogs that got too close, but he didn't dare do that with this one.

"Don't be afraid of him," said the Apache hunter—
a comment that startled Delgado, since the man rode
a little ahead of him and, as far as the soldier knew,
had not looked around, and so could not have seen
Delgado's predicament. "He can smell fear, and I
don't think he likes the scent."

"Easy enough for you to say," replied the veteran.
"After all, you are its master. You have little to fear
from him."

The Apache hunter shook his head. "He doesn't
have a master. Sometimes he travels with me and
sometimes he goes his own way."

"He killed the Netdahe who was trying to kill
you," Delgado reminded him.

"No, that isn't why. He hates Apaches. I don't
know why. But when we're together it's just a matter
of one of us making the kill before the other can get
it done."

Delgado was struck by how talkative the Apache
hunter was. He wondered if this was a consequence
of the man living so many months alone in the malpais. The veteran wanted to find out more about this
man, and saw this moment as a rare opportunity. He
had heard all of the stories. All of the legends. The
Apache hunter's story was known throughout the
northern desert. Or perhaps "stories" was more accurate, since there were so many versions. One element
that was consistent in all of them was that the
Apache hunter had lost someone very dear to him—
a loss that continued to fuel, after all these years,
his incessant yearning for vengeance. Because, people
said, it had been a Netdahe who killed the loved one

of the Apache hunter. Now all Netdahe were his prey, and he would not stop until all of the Avowed Killers were gone from the face of the Earth.

That this man had spent many years tracking down and killing the Netdahe—the most feared of all Apaches—was the source for the awe in which he was held. Some said he was in league with the devil, or even the devil himself, since no ordinary human could do what he had done. When he looked at the Apache hunter, Delgado did not see a devil. An accomplished hunter and killer of men, yes. Yet just a man, for all that. A tired and somewhat lonely man, perceived Delgado.

As they drew near the commandant's office, Captain Menendez emerged. He smiled broadly and extended his arms in a symbolic embrace.

"Ah, senor! It is good to see you alive. Every time we meet I wonder if it will be the last time."

Delgado could sense that the captain's joy was authentic. Rumor had it that Menendez and the Apache hunter were, if not friends, acquaintances of many years, and that the captain was among the select few who knew the Apache hunter's identity.

"I'm still above snakes," replied the Apache hunter, in a tone that betrayed considerable indifference.

The men left the office. Menendez went to the horse carrying the dead Apache and, lifting one end of the blanket, briefly and impassively examined the remains of the Netdahe.

"It's taking you much longer to find them, eh?"

"This one found me."

"You know, of course, that *officially* there are no

more wild Apaches in the Sierra Madre. That's what the government says."

"If this is true, then why are you still posted here?"

Menendez shrugged. "The people don't believe the government. So we are here to make them feel more secure. It looks bad, amigo, you bringing these Netdahe in and making liars out of us." He flashed a disarming grin.

"Well, don't go anywhere," advised the Apache hunter. "Geronimo and his kind won't stay long on the reservations. They'll be back."

"So you say the war with the Apache, it is not over. Wishful thinking on your part, maybe?"

"No. I don't want war. War just gets in the way of what I have to do."

"What you *have* to do," murmured Menendez, with a slight shake of the head. "Come inside, amigo. Have a drink with me. First, though, tell Delgado what you wish to do with this body, which does not, officially, exist."

"I don't care," said the Apache hunter. "Bury it Or leave it outside the wall for the coyotes to haul off."

"I think we will bury it." Menendez nodded at Delgado, then glanced uncertainly at the wolf-dog, which sat on its haunches watching every move that anyone made. "And what about this one, amigo?" he asked the Apache hunter. "He won't attack my men, will he?"

"Not unless they attack me first."

"I don't think we have to worry about that," said the captain wryly. "Come, then. I have something important to give you."

He went inside, and the Apache hunter followed.

Delgado looked with distaste at the Netdahe corpse. Then he remembered the new recruit and smiled. One of the benefits of being a mentor was that he could give the unpleasant jobs to the protégé. He took up the horse's rope and remembered just in time how possessive the wolf-dog could be where the Apache carcass was concerned.

"Why don't you come with me, then?" he said, using a very reasonable tone of voice. "You can help dig the hole. We need to bury this stinking Netdahe."

The wolf-dog watched him intently, cocking its head slightly to one side. Bracing himself, Delgado gingerly took up the rope. The wolf-dog didn't react. The old soldier proceeded with slow and casual steps toward the gate, bringing the horse along behind. He could not bring himself to look back to see what the wolf-dog was doing. A moment later the beast fell in step beside him. Delgado was relieved, and greatly elated. *You see*, he told himself, *all you have to do is treat this creature with respect. Just like its owner. And everything will be okay.*

He almost believed it.

Inside the commandant's office, the Apache hunter found to his surprise that Captain Menendez had turned what must have been a bleak and dusty room into a comfortable sanctum. There was a small case of books under a window framed with curtains, and the Apache hunter could tell that the books weren't there just for show—they were well-read, all of them. The captain's desk was clean and polished, and the chair into which the Apache hunter lowered his lanky frame was more comfortable than most that one found on the frontier. Menendez sat down behind the desk and took a bottle of tequila and two glasses out of one of the drawers. He filled one glass nearly to the rim, while pouring just two fingers' worth into the other. The full glass he handed across the desk to the Apache hunter.

"To better days," Menendez said and knocked his tequila shot back in one gulp.

After the men returned to Menendez' office, the Apache hunter took a long drink, gasping as the liquid fire seared his throat and exploded in his belly.

"You are welcome to take the bottle with you when you go," said Menendez.

"No. No, I can't afford to make mistakes out there."

"Of course. Well, you must at least take any provisions and all the ammunition you need, as usual."

"Thanks."

Menendez waved away the gratitude. "This is the least I can do for a man who is cleaning the last of the rats out of their holes. Perhaps one day what the government says about the Apaches will actually be true. And then maybe I will be fortunate enough to be posted elsewhere." He glanced around the room with disgust.

The Apache hunter didn't say anything. Menendez looked at the man across the desk. There was an understanding between them. Officially, the captain adhered to the government's line that there were no more Apaches in the Sierra Madre. Yet even without the proof periodically provided by the Apache hunter, he would have known better. He would not mention the dead Netdahe in his reports. He never made mention of the dead men whom the Apache hunter brought to him. There was no need for the Apache hunter to bring them here at all. The captain assumed that by bringing them the Apache hunter felt he was justifying taking the food and ammunition that Menendez always offered. The Apache hunter was not the type of man who would take charity, no matter what the circumstances. Menendez was happy to help, but he could not consider the Apache hunter his friend. They did not know each other that well. He knew the man's story, though. He understood his obsession and felt sorry for him. Since the government no longer paid a bounty for Apache scalps, and killing Netdahe was the Apache hunter's sole vocation, he had no means to support himself. And so Menendez accepted the Netdahe corpses, which did not exist, disposed of them, and gave in exchange the Apache hunter the supplies he needed.

"A few months ago," said the captain, opening another of the desk's drawers, "I received this letter. It is from a gentleman named Tom Horn. Do you know this man? Because apparently he knows you."

"I met him once, several years ago," said the Apache hunter.

Menendez opened the brown envelope and removed the letter. "It is addressed to the commanding officer, Mexican Army forces posted at or near Dolorosa, and it is signed by Senor Horn, who asks if, in the event I see you, that I inform you of his desire to meet with you as soon as possible."

"Meet me? How come?"

"He does not say."

The Apache hunter finished off the tequila in his

glass. The captain pushed the bottle across the desk, and his guest poured himself another shot—filling the glass only halfway.

"I can speculate, of course," continued Menendez. "I too have heard of Senor Horn. He and the half breed, Mickey Free, ride as scouts for Al Seiber, who is now chief of scouts for the United States Army. I also know that, while the Apaches have remained fairly quiet on their reservations for several years now, the United States government has pursued the negotiation of what has been called the Hot Trails Treaty with my government. This agreement will allow your cavalry to pursue hostile Indians across our common border without first acquiring permission. And, if such were to occur, Mexican troops could give pursuit into the United States."

Menendez grabbed the bottle and poured himself another two fingers. "Obviously, your government believes there is a distinct possibility that at some point Apaches will flee the reservations and seek refuge in Mexico. Just as obviously, if such an event occurs, the Apaches will head straight into the Sierra Madre. Where else would they go? The mountains have been their sanctuary for centuries. It follows, then, that they want to at least talk to you, amigo— if not enlist your services—since no one who is not Apache knows the Sierra Madre better than you."

The Apache hunter took a drink. His eyes were hooded, his brows knit. "They're smart to be taking precautions. Because it *will* happen. But I want no part of it. I wouldn't blame the Apaches for jumping the reservations. That's not how those people were meant to live."

"You must admit," said Menendez with a smile, "that that's a strange sentiment coming from an Apache killer."

The Apache hunter's eyes turned another shade of bleak. " My wife was Apache. The daughter of Cochise, who was a great man, in my opinion. I don't hate all Apaches. Just the Netdahe. The renegades. The Avowed Killers."

Menendez nodded. *The ones like you*, he thought, wondering if the Apache hunter comprehended the supreme irony of his situation.

"The one who killed your wife," said the captain softly. "You killed him, didn't you?"

"I don't know. I think so. But I never found his body."

Menendez wanted to ask for more details, but thought it wiser, based solely on the other's expression, to change the subject. "So what of this letter? Do you intend to meet with Tom Horn?"

The Apache hunter shrugged. "I might as well. Could be I'll learn something useful."

"He might want to recruit you as a scout, you know."

"He'd be wasting his time."

"Well, I'll send a rider to the telegraph line and convey to them that you'll meet. The U.S. Army has established a fort on the border."

The Apache hunter shook his head. "No. I'll meet Horn on this side of the border. But I won't go to an army outpost."

Menendez didn't press for reasons. He knew something of the man's history. He'd once been an officer in the United States Army. But, to prevent an injus-

tice to peaceful Apaches, he had disobeyed orders
and then gone absent without leave. A dishonorable
discharge had resulted. That was all Menendez
knew—or needed to know—to understand the
Apache hunter's aversion to a U.S. Army post.

"You could meet in Santo Domingo," he said.
"You remember the place, I'm sure. It isn't far from
the Yankee fort."

"Yes, I remember." The Apache hunter finished off
his tequila and stared moodily into the empty glass.

"Do you remember the woman there? What was
her name? I know—Angevine. Her husband was one
of the scalphunters you killed."

The Apache hunter looked up from the empty
glass and glowered at Menendez. The captain realized he was taking the conversation where his guest
didn't want it to go, but he decided to press his luck.

"I wonder if she is still there," Menendez said, as
though he were just talking to himself. "She's probably married again, by now. A woman like that
wouldn't be alone for long."

Still, the Apache hunter didn't say anything.

Menendez shrugged, then sat forward in his chair.
"But I'm sure the people of Santo Domingo will be
happy to see you again. You were quite the hero to
them after you killed those scalphunters."

The Apache hunter put the glass on the corner of
the desk and stood up. "I'll be moving on. Thanks
for the drink, Captain."

Menendez stood up too and came around the desk
to proffer his hand. "Goodbye, Senor Barlow. *Vaya
con Dios.*"

A quarter of an hour later, the Apache hunter was

leaving the outpost, the mochilla tied to his saddle bulging with ammunition and a burlap sack filled with provisions lashed to the other side of the hull. The wolf-dog was sitting on a rock not far from the gate, watching Delgado, who in turn was watching the new recruit. The latter was finishing up with the chore of burying the Netdahe. The wolf-dog was on the run as soon as he saw the Apache hunter, and it was this reaction that caught Delgado's attention. He turned and saw the lone rider coming toward them. Without a word, the latter gathered up the pack-horse, spared the grave an uninterested glance, and then nodded to Delgado. The old soldier wanted to say something in parting, well aware that he might never see the Apache hunter again. He felt saddened, infected by the great tragedy that surrounded this killer of men, a tragedy that emanated not only from the man's past, but from his future, as well. In the end, though, Delgado merely raised a hand. The Apache hunter didn't respond, turning his horse and riding away, the packhorse in tow and the wolf-dog loping alongside.

Chapter 2

When the morning sun struck the limestone ledge halfway up a steep and rugged slope in the Sierra Madre Mountains, the Netdahe Apache called Kiannatah crawled like a snake on his belly out of the cold, dark cave that was his home and into the warmth and light of a new day. The cave entrance was nothing more than a lateral crevice about eighteen inches high. You could walk along the ledge and pass within a few feet of the cave and not know that it existed. The cave itself was about twenty paces deep, and the ceiling was high enough so that Kiannatah could stand fully upright in most of it. At the rear of the cave was a small natural vent, caused by centuries of water seepage; the chute—too small for a man to negotiate—twisted and turned up through the mountain, opening near the rimrock several hundred feet above the cave. Kiannatah built his cook fires below the chute so that the smoke was drawn up into it; by the time the smoke reached the top of the chute it had dissipated to the extent that no one, even someone close by, could have seen it.

Such matters were of great import to Kiannatah, for he was the most wanted man in Mexico. Every-

one was his enemy. He was even an outcast from the
Netdahe, who were themselves outcasts among the
Apaches. The Mexicans would kill him on sight. His
former mentor, Geronimo, had given the other Netdahe permission to kill him. And the entire Chiricahua band had adopted a blood feud against him, in
honor of their former chieftain, Cochise. Kiannatah
had kidnapped and then murdered Cochise's daughter, Oulay, and since Cochise had been unable to
carry out a vow of vengeance during his lifetime, the
entire Chiricahua clan had taken up that vow.

Then there was the white man, the one who had
been a yellow-leg officer when he'd taken Oulay as
his bride. The one who now roamed the Cima
Silkq—the Sierra Madres—killing any Netdahe he
could find. As isolated as he was—and had been for
nearly ten years—Kiannatah had heard rumors of
this Apache hunter. They had met before—the Kiannatah had barely escaped with his life. Many were
the days he had spent prowling the mountains, hoping to meet the man again. But the Sierra Madre were
vast and rugged, and it wasn't easy finding one man
in them, especially a man who was as skilled as an
Apache at traveling unseen.

Kiannatah sat cross-legged on the ledge in front of
the cave, soaking up the warmth of the early sun,
breathing deeply the crisp mountain air. The cave
was dark and dank, and he spent as little time as
possible within it. He could have built a jacal, but a
jacal would have been easy to spot, and so was a
luxury Kiannatah could not afford. That he lived in
a cave like a wild animal was of little consequence
to him anyway. The only material possessions he

had, or cared about having, were his rifle, his bow, and his knife. These were all he needed. The tools of his trade.

Not that he practiced his trade much anymore. In his time Kiannatah had killed many people. He had never kept track, but the sum total had to be in the hundreds. In recent years, though, he had claimed relatively few victims. In the old days he frequently had come down out of the mountains on a bloody rampage, killing just about anyone unfortunate enough to cross his path—since everyone was his enemy, he did not have to pick and choose. He had been bold, sometimes to the point of carelessness, driven by a terrible and unrelenting hatred that was, in turn, fueled by an unremitting need for revenge.

That need was no less strong today. He assumed he would take it to his grave. As a boy he had witnessed the massacre of his entire family by the Nakai-Ye, the Mexicans, in the village called Dolorosa. From that day he'd had but one purpose in life: to destroy the enemies of his people. Of course this was a job that he could never complete; the Apaches had far more enemies than they had friends. Not just the Nakai-Ye, but the Pinda Lickoyi—the White Eyes—as well, who numbered more than the grains of sand in the desert, or at least so it seemed to the Indians, who had been pushed off their homelands by the tidal wave of Americans. Most of the other Indian tribes feared and hated the Apaches, as well, and had long made war against them. There were even a few Apache bands, such as the White Mountain, who from the beginning had sided with the Nakai-Ye or the Pinda Lickoyi against their own kind. All of these called Kiannatah their enemy. Time and time again he had demonstrated just how fearsome an enemy he would be.

It was when Geronimo had become his enemy that everything changed for Kiannatah. The renegade leader of the Netdahe—the Avowed Killers—had been Kiannatah's mentor, the closest thing to a father he'd had since his very early years. Geronimo had been just like him, a killer motivated by vengeance—he too had lost his family to the treacherous Nakai-Ye. For many months Kiannatah had ridden with Geronimo and the other Netdahe. Then Geronimo had turned against him—had given the other Netdahe leave to kill him. And since he had always been Geronimo's right-hand man, smarter and stronger than any other Netdahe, they had resented him all along, and the resentment had transformed into hatred, and they had been enthusiastic in their efforts to take his life once Geronimo gave the word. So Kiannatah had become an outcast among outcasts, hunted by his own kind. Betrayed by his mentor, the embittered Kiannatah had sought refuge in the isolation of the most remote parts of the Cima Silkq. Rarely did he venture out of the mountains. And since neither the Nakai-Ye nor the Pinda Lickoyi often ventured into the Sierra Madre, Kiannatah's killing sprees became, for many years, very few and far between.

Lately, though, the Nakai-Ye had begun to filter into the mountains again. The Mexican government had declared the Apache menace over. Indeed, most of the bands had surrendered to the Americans and were now living on reservations. (Kiannatah had

nothing but contempt for those who had succumbed
to the Pinda Lickoyi because now they were like cattle, fenced in, no longer free. They were prisoners on
their own land. Or a portion of their land—that portion which the Pinda Lickoyi, for one reason or another, had not claimed for their own.) There were
tremendous deposits of gold and silver in the Cima
Silkq—deposits that had gone untapped for generations while the Apaches held sway in the mountains;
during that time a Nakai-Ye who entered the Cima
Silkq was not expected to come out again. Today
there were mining concerns scattered throughout the
mountains. And every now and then, more out of
boredom than anything else, Kiannatah would kill a
few of the Nakai-Ye who either worked at or did
business with the mines. Not enough, as it turned
out, to raise widespread alarm. The Nakai-Ye were
not fools. They knew—the government's declarations
to the contrary—that the mountains were still home
to a handful of die-hard wild Apaches. But the allure
of gold and silver overcame their caution.

Kiannatah sat in the sunlight, his bronze flesh glistening with sweat. Even though it was still very early
in the day, the temperature was rising quickly. In a
couple of hours the sun would be a blazing inferno
high in a brass-colored sky. Kiannatah didn't care if
it was hot or cold, sunny or raining. He paid little
attention to physical discomfort. His entire life had
been anguish of one sort or another, and he was as
impervious to pain as a human could become. His
eyes were closed as he sat cross-legged on the high
ledge. An observer might have assumed he was
asleep, since he hadn't moved in an hour. But Kian-

natah had made a habit of conserving his energy; he made no unnecessary movements. Even in apparent repose, though, his senses were acute. He heard the faintest of sounds—a sound so small that most men would have discounted it as unimportant, or not heard it at all. Kiannatah's eyes snapped open. Without turning his head—an unnecessary movement— he looked to his right just in time to see a rattlesnake land on the ledge ten feet away. The snake was large, even by Sierra Madre standards—at least four feet in length and as thick around as Kiannatah's wrist.

The slope above the ledge was sheer, rising on the vertical more than fifty feet before beginning to angle steeply to the rimrock high above. Kiannatah deduced that the sound he had heard was the whisper of scales on stone, so he assumed the snake had fallen from the slope above. How and why it had been on the vertical slope in the first place was a mystery, one that Kiannatah did not spend much time trying to understand. He was an intensely superstitious man. As any Apache knew, the Great Spirit often communicated to humans through signs. These communications took varied forms. The way lightning traveled across the sky during a storm. The way the flames of a lodge fire flickered and danced. The way one stick lay across another on a path. Or in the sudden appearance or uncharacteristic behavior of an animal. The key was to be receptive to the communication, and to decipher it correctly. The meaning could be quite apparent, or extremely obscure.

In this case, there was no question in Kiannatah's mind what the unusual appearance of the rattler signified. Not surprisingly, the rattlesnake represented danger. The sudden and unexpected manner of its arrival meant that danger was coming soon—and from an unexpected source or direction.

The rattlesnake immediately coiled and began to give warning. Kiannatah didn't move a muscle. He wasn't afraid. He was confident that he could kill the snake before it could strike. Assuming, of course, that it was real, and not a spirit snake. Since there was no movement on the ledge, the rattler soon uncoiled and slithered across the ledge and into the crevice, seeking respite from the sun's heat in the cool shade of the cave. Kiannatah wasn't worried by the fact that the snake was intruding into his home. If the rattler was still there when he returned, he would dispose of it. He was fairly certain, though, that the snake would be gone.

As always, he had his weapons with him. There was the Winchester repeating rifle that he had taken from the dead hand of a gunman who had worked for the Overland Company, back in the days when he and Geronimo and the other Netdahe had been raiding the stage line. Kiannatah recalled those days as some of the best of his life. He had been young and strong, at the peak of his powers. He had been admired by none less than Geronimo, the man he had most admired. And he had felt as though he had been engaged for a time in work—bloody work— that struck a serious blow to his enemies, the Pinda Lickoyi, since the Overland was an important lifeline back east for the White Eyes who had invaded Apacheria. The Winchester was a fine rifle, durable and accurate. Kiannatah, however, seldom used it, since ammunition was extremely hard to come by; at the moment he had but three cartridges.

His bow had been crafted from bois d'arc wood. In his hands it was nearly as powerful and accurate a weapon as the Winchester long gun. He took intricate care—and sometimes spent many hours in the day making his arrows, for he did most of his hunting with the bow in order to conserve his cartridges. With either bow or rifle he rarely missed, even at long range or poor light.

The knife sheathed at his side had belonged to a buffalo hunter—a man Kiannatah remembered as being the most foul-smelling human he had ever met. The one-sided blade was twelve inches long; bone-handled grips had been secured to the steel with generous wrappings of rawhide, which, over the years, had hardened to the consistency of iron. The knife was long enough and heavy enough so that Kiannatah could crush an enemy's ribs and pierce his heart with a single thrust. He preferred a quick kill. His goal had never been to inflict pain. He wasn't a sadist. His sole purpose was to kill his enemies. Nor did he indulge in the disgusting art of torture, of which so many Apaches were overfond. In Kiannatah's opinion, torture was the avocation of cowards who felt better about themselves if they could force brave men to scream in agony or beg for mercy. Kiannatah was as hard of heart as the worst torturer; and he was not a merciful man by any means. He just believed it best to kill as swiftly and efficiently as possible.

No doubt lingered in his mind regarding the meaning of the rattlesnake's appearance. The only question was what to do about it. Kiannatah did not ponder long on this matter. He was not one to sit and wait for an enemy to find him. No, he would go and find the enemy. He would meet the enemy on his terms, on ground of his choosing.

For Kiannatah, thought was action. He rose in one fluid motion. A steep and narrow trail led from the ledge down to a place where a spring—his usual source of water—came trickling out of cracks in the stone face of the mountain. The water had, through the ages, carved a steep ravine in the mountain flank, a ravine now filled with boulders, detritus, and some wind-twisted cedar. Kiannatah made his way down this cut to the base of the slope. At times the descent was a treacherous and difficult one, but he was sure of foot, and had passed that way so many times in the past that he could have negotiated the entire route with his eyes closed and still not missed a step.

Danger was coming. Of this he was certain. Nothing in the omen of the snake, however, alerted him as to what form the danger would take, or whence it would come. He decided that the most likely source of the peril would be human, and if this were the case, the most likely place to find it would be a canyon trail less than a mile to the north. This trail was often used by those traveling to or from several mines located deeper in the Sierra Madre. Loping with the ease and stamina of a wolf across the broken terrain, Kiannatah headed in that direction.

Two hours later he was stationed on the canyon rim, well concealed in an outcropping of rocks, and in a place from which he could see a fair distance both up canyon and down. Like any hunter, he was accustomed to waiting for long periods and without any assurance that his prey would appear. Kiannatah's patience was infinite. He did not plan to remain in this location for a certain number of hours before moving on. Nor did he plan to return to the cave at nightfall. He made no plans whatsoever. He was prepared to respond to whatever might occur.

He did not have long to wait. They came from the east, moving up canyon, and he heard them long before they came into view. A single wagon, pulled by a team of mules. The creak and rattle of the wagon and the clatter of shod hooves on stone were interspersed with the brutal percussion of a bullwhip and explosive epithets uttered by a man—a Nakai-Ye. Kiannatah remained motionless among the rocks until the wagon came round a bend in the canyon and into view. Then he leaned an inch to the left for a better view through the space between two boulders. He knew immediately that the wagon belonged to a trader. Items of merchandise like pots and pans and bolts of fabric were lashed to the sides of the wagon, indicating that there was no room for them under the canvas. Kiannatah could see two men, one driving the wagon and one riding an extra mule alongside. And there was one woman—or perhaps just a tall girl; it was hard to tell at this distance—walking at the head of the mule team. He doubted that there were any other people in the wagon, but he would work under the assumption that there *might* be. To do otherwise could be a fatal mistake.

The man in the wagon box was the one using the bullwhip and shouting the epithets; every minute or so, he cracked the whip over the heads of the lead mules, urging them to greater exertion. From as far away as the rimrock, Kiannatah could see that the animals were exhausted, lathered in their traces, and there was not much more that they could give. Once, the driver missed and laid the twisted leather of the whip across the flank of one of the mules. The woman or girl whirled and shouted angrily at him. He shouted back at her. Then he let loose with the whip again—and this time laid open the flank of the other lead mule. With what Kiannatah thought was admirable quickness, the woman grabbed the end of the whip and tried to pull it from the driver's grasp. He was a big man, though, powerfully built, and three times her weight. He pulled back, and she went sprawling in the hot yellow sand of the canyon bottom. In an instant she was on her feet and leaping up into the wagon box, attacking him. The driver backhanded her, and she went flying off the wagon, landing sprawled on her back. She lay still, and Kiannatah wondered if she was unconscious. Not that he really cared.

By this time the wagon was almost directly below his vantage point. Kiannatah did not give much thought to whether the three Nakai-Ye in the canyon below had anything to do with the danger heralded by the snake omen. They were Nakai-Ye, and they were available for the killing. It was so routine that he scarcely gave it a thought. He took an arrow from the quiver and fit notch to bowstring. He had participated in too many ambushes to have to ponder long over the strategy he would employ. The first order of business was to make escape difficult for his prey. To that end, his first target was one of the lead mules.

From this extreme angle, his first arrow entered between the haunches. Not a mortal wound, but one sufficient to drop the mule in its traces. Kiannatah had another arrow notched and away almost faster than the eye could follow. This one pierced the mule's neck, killing the animal in a matter of seconds.

Dropping the mule brought the wagon to a halt, and the rest of the mule team immediately became entangled in their traces. Kiannatah turned his attention to the two Nakai-Ye men. The one on the mule had jumped off the extra mule and, running to the wagon, threw open a supply box attached to the outside of the bed and pulled out a rifle. All of this took time—a quarter of a minute. It was the last quarter minute of the man's life. Kiannatah's arrow caught him right between the shoulder blades, and struck with such force that the shaft was driven completely through the body, piercing the heart in passing, and the arrowhead lodged in the wooden box, so that the dead Nakai-Ye was pinned to the wagon like a butterfly to a display board.

The wagon driver bleated with incoherent fear as he hurled himself from the box and sought cover behind the wagon. The woman, on the other hand, gave no thought to her own safety; she went to the mules tangled in their traces and, using a knife that she produced from somewhere, began to cut them free. Kiannatah had already decided to kill her last. The fact that the second Nakai-Ye man was cowering behind the wagon, where arrows could not reach, annoyed the Netdahe. Kiannatah did not mind close-in killing work. He simply preferred to do the job quickly, efficiently, and with minimum effort.

Shouldering the bow, he proceeded down the slope, moving quickly and with the agility of a mountain cat, never losing his balance even though the incline was steep and the going was often treacherous. He did not bother trying to remain concealed. There was a rifle down there—it lay in the dust on the nearside of the wagon—but he doubted that the remaining Nakai-Ye man had the nerve to expose himself in order to retrieve it. And there could be other firearms down there, but since no one had yet fired a shot at him, Kiannatah wasn't overconcerned. He had been shot at far too many times to be deterred by such worries.

Reaching the canyon bottom no more than a stone's throw from the wagon, Kiannatah paused to catch his breath and then darted across the open to seek cover on the other side. He heard a shout from the direction of the wagon, indicating that the driver who cowered behind the wagon had spotted him. A moment later the Nakai-Ye broke cover and began running. Kiannatah muttered a curse. He had hoped to save his precious few cartridges and make the kill with knife or arrow. Now, though, the driver was fleeing down the canyon away from him, and even though the man was large and lumbered along like an elephant, Kiannatah didn't want to waste the time or expend the energy tracking him would require. The Winchester repeating rifle was slung on his back with a long length of rope serving as a shoulder strap; the Netdahe unlimbered the long gun and fed one of the cartridges—which he carried in a small pouch—into the breech.

It was conventional wisdom in the United States

Army that most members of the western Indian tribes were not very good shots. Had he been asked, Kiannatah would have agreed with this assessment. For many tribes, getting firearms was difficult enough—getting sufficient ammunition to practice to the point of acquiring a certain proficiency with such weapons was rare, indeed. Kiannatah was an exception. He was a crack shot. From his earliest kills, he had made a habit of taking his victims' weapons and all the ammunition he could find, and he hadn't hesitated in expending hundreds of rounds in practice, secure in the knowledge that all he needed to save was one bullet to make his next kill, from which, with any luck, he could acquire more guns and cartridges. In addition, he had more experience than most in hitting human targets.

So, even though the Nakai-Ye driver was getting farther and farther away with each passing second, Kiannatah took his time loading the Winchester and aiming and drawing a bead and squeezing the trigger. As soon as the Winchester recoiled against his shoulder, he stood and moved out into the open—and away from the drift of eye-burning powder smoke—confident that he had hit his mark. He really didn't even need to look to confirm that the Nakai-Ye was down. Later he would go to where the body lay to make sure—he wasn't one to leave anything to chance, and he had seen men survive what had appeared to be mortal wounds. At the moment, though, he had more pressing business. There was one more Nakai-Ye to kill.

Slinging the rifle back on his shoulder, Kiannatah moved in a crouching run to the back of the wagon.

Just because his next victim was a woman did not mean he would lower his guard. Drawing the knife from its sheath, he moved cautiously around the wagon, expecting either to be attacked by the woman or to find that she, like the man, was fleeing. He was surprised, then, to find that she was still working to free the mules; as he reached the front of the wagon, she was cutting the last one loose. The mule, standing between them, bolted, and she found herself face-to-face with the Netdahe. Fear flashed momentarily in her eyes. Then, as he watched in growing astonishment, a calmness overcame her, evident in her eyes and in her expression and in her posture. She lowered the knife with which she had been cutting the traces and which, without conscious thought, she had brandished in front of her when Kiannatah appeared.

He observed that she was young, perhaps fifteen or sixteen summers old, passing through that mysterious realm between childhood and womanhood. She was slight of build, exceedingly slender—he reflected that he could snap her forearm as easily as if it were a twig. She had large eyes that were alert and intelligent—and now serenely unafraid, which was most remarkable under the circumstances. She wore a plain, somewhat ragged dress, and there were no shoes on her feet. Despite her tender years, there was a toughness about her that Kiannatah recognized. Apache youth had that same sort of toughness, derived from growing up accustomed to certain hardships.

The woman child looked around—at the man who lay impaled against the wagon close at hand, and then at the other one, who lay motionless in the hot sand of the canyon bottom about two hundred fifty feet away. Several of the mules stood a little distance off. Watching her, Kiannatah could almost see her calculate her chances if she made a run for one of the mules, in hopes of getting on it and riding to safety. But she was smart enough to realize that she had no chance at all, regardless of whether she tried to run away or stood her ground. Finally, as this realization sank in, she turned back to him and looked him in the eye, and once again Kiannatah marveled at her lack of fear.

"I know who you are," she said.

He spoke her language perfectly, and still he wondered, at that moment, if he had misunderstood.

"You are one of the Netdahe," she continued—and then he understood. She did not know his identity but only his type, a reasonable conclusion for a Nakai-Ye to make, considering the situation.

When he made no response, she continued, quite calmly, almost as though she were making idle conversation.

"The government says there are none of you left in these mountains, but we all know better." She pointed with her chin at the body of the driver, which lay farther down the canyon. "Even that pig of a man knew better. But he had to sell his cheap goods and his cheap whiskey to the men at the mines."

Kiannatah's curiosity got the better of him. "Your father?" he asked.

That he spoke her tongue surprised her, but she recovered quickly. "My father? No! But my father, he was just as bad. He sold me to that pig of a man for a case of whiskey. I am glad he is dead. I . . . only wish I did not have to die with him."

"You should have run away."

She gave him a who-are-you-kidding look. "You would have caught me. Besides, I had to set the mules free. They deserved to be free. They didn't ask to be here."

Any more than you did, mused Kiannatah. He looked at the knife in her hand, now held down by her side. "You could try to kill me first," he suggested.

She looked down at the knife, her expression one of mild surprise, as though she had forgotten that she held the weapon. Then she smiled faintly and shook her head. The utter futility of trying to fight the Apache warrior was so immense as to be almost laughable.

"I know why you keep fighting," she said, looking up quickly and earnestly into his eyes, "even when you do not care for life, yours or anyone else's. I can see it clearly. It is because you cannot let them defeat you. If they kill you, they win, and you won't let them win. So you keep fighting to live, even though there is nothing left in life that gives you pleasure."

Kiannatah felt a chill run up his spine. The woman was right. But how could this be so? And one sentence reverberated in his mind: *I can see it clearly.* Did she, like Geronimo, have some sort of second sight, some powerful magic? Could she see into men's hearts? Into their pasts? Into their futures? Kiannatah believed that some people had such a gift. He had witnessed it in Geronimo. He had been there when Geronimo predicted exactly what would, in fact, transpire in the hours or days to come. He had heard—and believed, as did many other Apaches—that at one point Geronimo had summoned all his powers to stop, for a brief time, the sun in its travels across the sky. No one who knew Geronimo could doubt that he was a man who had frequent visions and spirit visitations. Certainly, this woman was a strange one. Any other woman—and most men—in her predicament would have been petrified by fear, or begging for mercy, or trying to run no matter how hopeless escape might be. But not this one. She was different. Perhaps, he thought, she really could see the future—and saw that he was *not* going to take her life. He realized, then, that he wasn't going to kill her. What intrigued him was that she might have known this even before he did.

Once the decision to let her live had been made, Kiannatah understood clearly that the wisest course was to let her go. But he didn't want to—and wasn't sure why. There was nothing sexual about it. He didn't want to rape her. Ever since he had witnessed the rape of rancher John Ward's daughter by several of his fellow Netdahe—an event that had occurred on a raid many years ago—he had eschewed that sort of thing, because he was better than other Netdahe. Better in some ways—and worse in others. In his entire life he had truly desired only one woman: Oulay, the daughter of Cochise. He had wanted her so much that he'd killed her rather than lose her to a Pinda Lickoyi army officer—the very same Pinda Lickoyi who was now known as the Apache hunter.

Keeping this woman child with him made no sense. In fact, it was dangerous. She would just slow him down. And there was still the danger, signified by the snake omen, out there—somewhere. Kianna-tah was certain now that this small party of Nakai-Ye did not represent that danger. The two men he had just slain had been no greater threat to him than this woman child, and she was no threat at all. The Netdahe was suddenly overwhelmed by the urge to move, and move quickly. He had been in this canyon too long. Eyes narrowed, he swiftly scanned the rim-rock. Perhaps it had been the thought of the Apache hunter that had sparked this anxiety. Whatever the source, he would, as always, respond to his intuition.

"You will come with me," he told the woman child. "Pick one of the mules to ride. Leave the rest."

Her expression was unreadable as she began to turn away.

"Wait!" he snapped.

She turned back to face him, looking him straight in the eye, and there was not even a trace of fear to be seen. Again—and this would happen to him many more times in the days to come—he was struck by how odd it was to find someone who had no fear of him. Everyone feared Kiannatah. Even Geronimo had learned to be afraid of him. But not this wisp of a girl, with the raven black tendrils of hair hanging like a veil across her face.

The Netdahe held out a hand. "Give me the knife."

She raised her arm, and when it was parallel to the ground, she flicked her fingers, flipping the knife over so that the handle, rather than the blade, was pointed at him. Kiannatah took the knife, and with-out a word, she turned away and went to the nearest mule and, with a light and sinewy grace, mounted it. He waited until she was aboard the mule and then began to lope with long, easy strides up the canyon. He knew this place well and remembered a game trail a half mile or so away that he was confident the mule could negotiate all the way to the rim. He did not even glance at the corpse of the Nakai-Ye driver as he went by. But he heard the woman child hawk and spit as she passed—a final demonstration of her supreme contempt.

Kiannatah could not help himself. He smiled.

Chapter 3

Charles Summerhayes, Lieutenant, United States Army, was shocked and disappointed when he arrived after a long journey at Camp Bowie in the Arizona Territory. Not because of the appearance or the location of the outpost; though he had resided back east for some time now, the memory of life on an army outpost in Apacheria remained fresh in his mind. Such experiences were never forgotten. For such a famous post, one that was often mentioned in the Eastern newspapers, Camp Bowie looked dusty, small, and unimportant. A low adobe perimeter wall encircled several rows of adobe huts, most of which faced a sun-hammered parade ground. Inside the encampment were some drought-stunted trees and a couple of pitiful vegetable gardens, but this country was far better suited to the propagation of sagebrush and Joshua trees—both of which dominated the flats stretching off in three directions from the camp—than to the growing of tomatoes and strawberries. A range of rugged mountains loomed over Camp Bowie in the fourth direction—the north—and up there in the high country, up where it wasn't hotter than hell with the hide off nine months out of the year, were some impressive stands of pine and aspen.

Summerhayes' first posting following receipt of his commission had been to a place very much like this one. Those long-ago days had been miserable ones for him. He hadn't wanted to make soldiering a career in the first place—a state of affairs that had only compounded the misery. Family tradition had dictated his course. He would have liked to look back on those years and be able to say that he'd made the best of a bad situation, that he'd possessed sufficient character to accept whatever life meted out and to triumph over adversity. The truth, sadly, was an altogether different story. He'd allowed self-pity and resentment to consume him to such a degree that he had very nearly been dishonorably discharged. All in all, mused Summerhayes, as he approached the main gate of Camp Bowie, that had not been his finest hour.

As boring and depressing as that first posting had been for him, Summerhayes could only assume that it was just as bad, if not worse, for the men stationed here. Because back then, at least, they'd had the prospect of action against the Apaches with which to spice up their miserable lives. The United States Army had not had an engagement against an Apache foe for several years now. All—or almost all—of the Indians were cooped up on reservations like San Carlos, which lay between this encampment and the mountains to the north. Apacheria was being overrun by white emigrants. Farmers, ranchers, miners, businessmen—you name it, and they were coming, now that the Apache menace was a thing of the past.

Summerhayes had been amazed at just how much this country had changed since last he'd seen it. Case in point was the burgeoning town of Tucson, whence he had come, riding in the wagon that the Camp Bowie commandant had sent to the railhead for the purpose of transporting him. A telegraph line strung up along the road Summerhayes had just traveled extended all the way from Tucson to the outpost, a distance of about sixteen miles; news and orders could reach Camp Bowie fairly quickly, by frontier standards, thanks to that wire. Of course, in the old days, nobody would have gone to the trouble and expense of erecting a telegraph line in this territory, since renegade Apaches would have torn it right down. Even the Overland Stage, which had loaded its coaches and way stations with heavily armed guards, had barely managed to survive the Apache scourge. Summerhayes knew this all too well—he'd once been assigned the impossible task of catching the Apache raiders who were plaguing the Overland.

Some things, then, had changed drastically in the years he had been away. But others had remained very much the same. Like life in a frontier garrison. Like the land itself, which was better equipped to kill you than be hospitable to you. But none of this was the reason for the lieutenant's shock and dismay as he neared the Camp Bowie gate. What caused that was the physical appearance of the Apaches who lived in jacales scattered along both sides of the wagon trace leading to the outpost.

There had been a time when Charles Summerhayes was deathly afraid of Apaches—back when he'd been a reluctant shavetail fresh out of the military academy at West Point and just assigned to Apacheria. Then he had fought them and, for a time, hated them as the most fierce and dangerous of foes. Finally, he had seen another side of the Apache. He learned more about their history, about their customs, about their way of life. He'd seen the human side of his enemy. Thanks in no small measure to his friend, Joshua Barlow, he had even come to perceive the Apache in a sympathetic light, as victims of Mexican skullduggery and American greed. The Mexicans had made a habit of luring bands of Apaches into ambushes with offerings of peace as the bait. Many of the most warlike of Apache leaders—Geronimo among them—had seen his loved ones butchered by the Mexicans in just such a fashion. Meanwhile, Summerhayes had watched his own people pour into Apacheria, taking whatever they wanted without the slightest consideration for the rights of the previous owners. He had no idea how many times he'd heard someone describe Apacheria as "free for the taking." In the minds of such people, the Apaches were, at best, nuisances or, at worst, vermin that needed to be eradicated, just like the wolf. Summerhayes had come to understand that, like so many other Indian tribes, the Apaches fought mostly just to hold on to what belonged to them. A noble struggle—and a futile one. For most Apaches, anyway. There were some, like Geronimo and the Netdahe, the Avowed Killers, who fought merely for vengeance, or because they liked to kill. In Summerhayes' opinion, they had been in the minority. Most whites would have vehemently disagreed, of course. Most whites would have been shocked to hear his point of view. Summerhayes was of the opinion that his lack of discretion in mentioning his changed views regarding the Apache had been instrumental in his eventual reassignment back east.

It was off, mused Summerhayes—perhaps "ironic" was a better word—that someone who had been so transparently ill-suited to service on the frontier had ended up missing Apacheria, with all its dangers and inherent hardships, during his many years on the safe other side of the Mississippi River. When he had received his quite unexpected orders to report to the commander of the military district that contained Camp Bowie, he had been elated. His years in the East had been prosaic and unrewarding, despite the fact that he had been promoted to his own (small) garrison command and had married a wonderful young woman who thought he had hung the moon. He found he could scarcely wait to return to the desert, even though it meant leaving his home and lovely wife behind. (She had wanted to accompany him, but he'd managed, with considerable effort, to talk her out of it.) Not because he expected action—everyone knew that the Apache threat was a thing of the past. No, it was just because he had missed the country and its people. And had been eager to see an Apache again.

But as the wagon drew within a hundred yards of the Camp Bowie gate, passing through the scattering of Apache jacales, and he saw the inhabitants of those squat, round mud-and-straw structures, Summerhayes stared with growing dismay. What had become of the proud people he'd learned to respect? These Indians were dirty, scrawny, haggard scarecrows in tattered and filthy dresses and himpers, the traditional garb for Apache males. No matter how desperate the circumstances, the Apache of old had always carried himself with dignity. There was nothing dignified in the way these people flocked to the wagon, begging for food. So needful and persistent were some of them that they got too close for the liking of the solider driving the wagon. He ordered them to back away, cursed them vigorously, and finally began lashing at them, with equal vigor, using the ends of the harness reins threaded through his fingers. Summerhayes almost intervened, but decided instead to do nothing. He didn't need to start his new assignment with the old "Indian lover" albatross around his neck.

"Goddamn filthy heathens," muttered the driver, shaking his head in disgust. He glanced at Summerhayes, just to confirm that the officer did not object to his profanity. "Can't figure out why the major let's 'em get in so close to the fort. But word is General Miles will put a stop to that pretty damn quick, now that he's in charge."

"Maybe they'll starve to death soon," remarked Summerhayes, with only the slightest trace of irony in his voice. "Then you won't have to worry about them at all."

The driver nodded enthusiastic endorsement of the idea. "Works for me," he declared.

They passed through the gate without delay—the lethargic sentry paid them little attention. Summerhayes looked over his shoulder to see what the Apaches were doing now that the wagon had entered the outpost. They stopped well short of the sentry, some turning back, dejected, to their jacales. Others simply stood there, forlornly staring after the wagon as though it had been their last hope for survival. The sentry didn't pay them much attention, either. He knew they were no threat to him and he didn't even bother brandishing the carbine that was slung over one shoulder. For their part, the Apaches knew they weren't welcome inside Camp Bowie. Knew too that most of the soldiers garrisoned there would use any excuse to shoot them down. There was an invisible but inviolable line past which they could not venture and expect to live.

Slightly sick to his stomach, Summerhayes turned back around as the wagon followed a stone-lined lane that ran along the perimeter of the parade ground, following this to the headquarters building—a structure, like all the others in the post, that consisted of thick adobe walls and a heavily timbered roof fashioned from lumber transported from a logging camp in the mountains to the north. There was a good deal of activity around this building, and as they got closer Summerhayes pegged the men loitering in and around the shade of the front porch as aides and orderlies assigned to high-ranking officers. Not that he recognized any of them. But he'd been in the army long enough to know the type. Perhaps the most telltale clue was their obvious commitment to regulations where their attire was concerned. A veteran of frontier service put comfort and utility above style when it came to uniforms, and whether he was "presentable" or not was usually the last thing on his mind. These men, though, looked like they had just stepped out of the War Department building in Washington. They were resplendent in dress uniforms flashing with brass and adorned with braid. And somehow, mused Summerhayes, in this place, they looked quite ridiculous too. He counted five of them and wondered just how many generals were congregated inside the adobe headquarters building.

The aides, engaged in conversation among themselves, stopped what they were doing and turned to watch the wagon as it pulled alongside the front porch of the headquarters building. Even before the wagon's team had come to a complete halt, Summerhayes was performing an agile jump out of the box; he circled round to the back of the wagon to retrieve his single valise, and thanked the driver, who managed a lethargic salute before whipping up the team to pull away. Summerhayes watched with some amusement as the dust, kicked up by the wagon wheels and the hooves of the four-mule team, swirled over him and began drifting toward the porch—and how several of the aides scattered in a vain attempt to escape it. For his part, Summerhayes didn't worry about the dust—he was already covered in it from head to toe. He approached the single guard stationed at the door of the headquarters building and identified himself. It wasn't necessary for Summerhayes to state the obvious; clearly he was here to report to the garrison commander.

"Just a minute, Lieutenant," said the guard. He opened the door a crack and called for the sergeant at arms.

As Summerhayes waited, one of the aides stepped up to him. "I say, old fellow," drawled the aide, affecting a British lilt—an affectation Summerhayes had noticed among many of his fellow officers back east and which, he supposed, was part and parcel of a growing infatuation in the United States Army's officer corps for all things Victorian. Queen Victoria's redecorated army was uniformly believed to be the best in the world—and had for decades been engaged in campaigns against enemies as exotic as camel-mounted Mamelukes and the wily Thugs of India. "I would advise you," continued the aide, "to clean yourself up a bit before presenting yourself to General Miles. He put stock in such things."

"Thanks, but I have my orders. I'm to report immediately upon arrival at Camp Bowie to the commandant, Major Bendix."

The aide was about to reply when the door flew open. Summerhayes identified the man who appeared in the doorway in an instant—even though many years had passed since last they'd met. The man recognized him right away too. His sun-faded blue eyes widened, reflecting his amazement.

"Well I'll be damned," he breathed. "Summerhayes!" Belatedly, he realized his error. "I mean, *Lieutenant* Summerhayes!"

"Sergeant Farrow. It's good to see a familiar face."

The aide in the fancy dress uniform, disgusted by this display of familiarity between a commissioned officer and a lowly sergeant, made a sound of disdain and turned on his heel. Farrow glanced his way, grimaced, and shook his head. Then he flashed a tobacco-stained grin in Summerhayes' direction.

"You don't know how happy I am to see you, sir," he said, sounding greatly relieved.

"And why is that?" Though they had served together—had seen action against the Apaches together—Summerhayes had never considered himself to be friends with Sergeant Farrow, and he had never wondered during his long sojourn back east how the sergeant was faring out on the frontier. So the fervor with which Farrow made his comment surprised Summerhayes.

"Because I was beginning to wonder," said the sergeant, his voice laden with scorn, "if they were ever gonna send an officer out here who'd actually *seen* an Apache before."

He spoke loudly enough for the aide in the resplendent uniform to hear, and the latter whirled, his cheeks reddening with a rising anger. Summerhayes reflected on how Farrow had always possessed an uncanny ability to get into trouble with superior officers.

"I'll have you know, Sergeant," sneered the aide, "that I served with General Miles in the campaign against Chief Joseph and the Nez Percé Indians."

"The Nez Percé, the Sioux, the Comanches, that's one thing, sir," said Farrow. "But the Apaches are something else entirely."

Summerhayes thought it best to intervene before Farrow said something else and really got into hot water. "The sergeant doesn't know what he's talking about—as usual," he told the aide. "I'll have a word with him."

"You do that," said the aide tersely. "Better see to it that your *friend* learns to keep a respectful tongue in his head."

Summerhayes nodded, as though he were in full

agreement. The aide rejoined his peers at the end of the porch.

"Damn, Lieutenant," muttered Farrow. "That struttin' peacock doesn't outrank you—and you let him talk to you like that?"

"Doesn't matter. Just keep your opinions to yourself. If that's possible."

Farrow was grinning again. "I'm too old a dog to learn many new tricks, sir."

"Do it anyway." Summerhayes brushed past the sergeant and entered the headquarters building. He found himself in a wide, short hallway. There was a door to the outside at the other end, and a single room on either side. The door to the room on his right was closed, and he could hear voices on the other side. Farrow took the valise from him—a small courtesy.

"I was ordered to report immediately to your garrison commander," said Summerhayes.

"Right. That would be Major Bendix. Him and his lieutenants are in there right now with General Miles. Hole up right here for a minute and I'll see if they'll let you join in."

Summerhayes nodded, and strolled down the hall to the other door and back again. By the time he'd returned to his starting point, Farrow had knocked discreetly on the door to the room whence the voices had come, entered upon being curtly summoned, and was now emerging to give Summerhayes the thumbs-up. Summerhayes went straight in.

There were five men in the room, all officers. Three were lieutenants—troop commanders stationed at Camp Bowie. The fourth was a short, broad-shouldered man with close-cropped gray hair and a bristling mustache. Summerhayes had seen renderings of the legendary General Nelson Miles, and though he had never met the man personally, he knew immediately that this was Miles. The man Summerhayes had served under while in Apacheria had shunned all the trappings of high rank; General George Crook had not even bothered to wear an army-issue tunic, opting instead for a buckskin jacket or blanket coat. But General Miles had an impressive amount of braid and a good many ribbons and medals adorning his immaculate blue tunic, not to mention the shiny general's stars on the tunic's epaulets. Miles had a barrel chest, short legs, bright dark eyes and a jutting chin—and he reminded Summerhayes of a bantam rooster.

By a process of elimination, then, he was able to presume that the fifth officer was the commandant at Camp Bowie, Major Bendix. Bendix was a tall, lanky individual with aquiline features—a hawkish nose, prominent cheekbones, gaunt cheeks, and a wide, thin-lipped mouth. When Summerhayes presented his orders, Bendix gave them a cursory going-over, and Summerhayes got the impression that this was a man who did not like to be bothered with small details.

"Lieutenant Summerhayes," murmured the commandant as he folded the orders, returned them to the pouch in which they had been transported, and tossed the pouch negligently onto a desk. "I've been expecting you. It's about time you got here. Matters are coming to a head."

Summerhayes bristled. He was as exhausted as

he'd ever been in his life, after a journey of nearly two thousand miles—by horseback, stagecoach, rivercraft, train, and wagon—from Washington.

"I got here as quickly as I could, sir."

"As I was telling General Miles, in my opinion we are on the brink of the last great Apache war."

He said it with such conviction that Summerhayes was perplexed. He'd heard nothing of an outbreak of violence in Apacheria. Nothing in the newspapers, nothing among his fellow travelers on the succession of trains he'd ridden nonstop for the past week.

"Has there been a raid, sir?" he asked. "Have some of the Apaches jumped the reservation?"

"Not yet," replied one of the lieutenants. "But it's just a matter of time, you know. As long as that troublemaker Geronimo is alive."

"Some of the ranchers in these parts have complained of someone killing their stock," chimed in another of the Camp Bowie officers.

Summerhayes was beginning to get the idea. "And you think the Apaches are responsible," he said.

"Well," said the lieutenant, with uncertainty, "not exactly, no. But who else . . .?"

Bendix abruptly intervened. "Lieutenant Summerhayes, I suspect, is about to suggest that we could be wrong in laying the blame on the Apaches. That maybe we have a rustling problem. I don't deny that there are a few gangs running irons in the territory. But they normally steal the cattle to sell for cash on the barrel head. They don't butcher the animal right on the spot and take the meat."

"If that's how it happens, then I don't doubt that Apaches are responsible," said Summerhayes. "I would hope, though, that the local ranchers wouldn't want a war to break out over a handful of cattle. The Apaches are obviously not killing the cattle to make an illegal profit. They're just trying to survive."

"The number of cattle lost is not the issue," replied Bendix curtly. "The Apaches agreed not to stray from this reserve without permission. They'll start with livestock. Then they'll become emboldened, and before you know it, you have white men dead, white women violated, and white children enslaved."

Watching Bendix, Summerhayes experienced a powerful sensation of déjà vu. Clearly, some things had *not* changed in this part of the country—particularly the attitude of most white civilians and solider towards the Apaches. As far as men like Bendix were concerned, Apaches were simply vermin that needed to be exterminated, and until such time as that end was achieved, there would be nothing but trouble in the territory. Any trouble that did arise could almost automatically be laid at the Apache doorstep. Summerhayes recalled the rancher named John Ward, who had occasionally lost a few head of cattle to his Apache neighbors. Ward had his brand on thousands of head, so he might have chosen to overlook the loss of a few dozen steers just to keep the peace. Peace, however, didn't matter to men like John Ward—or, apparently, like Major Bendix. The rancher had declared his own private war against the Apaches, which had escalated into an all-out conflict between red man and white throughout much of the territory. Many good men had died during that war. Summerhayes knew this to be true, since he'd been right in the middle of it. His first command in the field—and his first action—had been in defense of the Overland Stage route against marauding Netdahe Apaches led by Geronimo himself. As for John Ward, he had lost both of his children—kidnapped and murdered by the Netdahe—and then his own life before the bloodshed ceased. For his part, Summerhayes had learned a valuable lesson: In war nobody won.

General Miles seemed to sense the discord brewing among his subordinates—and stepped forward into the fray. His keen, unblinking gaze cut right through Summerhayes.

"Major Bendix has forgotten his manners, Lieutenant. We haven't been formally introduced, but I am assuming that you are Charles Summerhayes, the man my predecessor convinced the War Department to send. I understand you are an expert on the Apaches, and that you speak their language fluently."

"I was never fluent, but I used to be able to make myself understood. I haven't had much practice in the past ten years, however."

"And I'm told you know many of the Apache leaders personally."

"I knew some of the Chiricahua leaders back in those days. Some of them, like Cochise, are dead."

"How did this come about, Lieutenant, your familiarity with the Apaches?"

Alarms went off in Summerhayes' head. He knew he had to tread very carefully now. If he told the truth—the whole truth—then he risked being branded an Indian lover by these men. And one did not get on the bad side of General Miles if one cared

at all about a career. Miles was the darling of the
United States Army. The son of a Massachusetts
farmer, Miles had volunteered when the War Between the States broke out. He had been in the thick
of the action at Fredericksburg and Chancellorsville,
been wounded four times, won the Congressional
Medal of Honor, and risen to the rank of major general. After the war he had been assigned to the frontier, where he had participated in numerous
campaigns against the Indians. He had fought the
Cheyenne, the Kiowa, the Arapaho, the Lakota Sioux,
and in 1877 had commanded the force that pursued
Chief Joseph and the Nez Percé in their attempt to
escape into Canada. That much-celebrated campaign,
which culminated in Chief Joseph's surrender just
miles short of the Canadian border, had ultimately
brought Miles here to replace General George Crook.
Crook had managed to persuade the Apaches to
abide by new treaties that kept them confined to reservations, but Miles, the great Indian fighter, was the
man best suited, according to the War Department,
to deal with any problems that might arise. And
Summerhayes was aware that Washington fully expected problems with the Apaches.

He had served with Crook, and admired the man
many Indians respectfully knew as "Red Beard."
Crook had treated even those Apaches who fought
against him with respect, and he was willing to put
his trust in—and sometimes even offer his friendship
to—those who stayed off the warpath. The Apaches
had learned that Red Beard was one Pinda Lickoyi
they could trust. As far as Summerhayes was concerned, George Crook was the man most responsible

for the current state of peace that reigned in Apacheria. Why he had been replaced by Nelson Miles was a mystery.

Summerhayes had not read nor heard anything to indicate that General Miles was an Indian hater. But it was a safe bet that he would not be as sympathetic to the Apaches as Crook had been. So the last thing Summerhayes needed was to bring down on his head the animosity of Miles, or to give the general any reason to mistrust him. Unless, of course, he wanted his next assignment to be a remote outpost on the Alaskan frontier. Still, there was the little matter of integrity. Summerhayes was afflicted with a lot of that, and the more he thought about the condition of the Apaches he had seen at the Camp Bowie gate, the angrier he got.

"I have a good friend of mine to thank for that," he said in response to the general's query. His chin was raised at a defiant angle as he scanned the faces of the other officers in the room. "It may be that none of you know him by the name he used to go by."

"And what might that be?" asked Major Bendix.

"Joshua Barlow, sir. Formerly a commissioned officer. Now I understand that most people around here call him the Apache hunter."

"I've heard of him," said one of the other lieutenants. "Rumor has it that he's dead. Has been for a long time now."

"No," countered another. "He's not dead. He's down in Mexico, in the Sierra Madre, still looking for Apache renegades. Word is that every once in a while he'll come down out of the high country with an Apache carcass and the Mex government pays him a bounty, even though officially they don't offer to buy Apache scalps anymore."

"He used to be a friend to the Chiricahua," explained Summerhayes. "In fact, he became the son-in-law of Chochise. After he left the army, he ran a ranch for a while, up near the Mogollons."

"He married an Indian woman," muttered Bendix, shaking his head in disapproval.

"Yes, sir," said Summerhayes. "She was murdered by a Netdahe. Ever since then Barlow has been on the warpath. But for a time I was in charge of delivering Barlow's cattle, as part of the government's promised annuity to the Chiricahuas, to the Indian camps."

"Soldier, rancher, Apache killer, and squaw man," mused Bendix. "All your friends that colorful, Lieutenant?"

Summerhayes thought it wise to let "squaw man" go without comment. "If only they were, Major. If only they were."

"There are some who think Barlow is a deserter," said Bendix.

"Well," said Miles brusquely, "I frankly don't care what this man Barlow has done in the past. If he can be of use to us against the Apache, fine. That is why I gave Al Seiber permission to try to make contact with him."

"Al Seiber, sir?" The name was unfamiliar to Summerhayes.

"My chief of scouts," said Miles. "A Dutchman. I think he used to be a gold prospector. But I may be wrong." He shrugged, because it also didn't matter to him what Seiber—or anyone else, for that matter—had done in the past. If they could help him achieve his objective, that was all that really mattered. "Allow me to explain to you, Lieutenant, the situation that is responsible for bringing you, with your unique skills and experience, here to us."

"Thank you, sir."

Miles began to pace back and forth behind the commandant's knee-hole desk. His hands were clasped behind his back, and he gazed at the floor in front of him as he moved, glancing only occasionally at Summerhayes or one of the other men in the room. "The major is not the only one who believes we are on the eve of a major Apache outbreak. There are some in Washington—I should add, *high places* in Washington—who also believe this. And, in the two months that I have been here, I've heard many soldiers stationed here and many civilians who live here make the same prediction.

"Now you may or may not know that Geronimo currently resides among the Chiricahua. He is related in some way to the Chiricahua chief, Juh—"

"Geronimo is Juh's brother-in-law, sir," said Summerhayes. "The woman in question was killed by the Mexicans."

He regretted it as soon as the words passed his lips. Miles would not care one whit about Geronimo's murdered wife, and the comment could be construed as an attempt by Summerhayes to defend Geronimo's past actions. He wasn't trying to do that; if anything, he was hoping Miles would understand the kind of bond that had existed between Geronimo and Juh since that tragedy. If any thing, he was defending Juh's decision to provide Geronimo sanctuary among the Chiricahua.

Miles stopped pacing just long enough to give him a disapproving look. "Major Bendix reports that there are a number of the Netdahe among the Chiricahua living on San Carlos, as well. Now it is not within my purview to criticize the decisions of my esteemed predecessor, General Crook. But, to me, letting Geronimo and his killers live among the Chiricahua is akin to building a bonfire on top of a stack of powderkegs."

There was a pause—and Summerhayes, anxious to know what lay in store for him, and for the Apaches, inserted a question. "May I ask, then, what the general proposes to do?"

"I in tend to have Geronimo placed in custody. I want to remove the bad influence that lives among the Chiricahua. Do I believe this one action alone will avert an all-out war with the Apaches? I don't know. I don't know if the threat of war is as serious as the major here seems to think. But I do know that Geronimo himself is a threat, and I intend to eliminate that threat."

Summerhayes wasn't sure he liked the sound of the word "eliminate" in this context. But that was a minor issue compared to what he perceived to be a major problem with the general's plan. He glanced at Bendix and the Camp Bowie lieutenants, hoping to see in at least one face a shred of concern, but he was disappointed. So now he had a choice to make. He could keep his mouth shut and go along with the general's scheme—even though, in his opinion, it was exceedingly ill-advised—or he could recommend a more commonsense approach to the problem. If he did the latter, he ran great risks, career-wise. And, apparently, he would stand alone. None of these men were going to stick their necks out by disagreeing with General Nelson Miles. None of them were that foolish.

Once again, though, Summerhayes thought about the dirty, haggard, decrepit Apache scarecrows he had seen on his way into Camp Bowie. He had a hunch that it wasn't just Geronimo who would suffer as a consequence of Miles' plan—he really didn't care about Geronimo, and was willing to concede that the man was a troublemaker, and that both whites and Apaches would be better off if he wasn't around. Even innocent Apaches would suffer. Maybe the other men in the room didn't care about that. But Summerhayes did, and the prospect offended his sense of fair play.

"Begging the general's pardon," he said, "but the Apaches wouldn't need encouragement from Geronimo to kill a few cattle if their families were hungry. So how can we be certain that he is involved in these depredations?"

Miles stopped moving and wheeled and stared at him—and Summerhayes felt the eyes of every other person in the room fastened on him, as well. *Now you've done it*, he told himself ruefully. *You haven't been here even an hour and already you've marked yourself as an Apache lover, and there will be hell to pay from here on out.*

"You have made two erroneous assumptions, Lieutenant," said Miles coldly. "The Apaches do not have to steal cattle to keep themselves fed. The United States government provides them with an annuity of food, not to mention farming instruments so that they may grow their own food. The distribution of these goods is in very capable hands, I assure you. The problem, it seems, is that the Apaches believe that farming is beneath them. They would rather steal than expend sweat and toil to provide an honest living for themselves."

Summerhayes glanced out the window at the sun-hammered hardpack of the parade ground, and then down at the floor beneath his feet, which was covered with a patina of pale dust. He wondered how Miles expected the Apaches to farm this land. There were some arable sections of the territory; these, of course, had been grabbed up by white emigrants. The land left to the Apaches was the worst of the lot. The San Carlos agency was nicknamed Hell's Forty Acres, and there was a good reason for that. Apaches knew how to farm. They had done so for generations. But they didn't know how to farm rocks and dust, in a place where there was scarcely enough water to drink, much less irrigate.

"Your second mistake," continued Miles, "is to think that it matters whether Geronimo is involved in the killing of those cattle. That doesn't matter at all. This is merely an opportunity to remove Geronimo from the Chiricahua camp. Even if he hasn't indulged in any rabblerousing yet, one thing is certain. Sooner or later, he will. I want that man under lock and key. Watched at all times. This, it seems to me, is the only way to avoid, or at least forestall, the war that Major Bendix believes is inevitable."

"Yes, sir," said Summerhayes. "But if we ride into that Chiricahua camp and seize Geronimo by force, there *will* be trouble, General. That *is* inevitable."

"You mean from Juh."

"Not necessarily. Some Apaches have no use for Geronimo. But many admire him. Many believe he is a visionary. A prophet. They think he is a hero, of sorts, for standing up to the United States Army. They might object to our taking him away by force. They might rise up in an attempt to defend them. And then we will have instigated the war that we're trying to prevent."

Or, at least, that some of us profess *to trying to prevent,* he thought.

"Frankly," said Bendix, "I don't believe we should allow Apache feelings to dictate our actions, Lieutenant."

Miles made a curt gesture to wave away the major's comment. "Still, the lieutenant may have a valid point. Given that I am firm in my commitment to place this man Geronimo in custody, I am willing to give negotiation a chance. With that in mind—and your rather unique knowledge of the Apache, Lieutenant—you will proceed to the agency, pay a call on Juh at the Chiricahua encampment, and convince him to give Geronimo up to us. If he won't—or can't—do that, then you may, if you think the endeavor worthwhile, try to persuade Geronimo to surrender."

"Yes, sir," said Summerhayes, feeling like a condemned man who was being forced to put the hangman's noose around his own neck. Now he thought he knew why General Crook had sent for him. Old Red Beard had realized that, with the changing of the guard, there would need to be *someone* committed to maintaining the fragile peace now existing between red man and white in Apacheria. Unable to find anyone in the district who fit that bill, Crook had resorted to bringing him all the way from Washington.

"But you will *not* make any promises," warned Miles. "Juh must know—and Geronimo himself—that the surrender is unconditional."

"Yes, sir."

The general's tone became less harsh. "I am a man of war, it is true," he said. "As such, I know the value of peace. Anyone who witnessed the carnage of that terrible conflict between the states knows what I am talking about."

You don't know what carnage is, thought Summerhayes, *until you've seen what a broncho Apache on the warpath can do.*

"I will have your orders drawn up immediately," continued Miles. "You should depart for the Chiricahua camp as soon as possible. And you will take one man with you, in the event you need a post rider. Any questions, Lieutenant?"

"Just one, sir. How long do I have?"

"Not long. You have experience with the Apaches, Lieutenant, but I have dealt with a dozen different tribes, and I know that one thing is certain regardless of whether you treat with an Apache or a Lakota Sioux—they will attempt to drag out the negotiations. Then you wake up one morning to find they've pulled up stakes, or donned their war paint. Forty-eight hours. That's all the time I will give them. It's more than enough time for them to make a decision."

"Yes, sir. If it's all the same to the major, I'll take Sergeant Farrow along with me."

"Farrow," said Bendix gruffly. "He knows his way around this neck of the woods, General," he told Miles. "Knows the Apache too. I guess he ought to, since he was married to one once."

"He speaks their language too, sir," said Summerhayes. "Probably better than I do."

"Fine," said Miles, dismissively. "You'll have your orders shortly, Lieutenant, and I expect you to depart for the Chiricahua camp as soon as you get them. Good luck."

Summerhayes thanked him, saluted the general and the major, and left the room.

Farrow was waiting in the hall for him. "How'd it go in there, Lieutenant?"

"Do you have a last will and testament drawn up, Sergeant?" asked Summerhayes, as he walked briskly past the noncom.

"Wha'?" Farrow hurried after the lieutenant as the latter stepped out onto the porch of the headquarters building, squinting against the blinding glare of the hot sun.

"Don't worry about it," said Summerhayes gravely, having a little fun at the sergeant's expense. "You don't need one. You don't have anything anyone would want."

Farrow was squinting too but not because of the sun. He looked suspiciously at Summerhayes. "What are you trying to tell me, Lieutenant? Just spit it out, sir."

"Get two horses. Good ones. I'm going to the

agency to talk to Juh, and to get Geronimo to surrender. You're coming with me."

"Did you volunteer me, sir?"

"I did," said Summerhayes, fiercely trying to suppress a smile.

"Thank you, sir. I'm honored." Farrow did not try very hard to disguise the sarcasm in his tone.

"You look bored to me, Sergeant, so I thought I would do you a favor."

"Yes, sir. Two good horses. Fast ones too because I don't think we'll be bored while we're with the Chiricahua."

Summerhayes figured the sergeant was right about that.

Chapter 4

The day was on the wane as Chato approached the jacal of Geronimo. Dark shadows reached across the Chiricahua che-wa-ki located on San Carlos—the reservation that the Apaches called Hell's Forty Acres. This was Chato's favorite time, when the heat and hardships of the day were coming to an end, and his people were gathering round the cook fires with their families. Today, though, he could derive no satisfaction from the setting of the sun or the cooling of the air or the sight of the families around their fires. Foremost on his mind was the fact that there were soldiers in the che-wa-ki—and more yellow-legs on the way. The soldiers had come for Geronimo. And Chato feared that Geronimo, being the kind of person that he was, would not give himself up to the soldiers without a fight.

Not that Chato cared over much for Geronimo's fate. He was no friend to the Bedonkohe warrior who had become leader of the Avowed Killers. He had never agreed with Juh's decision to give Geronimo sanctuary among the Chiricahua, fearing that such generosity would sooner or later place the Chiricahua people in harm's way. Now he wondered if perhaps his fears were about to be realized.

He understood, though, the reason for Juh's decision. It wasn't just because Geronimo was Juh's brother-in-law, though that certainly had *something* to do with it; Juh no doubt felt obligated to assist Geronimo out of respect for the memory of his dead sister, Geronimo's wife, who had been murdered long ago by the Nakai-Ye. Part of it, believed Chato, was because Juh had always respected Geronimo as one of the true heroes of The People—one of the handful of Apache leaders who had never buckled under to the power of the White Eyes. Many Chiricahuas shared with their jefe this high opinion of Geronimo. Chato was not one of their number. Still, he kept in mind the possibility that some of his people might not stand idly by while the yellow-legs took Geronimo, their hero, away. That possibility, in fact, worried Chato most of all. He had no illusions about the outcome of a fight between the Chiricahua Apache and the Pinda Lickoyi. His people would be crushed.

As Chato drew within sight of Geronimo's jacal, he saw that a single Netdahe stood guard at the entrance. A half dozen of the Avowed Killers, fierce in their loyalty to their leader, had stayed with Geronimo during his self-imposed exile among the Chiricahua, and there was always at least one of them in close proximity to him. They stood guard over Geronimo not because they feared someone in the village would take his life; they watched over him, instead, because there were many in the che-wa-ki who wanted him to use some of his magic on their behalf. Because Geronimo had what the White Eyes called "big medicine." He sometimes had visions that foretold the future. Some said he had control over the elements. A popular story was the one in which Geronimo had caused the sun to stop for a couple of hours in its path across the sky. This—or so the story went—was so that Geronimo and his Netdahe raiders would have enough time to catch up to a fleeing patrol of Nakai-Ye soldiers, who otherwise might have succeeded in eluding the Avowed Killers under cover of darkness. Of course, there were variations on the story, including one version in which Geronimo actually hastened the passage of the sun down the western sky so that he could escape a large contingent of Mexican *federales* when night fell. Such was the way with fables, mused Chato, who did not believe that Geronimo had special powers—who believed, instead, that Geronimo cultivated such fictions because it contributed to his mystique.

Chato did not approve of Geronimo's presence in the che-wa-ki, but he liked the presence of the Netdahe even less. They had no allegiance to the Chiricahua band. At least Geronimo tried not to make trouble for his brother-in-law. The Avowed Killers were no respecters of tradition, either. So far, they had minded their manners, but only because Geronimo had told them to do so. Chato had worried since the beginning of their sojourn here at San Carlos that one or more of them would eventually act counter to Geronimo's wishes. They followed Geronimo. They were loyal to him. But that didn't mean, necessarily, that they would obey him without question in every instance.

As Chato reached the small stone-ringed fire beside which the Netdahe warrior sat, he noticed the deep, ugly scars on the man's cheeks. These were self-inflicted wounds. The marks were meant to demonstrate that the Netdahe warrior was heedless of his own welfare, and they added to the ferocity of an Avowed Killer's demeanor. The Netdahe looked up at him without expression. He did not appear to care why Chato was here. Chato noticed that he was heavily armed. The Avowed Killers were always so. This one had a repeating rifle on a sling over his shoulder, a revolver in a Mexican army holster on one hip and a sheathed knife on the other.

Sitting on his heels at the fire opposite the Netdahe, Chato said, "I need to speak with Geronimo."

He did not elaborate. He did not stress the urgency of his request. None of that would have made an impression on the Netdahe. Chato could only hope that his standing as a great warrior among the Chiricahua—a man who could legitimately claim to be one of the leaders of his band—would compel Geronimo's Netdahe gatekeeper to let him pass. But there was nothing in the Netdahe's expression to give Chato hope. The Avowed Killer said nothing in response. He merely gazed impassively at Chato for a moment. Then, abruptly, he rose in one impossibly fluid motion. As was to be expected of an Avowed Killer, this one was a superb physical specimen, forged in the crucible of a lifetime of desert warfare. It was said of the Netdahe that they could run from sunup to sundown without stopping, and without food or water.

The Netdahe went to the jacal, pushed aside the

dust-heavy blanket that covered its entrance. Chato heard him say something, but could not make out the words. Presumably he was speaking to Geronimo, informing the Bedonkohe outcast that he had a visitor. Chato had second thoughts—perhaps he should have told the Netdahe that he wanted to talk to Geronimo because the yellow-leg soldiers had come. But he was here to prevent an outbreak of violence, and telling an Avowed Killer that the bluebellies were coming did not strike him as a step in the right direction.

A moment later the Netdahe returned to the fire and resumed his position, sitting cross-legged opposite Chato. This time too he did not speak—only gave a curt sideways nod of the head to indicate that Chato could proceed into the jacal.

Since the Netdahe put such little stock in the spoken word, Chato said nothing more. He stood and moved to the jacal and, since he had already been announced, entered unbidden.

The jacal's interior was dimly lighted by a small fire. Geronimo sat near the fire, facing the entrance. Chato surveyed the shadowed recesses of the jacal to confirm that they were alone. The firelight cast Geronimo's cruel, deeply lined face in sharp relief and reflected in his small black eyes. The Bedonkohe's hair fell loose around his shoulders, and Chato noted that there was much gray among the thick black strands. Sitting there, a blanket thrown round hunched shoulders, Geronimo looked as old and weathered as the mountains.

"Chato is welcome here," said the Bedonkohe, his voice no more than a raspy whisper.

Chato took that for what it was—an invitation to sit down. "I have something important to tell you," said Chato. "Two soldiers rode into the village a little while ago. They talk now with Juh. I was there when Juh invited them into his jacal, and I heard one of the soldiers, the lieutenant, mention your name. He said they needed to talk to Juh about you."

Geronimo's body stiffened at mention of the yellow-legs. It didn't matter that the Apache and the Pinda Lickoyi were technically at peace; the United States Army was Geronimo's mortal enemy and always would be.

"Only two soldiers," he murmured.

"More are coming. Before the two got here, a scout reported a column of about twenty soldiers. They do not ride with the first two, but follow their trail."

Brooding over this information for a few moments, Geronimo sat silently gazing into the fire. Chato had more to say, and was impatient to say it, but held his tongue. Finally, Geronimo said, "I have expected this. I had a dream. I was warned that the yellow-legs were coming for me."

Chato kept his skepticism in check. It was too easy, he thought, for someone to claim to have had a vision about something they'd already been informed about.

"You should go," he said. "Leave the che-wa-ki. Take your Netdahe with you."

Geronimo gave him a long look. The corner of his knife-slit mouth curled in the semblance of a smile. "You have never wanted me here, Chato. Now you see an opportunity to be rid of me."

"I won't be sorry to see you go, it's true," conceded Chato, "because your presence among us puts every Chiricahua woman and child at risk."

"Every Chiricahua woman and child is already doomed, as long as the White Eyes remain on our land."

"You *know* you cannot defeat them."

"You cannot live in peace with them, either," retorted Geronimo. "They break the very treaties they make you sign. And yet men like you and Cochise try to live in peace with the enemy. You put your lives in the hands of people who do not want you to live. This is foolishness."

Chato sighed. He did not want to waste time engaging in a debate with Geronimo over how best The People should meet their doom. The Bedonkohe was right. It *was* foolish to depend on the integrity of the White Eyes, because they had none. Most of them did not act in good faith. But in Chato's opinion, it was *more* foolish to wage war against an enemy who could not be defeated. The whites were often easy to kill, and an Apache could take many Pinda Lickoyi lives before losing his own on the battlefield. But there were always more whites to take the place of their fallen. The same could not be said of The People. It was a matter of simple arithmetic. If one Apache perished for every ten White Eyes, then the white Eyes still won.

Leaders like Cochise—a man Chato had admired above all others for his courage and wisdom—had understood this fact, and knew it to be irrefutable. For that reason Cochise had tried to live in peace with the Pinda Lickoyi. Men like Geronimo knew the truth of it too. Only they believed that The People, since they were doomed, regardless, should die honorably, resisting the white interlopers. Chato put his faith in the first approach. His hope was that it would delay the inevitable. Every day of peace—and life—that could be purchased for Apache children was worth any sacrifice. Even the sacrifice of horror.

"Will you go?" he asked. There was no time to waste. He wasn't going to change Geronimo's mind, any more than Geronimo could change his.

"You have fought our enemies," said Geronimo. "But you have never been hunted. Never lived the life of an outlaw, as I have. I know how the yellow-legs do things. They have sent the two soldiers into our camp like dogs trying to flush a bird out of the brush. And when the bird takes flight, the others shoot it down."

"In the night you can make good your escape." No one had ever been so elusive as Geronimo. At times, hundreds of Mexican and American soldiers had been on the hunt for him. And he had never been captured.

"But I have done nothing wrong. Why should they come for me now?"

Chato shook his head. Making sense of what the White Eyes did was never an easy matter.

Geronimo stood up. "No," he said, brusquely. "I will not go—unless Juh himself asks me to."

With that he abruptly left the jacal. Chato scrambled to his feet and passed through the blanketed entrance into the deepening night in time to see Geronimo moving with long strides in the direction of Juh's jacal. His Netdahe bodyguard followed along behind. Chato grimaced. Geronimo was going to confront the two soldiers. He was going to force Juh to make a choice—either lose face by surrendering his brother-in-law to the Pinda Lickoyi, or put the lives of his people at risk by standing up to the yellow-legs. Chato had feared as much.

Reaching the vicinity of Juh's jacal, Chato saw that a crowd had congregated—perhaps as many as half of the inhabitants of the che-wa-ki stood about. They knew that something of great importance was happening inside the jacal. The word had spread quickly that two American soldiers had arrived, seeking a parlay with the Chiricahua jefe; Chato suspected that most if not all of them also knew that the soldiers were here to discuss Geronimo. They waited on the chance of learning the outcome of the talk between Juh and the yellow-legs. They were very quiet, and a pervasive tension underlay their silence. There was a ripple of surprise that passed through the crowd as Geronimo arrived on the scene, but the sound was short-lived. If anything, the Chiricahua spectators became even more quiet as Geronimo walked straight into the jacal of their jefe. Even more startling was the fact that the Netdahe warrior accompanying Geronimo followed the Bedonkohe into the jacal. It was simply a matter of demonstrating respect for any Apache to ask for permission to enter a jacal, or to at least announce one's intention of entering. This was especially the case where the jefe was concerned. But Geronimo acted as though the jacal was his own. The people, knowing the history of animosity that existed between Geronimo and the Pinda Lickoyi soldiers, became even more tense. Some, thought Chato, probably expected violence.

Under the circumstances, Chato himself acted discourteously. So apprehensive was he of Geronimo's intentions that he too entered Juh's jacal without asking permission. Once through the blanket he paused, surveying the scene. The interior was crowded. Juh, long and angular, with his gaunt cheeks iron gray hair, sat cross-legged at the fire. Across from him sat two American soldiers. One of them was a lieutenant, the other a sergeant. This Chato could immediately discern from their dusty uniforms. Off to one side sat two Chiricahua subchiefs—men who were, more or less, Chato's peers, established and respected leaders of the band. One was Dijiji, the other Naiche. By their position in the jacal, away from the fire, where Juh and the soldiers were located, Chato thought it safe to assume that they were here merely as witnesses, or observers, rather than active participants in the discussion. And then there was Geronimo and his Netdahe guardian, neither of whom had sat down by the time Chato entered.

Geronimo was staring balefully at the two soldiers. Neither of the yellow-legs, however, seemed afraid. The lieutenant steadily returned Geronimo's gaze. The grizzled sergeant, who sat beside the lieutenant, looked like he would just as soon kill the Netdahe warrior as look at him.

"I am Geronimo," said the Bedonkohe, his gravelly voice pitched low.

"I know," said the lieutenant. "I spent months chasing you some years ago, when you were leading raids against the Overland Stage."

"Are you still chasing me?"

"You're no longer running away."

Geronimo turned his gaze upon Juh. "You should have sent for me, brother. I always sit by your side at the big talk."

"Naiche is here," said Juh. "He speaks English."

Geronimo stared with disapproval at his brother-in-law. Chato was aware that the Bedonkohe jealously guarded his unofficial position as Juh's translator. He spoke English and Spanish fluently, and Juh did not. Further, Juh was afflicted with a speech impediment, and at times it seemed that Geronimo was one of the few people who knew what he was trying to say. Acting in this capacity did two things for Geronimo. It kept him informed of important matters, and it left the impression with the Chiricahua people that he was a part of the decision-making process. So far as Chato knew, Juh did not often, or ever, consult with Geronimo about things that concerned the Chiricahua.

Chato too disapproved of the way Juh was handling the situation. In his opinion, the Chiricahua jefe needed to be brutally honest with Geronimo. Needed to tell the Bedonkohe that, even though the discussion with the soldiers might determine his fate, he was not welcome to participate in it. Instead, Juh's tepid and dissembling response regarding Naiche's ability to act as translator, gave Geronimo the high moral ground.

"They have come to arrest me," said Geronimo, with haughty indignation. "Is this not so?"

Juh was reluctant to admit as much. He glanced at the lieutenant. Chato thought he remembered this officer from many years before. But he couldn't be sure.

"I'm hoping you will give yourself up," said the lieutenant, and Chato was impressed by the man's forthrightness and courage—he looked Geronimo straight in the eye as he spoke.

Geronimo sat on his heels across the fire from the soldiers. The Netdahe bodyguard remained standing behind him, his black eyes glittering like polished onyx in the firelight as he kept an eye on the yellow-legs.

"Why?" asked Geronimo. "Juh knows that I have done nothing to make him regret giving me a home among his people. I have held to the conditions he set when first I came here. I have seldom even left the village, and have never set foot beyond the reservation boundary. I have not made trouble for the Pinda Lickoyi. So why do they want to arrest me?"

The lieutenant glanced at Juh this time—a silent request for permission to answer. Juh gave an almost imperceptible nod. Chato noticed that the Chiricahua jefe could scarcely look his brother-in-law in the eye, and his opinion of Juh, which had never been high, began to sink. This yellow-leg lieutenant had more courage than the leader of the Chiricahua Apache! Chato was ashamed.

"There have been a number of raids recently," said the lieutenant calmly. "Chiricahua have killed some cattle on ranches hereabouts. Our new commander, a general named Miles, among others, believes that you are responsible. They think you've encouraged the young Chiricahua men to conduct these raids."

Geronimo smiled coldly. "It is the empty bellies of their families that encourages them to kill the White Eyes' cattle."

The lieutenant nodded, as though he commiserated. "I don't doubt that's true. And I don't doubt that you've had nothing to do with this trouble. But we're not talking about what's true and what's not. Or what's right and what's wrong."

Geronimo turned to Juh. "Did he tell you that many more soldiers are coming? Chato's scout has seen them."

"Chato sent word to me," said Juh. "The lieutenant said he did not know. I believe him."

"Yes, the yellow-legs always tell the truth," said Geronimo sarcastically.

"I didn't know," said the lieutenant firmly, "but I'm not surprised. All the more reason for you to surrender peaceably. The last thing I want is bloodshed. What about you?"

Geronimo gave him a withering look, then turned his gaze on the dancing flames of the fire. For several minutes he sat there in brooding silence, apparently oblivious to the others, and to the fact that they waited, almost breathlessly, for him to give the lieutenant his answer, because on his answer hinged the fate of the Chiricahua band.

When he finally spoke he did so slowly, softly, as though talking aloud to himself. "I was warmed by the sun, rocked by the wind, and sheltered by the trees, just like all other Apache babies. I lived peacefully until the Nakai-Ye stole the lives of the ones I loved. I did then what any warrior would do. I sought vengeance. Because of that, people began to speak badly of me. I became an outcast in my own land. I cannot eat well or sleep well. I cannot go anywhere and have a good feeling.

"I sometimes wonder if the Apache must go the way of the buffalo. The buffalo, the wolf, the Apache—must we all perish from the face of this land, which was once our own? I cannot believe that we are useless, or Ussen would not have created us in the first place. The sun, the darkness, the wind, all used to listen to what we had to say. Now, though, when we call out, nothing hears us."

He fell silent again. Several more minutes passed, and as before, no one else in the jacal moved or made a sound.

"When I was a child," murmured a pensive Geronimo, "my mother taught me to pray to Ussen for strength and health, wisdom and protection. Sometimes I prayed in silence. Sometimes I prayed aloud. And sometimes an old person prayed for all of us. In those times, we knew that Ussen listened. I was born on the prairies, where the wind blows free and there is nothing to break the light of the sun. But now the Pinda Lickoyi come, and they want to change everything, even the land itself. I think Ussen is angry at The People because we have let the Pinda Lickoyi change the land. I think that is why the wind and the mountain—and Ussen Himself—no longer listens to our prayers."

Geronimo raised his head and turned his gaze once more upon Juh. "Brother, you have given me shelter, and I thank you for it. I will not repay your kindness by bringing the wrath of the yellow-legs down upon the heads of your people. I have done nothing wrong since I came here. But then, the yellow-legs do not want to arrest me because of a few dead cattle. They are here because of what I have done in the past.

And for *those* things my enemy *should* want to kill me."

"They're not going to kill you," said the lieutenant. "I've given Juh my word that you will be delivered safe and sound to Camp Bowie, where I will see to it that charges, if any are brought, will be brought in a timely manner. You'll be given a fair trial, which is your right under our law. I will not let them keep you to languish with iron on your wrists unless they can prove a case against you."

"These are good words," said Juh gratefully. While he spoke thus to Geronimo, Naiche translated his words into English for the benefit of the soldiers.

"Yes—and you believe him," said Geronimo dryly. "I believe the lieutenant means what he says. But he does not command this situation. If he is to be believed, he did not even know that more soldiers have come to take me by force."

"You're right," said the lieutenant. "I'm not in command. I will ride out to meet the detachment. I will talk to the man who *is* in command. I will request that he come no closer to this village. That he wait until daybreak tomorrow for Geronimo to voluntarily give himself up."

All eyes turned to Geronimo. It was time, thought Chato, for the Bedonkohe to make a decision. No more talk of wind or mountain or Ussen. And Chato was pretty certain which course Geronimo would take. The Netdahe had never cared what degree of hardship or peril their actions might bring down upon the heads of peaceful Apaches. They didn't care if Apaches died, so long as enemies of The People also died. And the Netdahe philosophy had been forged by Geronimo. Chato had never believed that Geronimo's intent was to give up fighting forever. In his opinion, the man's sojourn among the Chiricahua was simply a temporary affair.

And so Chato was astonished when, after a moment more of brooding silence, Geronimo rose slowly and announced that he would surrender peaceably to the yellow-legs. Chato looked at Juh, who was obviously just as surprised—and immensely relieved. The jefe had wanted to avoid at all costs being put in the position of handing the famous Geronimo over to the soldiers. On the other hand, Chato was certain he had not been willing to take his people to war in order to defend his brother-in-law. Geronimo's decision had let him off the hook.

But Chato's suspicions where Geronimo was concerned ran deep. Was the Netdahe leader sincere? Did he have some treachery in mind? Perhaps he was just trying to fool the whites into lowering their guard long enough for him to make good an escape. Chato decided that it didn't really matter, tonight, what Geronimo's true motives actually were. What mattered was making sure Geronimo did what he said he was going to do, regardless of whether he was sincere.

"I will go with Geronimo to Camp Bowie," he said, and all eyes were turned on him. "I think the lieutenant speaks from his heart, and his words are true. He will try to keep Geronimo from harm. But he is only one man. There is only so much he can do. If I ride to Camp Bowie, that will be one more set of eyes to watch over your brother-in-law, jefe."

Juh nodded and thanked Chato profusely. All

Apaches knew that the great Bedonkohe chief Mangas Colorado had been murdered by the yellow-leg soldiers while he was in their custody. Of course, the soldiers claimed he'd been shot while trying to escape. But no one believed that for a minute. Cochise himself had once nearly met the same fate. Chato wanted to do all he could to guarantee no harm would come to Geronimo while he was a prisoner of the Pinda Lickoyi, because his murder by the White Eyes might be the one spark needed to ignite a widespread Apache uprising.

The lieutenant thanked Juh for his hospitality and said he would ride immediately to the column and return as soon as possible to report the decision of the detachment's commander. He and the sergeant left the jacal. Chato waited until Geronimo and his Netdahe guardian went outside before taking leave himself. He headed for his own jacal, burdened with a fresh set of worries. He hadn't planned on accompanying Geronimo to Camp Bowie—he hadn't expected the Netdahe leader to surrender in the first place. The offer to do so had been spur of the moment. And now he had to explain that decision to his wife. Apache women tended to be outspoken, and Chato's wife had always been even more adamantly opposed than he to Geronimo's presence among the Chiricahua. She would be thrilled to hear that the Bedonkohe troublemaker was being taken away by the soldiers, but she would *not* be happy to hear of Chato's promise to see Geronimo safely to Camp Bowie.

Fortunately for Chato, he did not have to long endure his wife's tirade. Before long a young warrior

named Massai—one of Chato's protégés—arrived
with the news that the two yellow-leg soldiers had
returned. Chato's horse was ready. He had already
said his farewells to family. He went immediately to
Juh's jacal. Another crowd had gathered. The two
soldiers were standing outside the jacal with Juh and
Naiche. But there was no sign of Geronimo. Chato
felt a knot in the pit of his stomach. He wondered if
he should have kept an eye on Geronimo. What if
the Bedonkohe had agreed to surrender only as a
ruse, to buy time in order that he might escape under
cover of darkness? This was what Chato had expected him to do; indeed, it was the very thing Chato
had suggested only hours earlier. Now, though, the
situation had changed. Now, if Geronimo had fled,
the Americans would suspect that Juh and his people
had been party to the ruse. They would be angry.
And they might take their anger out on the inhabitants of the Chiricahua che-wa-ki.

Chato was about to send Massai to Geronimo's
jacal when a murmur of excitement rippled through
the crowd. He turned to see the Netdahe leader coming forward, leading an old swayback mule. Geronimo looked ten years older than he had just an hour
or two ago. His shoulders were hunched beneath a
ragged brown serape. He wore a flat-brimmed hat
pulled low over his face. He looked beaten down,
disheveled. He looked like an old man, weary of life,
waiting for death, rather than the most feared
Apache raider of them all, the bringer of death to so
many of The People's enemies.

A profound silence fell over the watching Chiricahuas as Geronimo presented himself to the soldiers.

Most of them, mused Chato, knew that they were in the presence tonight of history in the making, and were perhaps awed by the significance of what they were witnessing. There was a tangible emotional tension running through the scene, and Chato felt the sudden urge to get Geronimo out of the che-wa-ki as quickly as possible.

"I am ready," Geronimo told the lieutenant.

"Where are your Netdahe followers?" asked the officer, giving voice to the question foremost in Chato's mind. Only six Avowed Killers had joined Geronimo in his self-imposed exile among the Chiricahua, but six Netdahe could kill a lot of people very quickly. They could ruin everything.

"I have instructed them not to interfere," replied Geronimo. "They will not surrender. But they will cause you no trouble. You have my word."

The sergeant was suspicious. "I better make sure he ain't hiding no guns or knives under that blanket, Lieutenant."

The lieutenant glanced at Juh, and then at the ring of Apache faces. "Check him later. Not here."

Chato was still wondering about the Netdahe. Would they obey Geronimo and not interfere? He wasn't sure. But he was confident that the Avowed Killers would not long remain among the Chiricahua with Geronimo gone. At least he hoped that would be the case.

He noticed that Geronimo spoke no parting words to Juh. In fact, he acted as though he wasn't even aware of Juh's presence. He was angry and disappointed, assumed Chato, that Juh had not stood up to the soldiers or been more resistant to the notion of

Geronimo's surrender. For his part, Chato had more respect for Juh than he'd ever had. Because, in a way, he had stood up to Geronimo, which was more difficult than standing up to soldiers. And he had done so for the sake of his people, even though he knew that some of his people would be critical of his decision.

The soldiers climbed aboard their horses, and Chato mounted his pony. Geronimo got on the mule. Looking at him now, one would be hard pressed to believe that this man had struck fear in the hearts of all Nakai-Ye and Pinda Lickoyi. He looked like a harmless old man, forlorn and a little ridiculous on the swayback mule.

The four of them left the che-wa-ki heading south, and had gone only a couple of miles before Chato saw dark shapes moving near a clump of man-tall ocotillo.

"Don't shoot, damn it," breathed the lieutenant, checking his horse.

"Who goes there?" The raspy whisper came from one of the shapes.

"Lieutenant Summerhayes, Sergeant Farrow. We have Geronimo with us."

The two shapes moved closer, until Chato could see, even in the gloom of a moonless night, that they were troopers, both armed with carbines held at the ready. The one in the lead spared Geronimo only a glance before moving over to Chato, who had been bringing up the rear of the party.

"So this is the famous killer Geronimo," said the trooper, sarcastically. "He don't look like all that much to me."

"I am Chato. *That* is Geronimo," said Chato.

"What'd he say?" asked the sentry.

"He said he's Chato, and that one on the mule is Geronimo," translated Farrow.

The sentry looked at Geronimo in utter disbelief. "Somebody's pulling my leg," he decided. "This old man is Geronimo? Can't be!"

The lieutenant was growing weary of the trooper's attitude. "Let's get going. You first, soldier. I don't care to be shot by some of your trigger-happy friends."

The two troopers led the way, calling softly into the darkness to alert other pickets. Chato had the eyes of a cat, but even he could see little, so dark was the night. Presently they found themselves in the midst of a large number of yellow-legs. Another lieutenant approached Summerhayes. Chato noticed that the cavalry horses were still saddled, the riders sticking close to their mounts.

"So you were right, Summerhayes," said the lieutenant, after being informed that Geronimo was in his presence. "He *did* surrender. Never thought the great Geronimo would give up so easy."

As with the trooper moments before, Geronimo completely ignored the lieutenant. Chato was sure that the Bedonkohe detected the contempt in the lieutenant's voice, but he betrayed no emotion. Acting as though his captors did not even exist was a prisoner's way of demonstrating his own contempt.

"Her didn't have many options," said Summerhayes.

The other lieutenant gave him a quizzical look. "Almost sounds like you feel sorry for him."

Summerhayes stiffened. "No, of course not."

"I *hope* not. This man is murdering scum."

Summerhayes didn't respond.

"Well," said the other, "let's get moving. I want to put a few miles between me and that Chiricahua village before we stop for the night. Juh might change his mind and decide to set Geronimo free. Sergeant, go find Corporal Stone. He's got some iron bracelets for our guest here."

Chato half-expected Summerhayes to speak out against shackling Geronimo. But once again Summerhayes said nothing. Chato had mixed feelings on the matter; he didn't like to see chains on any Apache, but he could understand why the yellow-legs would want to take such a precaution with the Netdahe leader.

He watched as the soldiers fastened the iron on Geronimo's wrists. The Bedonkohe showed no reaction, sitting motionless on his mule and staring off into the darkness as though completely oblivious to the treatment he was receiving. Their prisoner shackled, the soldiers moved out. The terrain was rugged, the going slowed further by the darkness of the night. By the time the moon rose to shed its soft silver light across the malpais, they had halted for the night. The lieutenant in charge of the detachment sent out numerous pickets. He forbade the building of fires for either cooking or warmth; as the night wore on, the temperature plummeted. Geronimo's hands had been shackled in front of his body for the duration of the night ride; now the irons were unlocked long enough to place the prisoner's hands behind his back. They were camped beneath some scrawny cottonwoods along a dry creekbed, and a stout rope was secured to the thickest of the tree trunks, then looped several times around the chain holding the shackles together. With Geronimo's back pressed against the tree, the rope was then passed several times around his waist before being tied off. The Bedonkohe legend suffered in stoic silence. Two troopers were ordered to stand guard within ten paces of the prisoner. Chato fetched his only blanket and was about to drape it over Geronimo's shoulders when one of the troopers stepped quickly forward, leveling his carbine.

"Stand clear," he rasped.

"It is just a blanket," said Chato. "He is cold."

He expected the soldier to continue with his objection, even though there was no harm in giving Geronimo a blanket, but rather because the typical yellow-leg would not want the Netdahe leader to be comfortable. He was surprised when the soldier said nothing more and backed away.

As Chato placed the blanket on Geronimo's shoulders, the Bedonkohe shrugged it off. He fastened his glistening black eyes on Chato.

"You should not be here," whispered Geronimo. "Go away."

"I will keep my word to Juh." Chato could tell that Geronimo wasn't concerned for his welfare. He just wanted to be left alone. Or perhaps he did not want Chato to witness the humiliation he was suffering now—and would suffer in the days to come.

Chato put the blanket back over the Netdahe leader's shoulders, and this time Geronimo made no attempt to remove it. He simply turned his face away from his benefactor, saying nothing more. Chato moved to a nearby tree and sat there with his back to the trunk. This was a vantage point where he could watch Geronimo and the two guards as they strolled back and forth on either side of the prisoner. The moonlight slanted like the blades of silver knives through the cottonwood canopy, and all Chato could make out were shapes. The other soldiers were scattered up and down the dry creek, and he couldn't see any of them. Off to one side a horse whickered softly. A man coughed. These men weren't talking, though. They had been instructed not to. They felt themselves to be in enemy territory, and were taking every precaution tonight to escape detection. But Chato was confident that their thoughts were on one thing: the presence of Geronimo in their midst. The yellow-legs—most of them, anyway—hated the Bedonkohe. And who could blame them? Geronimo had run circles around them for years. He had made them look like fools. And he had killed many Pinda Lickoyi. Chato thought that tonight would be the most dangerous night of Geronimo's captivity. What if one of the troopers in this detachment had lost a friend or loved one to the Netdahe? Would he seek vengeance against Geronimo? Once he was confined in the guardhouse at Camp Bowie, he would be more difficult to reach. Until then, Chato intended never to take his eyes off Geronimo. He was tired, but that didn't matter. He wasn't going to let Geronimo meet the same fate as Mangas Colorado.

He remained vigilant through the long night. When dawn light began to insinuate itself beneath the cottonwoods, Chato stood up and stretched. Geronimo's chin was resting on his chest; he seemed to be still asleep. There were still two sentries standing watch over him—two different troopers, since the guard had changed a few hours ago. Chato looked around, and was startled to see Lieutenant Summerhayes sitting against a tree not twenty paces away. Summerhayes saw Chato looking at him, gave a curt, embarrassed nod, and got quickly to his feet, brushing off the seat of his trousers. He gave the waking camp a long survey, his gaze ending up on Geronimo. Then he turned and moved away through the trees. Chato realized that the lieutenant had engaged in his own all-night vigil, watching over the prisoner. He didn't want anything to happen to Geronimo, either, and Chato presumed it was because he understood the possible consequences. So at least there was *one* yellow-leg who truly desired peace over war.

Noncoms moved through the rest of the camp, waking the troopers with well-placed kicks and whispered epithets. The lieutenant in charge had ordered the detachment on the move at once. There would be no morning cook fires allowed. No time for breakfasts of beans and hardtack and coffee. Geronimo was freed from the tree, and his hands were shackled, once more, in front of him—this, so that he could at least grasp the mane of the swayback mule while riding. Before the sun had completely risen they were on their way again. Chato calculated that, unless something happened, they would reach Camp Bowie in the middle of the afternoon.

Something *did* happen.

They had traveled only a mile or so when the Net-

dahe struck. The Avowed Killers literally rose up out
of the ground and attacked the column. It was an
old Apache trick—and a highly effective one. The
ambushers dug shallow holes, lay down in them, and
covered themselves with dirt. They breathed through
hollow cactus stems, waiting until they felt the vibra-
tions through the earth that told them that their prey
was close at hand. The sudden appearance of Apache
warriors caught the yellow-legs completely by surprise. Netdahe pistols and rifles spat flame and
smoke and noise; one cavalry mount went down
screaming in agony, and four other saddles were instantly emptied.

Chato rode near the head of the column, directly
behind Geronimo, who was flanked by a pair of
troopers. In front of Geronimo were the two lieutenants, a sergeant named Farrow, and a corporal. Geronimo acted as soon as the first shot was fired. One
of his guards was looking away, but the other had
the presence of mind to bring his carbine to his
shoulder and aim it at the prisoner. Moving faster
than the eye could follow, Geronimo grabbed the
barrel of the short rifle. Instead of pulling, as the
trooper expected him to do in an attempt to wrest
the weapon from his grasp, Geronimo gave it a hard
shove, and the butt of the carbine caught the trooper
a glancing blow across the left eye and temple. The
stunned and half-blind trooper fell sideways off his
horse, leaving Geronimo in possession of the rifle.
The Bedonkohe didn't waste precious seconds turning the gun around in his hands; instead, he used it
like a club on the other trooper, smashing the stock
into kindling as he struck with enough power to

shatter the soldier's skull. The man died sitting up in the saddle; his body convulsed, went limp, and slipped off the horse.

All of this took mere seconds, and Chato was momentarily paralyzed by shock. He had never seen the Netdahe in action before, though he had heard many stories involving their prowess in the art of killing. Now he could see it with his own eyes. After the first few volleys, they moved amongst their prey, fleeting figures in the dust and powder smoke, taking full advantage of the confusion their initial attack had wrought. The cavalry mounts were spinning and colliding; the few cavalrymen who had recovered sufficiently from their surprise to even think about trying to fight back had their hands full getting the horses under them in hand. Chato saw one Netdahe leap like a mountain lion onto the back of a turning cavalry mount and in one quick, violent motion slash the rider's throat. As soon as the trooper fell away, the Netdahe vaulted into the vacated saddle, kicked the horse into a forward leap, and drove the knife to the hilt into the back of another mounted soldier. Then, aware that he made too great a target aboard the horse, the Netdahe jumped to the ground and vanished once more into the melee.

The roar of a rifle in his ear jerked Chato's head around. Geronimo had given up the swayback mule and was now astride the horse of the man he had just killed. He no longer looked at all like a frail, defeated old man as he drew a carbine from its saddle stock and took aim at the officers. Finally Chato acted. He lashed out and struck the carbine's barrel aside just as Geronimo fired a shot that, but for

Chato's intervention, would have struck the detachment's commander squarely between the shoulder blades. Geronimo shouted a furious curse and struck back. The length of the carbine barrel caught Chato across the chest with such force that it sent him somersaulting off the back of his horse.

Dazed by the impact with the ground, Chato nonetheless saw Geronimo spin his horse back around, just as the detachment's commander, who was also turning his horse, took aim at the Bedonkohe with a pistol. They fired simultaneously at nearly point-blank range. The detachment commander dropped the pistol and clutched his throat with both hands. But that wasn't enough to prevent the shower of blood that gushed from his severed carotid. He fell to the ground, to thrash helplessly for a few agonizing seconds before death claimed him.

Summerhayes was preoccupied with a Netdahe who, rising up out of the ground, had killed the corporal outright before carrying Sergeant Farrow out of the saddle with a great leap. As the Avowed Killer plunged a knife into the sergeant's chest, Summerhayes fired down from his horse. But the Netdahe was already moving, and the bullet merely grazed his shoulder. Rising as he spun around, the Netdahe brandished a pistol—Farrow's pistol, taken from the dying man's side holster in the blink of an eye. Chato felt a fist-sized rock under his hand; without thinking about what he was doing, he hurled the stone at the Netdahe, who was no more than three strides away. The rock found its mark, striking the Avowed Killer in the side of the head and knocking him off balance even as he fired. Summerhayes fired at the same time—and missed. Even though thrown off by the rock, the Netdahe didn't miss. Not entirely. His bullet caught Summerhayes high in the shoulder. The impact twisted the lieutenant's body around; he involuntarily jerked the reins, turning his horse. The Netdahe disappeared into the cloud of battle. Chato got to his feet, still gasping for air after the fall, and reached the lieutenant's horse. He grabbed Summerhayes by the belt and pulled him out of the saddle, then dragged the wounded man into a narrow space between two slabs of sandstone. Crouching there for a moment, Chato noted that the din of battle was fading fast. He was aware that, as an Apache, he was a target for any trooper who saw him. The wisest course for him would be to slip away in the confusion. But he wasn't going to leave the lieutenant. This man Summerhayes had treated his people with respect. A White Eyes who did that was a rarity, and needed to be preserved, if possible. So Chato waited, crouching among the rocks, sheltering the half-conscious yellow-leg lieutenant, as the shooting died out, and then saw Geronimo, on foot, a cavalry carbine in one hand, the reins of a cavalry mount in the other, approaching through the diminishing smoke.

Geronimo saw him, but went first to the bodies of the detachment commander, the sergeant, and the corporal, all of which lay in a heap nearby. He prodded them with the toe of his n'deh b'keh, and then aimed the carbine at the head of the sergeant and pulled the trigger. Chato presumed that the sergeant had been still alive—the Netdahe leader would not waste a bullet on a dead man. Only then did Geronimo walk over to Chato. He looked past the Chiricahua at the lieutenant—and levered another round into the carbine's breech. Chato rose and positioned himself between the Bedonkohe and Summerhayes. For a moment they stood there, their eyes locked, Chato defiantly meeting Geronimo's fierce gaze. He noticed, even so, that the chain holding the Bedonkohe's shackles together had been shot apart. Geronimo was free—and many were going to suffer as a consequence.

"Why do you protect the enemy of your own people?" asked the Bedonkohe. "Stand aside."

"He is not my enemy," rasped Chato furiously. "*You* are."

Now that he'd had a few moments to reflect on what had transpired, Chato understood that it had all been a ruse, yet another bloody scheme dreamed up by this Bedonkohe trickster. He realized that Geronimo had never intended to surrender to the Pinda Lickoyi. Instead, he had lured them into an ambush. He had planned this bushwhacking all along. And in so doing, he had imperiled the Chiricahuas. Chato was furious.

Geronimo understood perfectly why Chato was defying him. He shrugged, indifferent to Chato's hatred—and indifferent to the plight of the people who had given him sanctuary all this time.

"Come with me, Chato," said the Bedonkohe. "You will have to fight the White Eyes now, even if you don't want to. Fight at my side, and you might live longer."

"No. I will go back to my people, and tell them of your treachery." *And try to prepare them for what is about to happen,* he thought, as he glanced past Geronimo to see the other Netdahe, roaming through the dead troopers and carcasses of horses. He wondered if any of the yellow-legs had escaped. How long would it take for the soldiers at Camp Bowie to learn of this ambush? How long before they came, in force, to the Chiricahua che-wa-ki?

One of the Netdahe approached, dragging a wounded soldier. The trooper was cursing a blue streak and clutching his bullet-shattered leg with both hands. He was covered in his own blood, and too weakened and crippled by the wound to put up an effective resistance.

"We found one who will live" was the Netdahe's dispassionate report to Geronimo.

"Good. We will take him." Geronimo looked at Chato, and smiled coldly as he lowered the carbine. "Keep your lieutenant, then. Stay here and die. We go to the Cima Silkq, and anyone who wants to join us and fight the enemy of the Chi-hinne is welcome to join us there."

"What about him?" asked Chato, nodding in the direction of the wounded trooper, who was presently being dragged away by the Netdahe warrior.

"Tonight they will kill him," said Geronimo. "Slowly. We will leave what is left on the trail for those who will be coming after us to find. When they see what has happened to him, maybe they will become less interested in catching us."

Chato watched the soldier, knowing that the man faced hours of torture before the bittersweet release of death. But there was nothing Chato could do about that. So he stood there, beside the man he hoped he *could* save, and watched Geronimo and the Netdahe, with their single captive, ride north. All of the Avowed Killers were astride cavalry mounts. These were far better horses than any an Apache could keep on San Carlos. Besides, the stolen mounts were all shod—which might make it more difficult for those who would pursue the Netdahe to distinguish their sign from another. Geronimo knew all the tricks. He left nothing to chance. Chato wondered how long it would take—and how many people would die—before Geronimo was once more in chains.

Chapter 5

When the Apache hunter rode into Santo Domingo, it was much as he had remembered it. Here was the same collection of modest—and, in some cases, miserable—adobe huts lining either side of a broad street of deeply rutted hardpack. The town was as unchanging as the malpais in which it was located. The Apache hunter supposed that the place had looked like this a hundred years ago, possibly even *two* hundred years ago. And it would look much the same a hundred years from now. He wasn't sure if that was a good thing or not.

Twice before his life's path had taken him through Santo Domingo. The first time, he had come in the company of a General O. O. Howard, a man representing the United States on a mission to strike a peace settlement with the Apaches. Howard had been a strange man, at least in the Apache hunter's opinion—the hero of several of the Civil War's bloodiest conflicts, a committed pacifist, and that rarity among white men, someone who preferred to treat Indians as equals.

It was during that first visit to Santo Domingo that the Apache hunter had met the young woman named

Angevine. She lived there with her young son. Though she was married, her husband had long been absent, and the Apache hunter had arrived, that first time, to find her the recipient of a lot of unwanted attention from Mexican troops. He'd intervened then—and again when, on his second visit, he discovered that Angevine's prodigal husband had returned, a man who was one half of a two-man scalphunting team that was holding Angevine—indeed, the entire town of Santo Domingo—hostage. The Apache hunter had killed both Angevine's husband and his partner, not just for her sake, or Santo Domingo's, but also because the two men had by the practice of their bloody vocation started an Apache war in which many innocents had died, including the Apache hunter's wife.

The town of Santo Domingo had hailed him as its savior. And Angevine had been grateful—one might say *more* than grateful. But while he'd been aware of her interest in him, the Apache hunter had not reciprocated. He was only just then beginning his new career as a killer of the Netdahe, and his grief over the loss of his beloved Oulay—a grief so strong that it almost choked the life out of him every time he thought of his slain Apache bride—was too fresh for him to even contemplate starting a new life with someone else. So he had gone away from Santo Domingo and never returned, until this day. Thoughts of Angevine had occasionally intruded in the interim. Occasionally he had thought about what it would be like to lead a peaceful life shared with someone he loved, and who loved him. But he'd had that once. His days with Oulay had been too few, yet he was grateful for them, aware that many men never knew such bliss, even for a day.

As he rode into Santo Domingo he wondered if Angevine—or any of the other villagers—would recognize him. Many years had passed. But such people normally lived and died in the villages of their birth, so many of those who had celebrated his killing of the scalphunters would still be here. The Apache hunter hoped they would not know him. Though he'd paid no attention to his appearance over the years, he was fairly certain that he was much changed.

The response of the villagers to his arrival was encouraging. They simply disappeared. The Apache hunter was amazed by how adept the Mexican peasant was at remaining out of sight and out of mind when danger loomed. Under normal circumstances, the villagers would have been the most gracious of hosts. They were a people generous to a fault. Though poor, they would give a welcome guest all that they possessed. That none came out to greet the Apache hunter as he rode down the one short, wide, dusty street of Santo Domingo was all the proof he needed that none knew him for who he was. Or rather, who he had been. Most of all, he hoped he would not run into Angevine or her son. He had a feeling that she might be the one person in the village who would recognize him regardless of all the changes that years as a manhunter had wrought upon him. It wasn't that he didn't want her to see him in his present condition. Or that she might in some way reveal that she'd forgotten all about him. Or that he was afraid to see how unkindly the years must have treated her. Rather, he simply didn't want any fresh, face-to-face reminders of how differently it all might have turned out.

As he rode through the seemingly deserted town, and drew near the well that marked the central square, or *zocalo,* he saw no sign of the man he had come to meet, the scout named Tom Horn. They had never met, but the Apache hunter didn't think recognizing Horn would be too difficult to spot in this environment. If Horn was an army scout, a hunter of Apaches too, then he would also have about him an aura of danger. The inhabitants of Santo Domingo would, if at all possible, avoid him like the plague, as well. The zocalo was the logical place to meet, or to wait for someone; a few scrawny cottonwood trees provided the only decent shade in town. Yet there was no sign of Horn, and the Apache hunter considered the possibility that communication had broken down somewhere along the way, and that Horn might not be coming at all.

At the well he checked his horse, gave the town a long, careful scrutiny, and dismounted. The wolf-dog put its front paws on the rim of the well and looked down into the cool dark hole, smelling water, and wanting some. The thirsty horse whickered softly. The Apache hunter dropped the well bucket, waited until the rope drew taut, signifying that the bucket had filled, and then cranked it up. The wolf-dog drank first. When its thirst was slaked, it circled the well with its nose to the ground, familiarizing itself with myriad new spoor, before finding a cool place under a tree whence it could keep an eye on the Apache hunter as well as most of the zocalo. The

Apache hunter let his horse drink a little before up-ending the bucket and pouring the rest of the brack-ish well water over his head. The cool wetness was a pleasant shock after long days of travel across the sun-hammered malpais. Life's little pleasures were few and far between, and he was lured by the pleas-ant sensation of the cool water to close his eyes for a moment. The wolf-dog's growl—so low that it was barely audible—alerted him. His eyes snapped open, and he beheld the small boy standing in front of him. The boy could not have been more than seven or eight years old. The well was taller than he, and, in fact, it was the well that had blocked his view of the wolf-dog. He too had heard the warning growl, and the sound had stopped him in his tracks.

"Buenos dias," said the Apache hunter.

The boy didn't speak. He simply gaped at the wolf-dog, which was on its feet now, head down, tongue hanging out of its mouth between inch-long canine teeth.

"Don't be afraid," said the Apache hunter. His Spanish was as fluent as his Apache. It was his native language that he wondered sometimes if he'd forgot-ten how to speak. "Fear makes him angry, because he doesn't understand it. He doesn't know you're just a boy. He just knows that you're a stranger."

The boy's eyes widened, and the Apache hunter detected the slightest movement of his narrow shoul-ders as he started to turn.

"Don't ever run," warned the Apache hunter. "He'll chase you if you run. That's his nature."

The boy obeyed. He stood there, rigid and trembling, not wanting to look at the wolf-dog but compelled to do so just the same. The Apache hunter looked at the beast and then at the boy—and swept the latter off his feet and onto a shoulder.

It was an action that caught the wolf-dog by surprise. Uncertain, it backed away. At the same time, the people of Santo Domingo appeared suddenly, as if by some kind of magic, in the square. They came from all directions, women as well as men. Some carried machetes or shorter knives, and all of them looked grim and resolute. The Apache hunter sensed immediately that he was in danger. But it took him a moment to figure out why.

The approach of the two dozen or so villagers alarmed the wolf-dog. Hackles up and tail held high, it circled the Apache hunter a few times, making a deep, huffing sound that indicated a high state of agitation. Seeing no escape route through the closing cordon of villagers, it took up a position on the Apache hunter's left side, and began to issue a series of warning growls.

The appearance of the wolf-dog—and of the man who traveled with it—caused the villagers to falter as they drew near the well. No one seemed eager to lead the charge. The Apache hunter scanned the dark faces encircling him, and spotted one woman whose expression answered the question foremost in his mind.

He put the boy down. "There's your mother," he said. "Go to her."

His release of the boy caught the villagers off guard. They exchanged glances and muttered comments, trying to figure out what to do next, as the boy ran into his mother's waiting arms. Santo Domingo had seemed deserted only moments before, but many eyes had been watching the Apache hunter's progress through the town. They had seen him grab hold of the boy—and that had brought them out of hiding. Concern for the boy's welfare superseded worries about their own safety. The Apache hunter instinctively understood that holding on to the boy as though he were a hostage or a human shield, if he had been the sort who might stoop to such a thing, would have been a deadly mistake. These people were fatalists, above all. They would assume that the boy was as good as dead, and their priority then would be to kill the stranger before he could harm another of their number.

The Apache hunter waited for the villagers to make the next move. He would defend himself if need be, but he didn't want to fight these people. He was worried, though, about the wolf-dog. The beast might attack at any moment. And then what would he do? Fight in defense of the half-wild animal? The wolf-dog would do—*had* done—no less for him.

One of the men who was armed with a cane knife took it upon himself to step forward—just one step closer to the stranger, no more.

"What do you want here, senor?" he asked.

"I'm not looking for trouble."

"There is trouble everywhere."

"Just came to meet someone. Another gringo. After that, I'll be moving on."

"There are no gringos here."

"There is one," piped up another man.

The others looked at him.

"*Es verdad,*" insisted the other man. "I saw him, last night, down at the cantina."

"You have a cantina here now?" asked the Apache hunter, surprised.

"A man—he is not one of us—came last year and took over a place down by the arroyo," said the villagers' spokesman. "He sells mescal and cheap whiskey."

"Why here?"

"Because we are near the border, senor," replied the spokesman, regretfully. "Many Mexican patrols pass through here now. And even some American soldiers."

"American patrols?" The Apache hunter was skeptical.

"*Sí.* This gringo you look for, you may find him at the cantina, if what Pedro says is true. But when he drinks, Pedro sees many things that aren't really there."

Some of the people in the crowd laughed. The Apache hunter was glad to hear the sound. It meant the tension was easing. He glanced down at the wolf-dog. The beast could sense the same thing, and looked somewhat less inclined to rip out a stranger's throat than he had a moment earlier.

"This beast," said the spokesman. He too was looking at the wolf-dog—with a great deal of dread. "Why do you travel with *el lobo,* senor?"

"Because we get along." The Apache hunter took up the reins of his horse. "I'll go along now and take a look down at the cantina."

The spokesman turned and spoke to the other villagers, who made way for the Apache hunter, who led his horse away from the well. The wolf-dog followed, glowering suspiciously at the crowd with his yellow-gold eyes. They were just about through the throng, and the Apache hunter was on the verge of breathing a sigh of relief, when a young man stepped in front of him. The Apache hunter thought he looked vaguely familiar, but couldn't place him.

"I know you," said the young man. "Don't I?"

The Apache hunter recognized him then. It was Manuel. Angevine's son. All grown-up. A stark reminder of just how many years had passed since last the Apache hunter had been in Santo Domingo. The Apache hunter had been thinking that at least some good had come from the confrontation in the square, since it had seemed that no one recognized him as the man who had rescued the village from a pair of scalphunters all those years ago. Now he knew he's been wrong.

"No," he lied, inscrutable. "You don't know me."

He spoke gruffly, as though impatient with this delay, and promptly pushed the young man aside and continued on his way. He caught himself wondering about Angevine. Was she here, in the square, somewhere? Had she changed at all? Had she found another man? It was all he could do to refrain from looking for her. Instead, he kept his head down and used long strides to carry him out of the zocalo.

The old cantina was located on the outskirts of the village, in an old adobe hut a stone's throw from a dry creekbed. At first glance the location didn't make much sense—why open a cantina out in the middle of nowhere? But the Apache hunter could see that nearby was a place where travelers could cross the steep-banked arroyo with relative ease. On one side, a narrow wagon trail led from rim to bottom, then angled across to a ravine, which provided access to the rim on the other side. Occasional flash floods had carved the arroyo deeply into the plain. The Apache hunter had not passed this way in quite some time, and so could not be certain, but he thought it likely that there was not a more convenient crossing for many miles in either direction.

He saw a single horse, a wiry black-and-white paint pony, ground-hitched a few yards from the cantina, and wondered if it belonged to the man he'd come to see. Approaching the adobe from the backside, he dismounted and drew his long gun from its saddle scabbard. Keeping all of his weapons close at hand had become a deeply ingrained habit. He noticed that the wolf-dog was sniffing at the air, no doubt picking up the stench of whiskey. With a quick—and, the Apache hunter imagined, reproachful—glance at its hukman companion, the beast then headed out into the malpais at a lope. It knew from past experience, mused the Apache hunter, that whenever they got close to a cantina there would be plenty of time to get a little hunting in before they moved on. Ruefully, the Apache hunter watched the wolf-dog disappear into the brasada; then he racked the repeating rifle on a shoulder and circled around to the cantina's entrance.

He entered and moved immediately to one side. This was habit too, derived from familiarity with cantinas and the sort of trouble that tended to gravitate to such establishments. The sideways movement kept him from being silhouetted for more than an instant against the bright daylight flooding through the door, which would have made him an easy target for someone inside. That shaft of daylight was the only illumination available, and yet the interior of the cantina remained wrapped in gloom. With his back against the wall, he waited a moment to let his vision adjust to the dimness. A tall, cadaverous Mexican stood behind the bar—a bar composed of a couple of weathered planks laid across a pair of barrels. The unlit stub of a cigar was clamped between the bartender's discolored teeth. The only other occupant of the cantina sat at a lopsided table in a back corner, a corner that the daylight coming through the door failed to reach, and where the deepest shadows lingered. This man was dressed like a gringo cowboy— a faded red checkered shirt, a yellow bandanna, leather chaps strapped to his trousers, and a high-peaked Montana hat. The battered brim of that hat was curled down low over his eyes. He had his feet propped up on the table, and shiny, big-roweled Chihahuan spurs stood in sharp contrast to his down-at-heel boots. A six-gun rode on the man's hip, and a Sharps .50 caliber Leadslinger lay across the table in front of him. It was the rifle of a man who preferred to do his killing from a distance. This, thought the Apache hunter, had to be Tom Horn.

"Hello, Barlow," said Horn, without looking up.

Hearing the name startled the Apache hunter. It sounded foreign to his ears.

Horn swung his legs off the table and kicked a vacant chair out. "Have a seat. And a drink."

There was a jug on the table, along with two

glasses. One of the glasses was half full of a cloudy liquid. The other one was empty. Horn picked up the jug and held it so that it rested on the back of his arm as he filled the empty glass to the rim. He chuckled—a soft and rasping sound—as he poured.

"Glad you finally showed up, pardner. That barkeep yonder's been thinkin' I'm plumb loco. Every day for three days now I've come in here and asked for two glasses."

The Apache hunter moved cautiously closer. That was pulque in the glass, the fermented juice of the agave plant, and he had acquired a taste for pulque above all the other strong spirits widely available in Mexico.

"Here's to better days," said Horn, and raised his glass. He kept it raised until the Apache hunter had picked up the other one. Only then did he knock the pulque back in one quick, violent motion, gasping as the liquid fire seared his throat and exploded in his belly. The Apache hunter took a cautious sip, followed by a long drink of his own.

"Some people think you're dead," continued Horn, offering the jug.

"Not just yet." The Apache hunter moved the chair so that he could sit with his back to a wall. From this vantage point he could see, from the corner of his eye, the cantina entrance as well as the bartender. The latter hadn't moved—he was still standing behind the bar, watching his two gringo patrons across the room.

"Well, ol' Seiber will be glad to hear it," said Horn. "Last thing he said to me was 'Tom, we need that man's help more than ever now.' And he's right. On

account of this new general of ours don't know horse
apples about fightin' Apaches. And it looks like we're
in for a big scrape. The last great Apache war. Which
is why, I reckon, they sent the great Nelson Miles to
run the show."

The Apache hunter appropriated the jug and filled
his glass. "What are you talking about? Have the
Apache left San Carlos?"

"Well, that's right. You don't know. How could
you? There's been trouble around San Carlos.
Apaches killin' cattle and what not. The thinkin' is
that Geronimo is behind it. That he's gettin' tired of
sittin' on his hands bein' a good boy with the Chiricahua, and that he's plannin' a big breakout. They expect him and his renegades to jump the reservation
any day now. Seiber thinks that when it happens the
Apaches will hightail it down to the Sierra Madre.
And General Miles is gettin' all set to go after 'em
when it happens."

The Apache hunter was skeptical. "Last time I
checked, the Sierra Madre are in Mexico. And American soldiers aren't too welcome down here."

Tom Horn cocked his head to one side and gave
the Apache hunter a quizzical look. "It's this new
treaty, hoss. They call it the Hot Trails Treaty. The
thing was just signed by Mexico and the United
States, couple of months ago. Good timing, if you
ask me. Guess there aren't a whole lot of people
dumb enough to believe that the Apaches would be
have themselves forever. Now the way I hear it, this
new treaty paper lets the United States Army cross
over into Mexico and stay as long as it needs to, just
so long as it's after Apaches. So it looks like we'll be

headin' down to the Sierra Madre someday soon, and word is nobody—no white man, anyway—knows those mountains like you do. And that, pardner, is why we're both here."

The Apache hunter finished off his second glass of pulque while Horn refilled his own. The potent liquor was soothing his nerves, taking away the aches and pains of a long trail.

"But I ain't introduced myself," said Horn. "Name's Tom Horn. I work for Al Seiber as a scout. Used to be a cowpoke, among other things. This kind of work suits me better. There's me and that worthless breed, Mickey Free." Horn grinned as he said it, and the Apache hunter gathered that, in truth, Horn didn't think this man Free was worthless at all. "There also used to be about twenty, twenty-five Apaches who worked for Seiber. Mostly White Mountains, with a few Coyoteros and a Mescalero or two thrown in for good measure. But not anymore. Just the three of us now. Mickey Free, me, and Al Seiber."

"How come?"

"Because the great and glorious General Nelson Miles is a fool—that's how come."

"He got rid of the Apache scouts."

"Sent every last one of 'em packin'. Said they couldn't be trusted to fight their own kind."

The Apache hunter scoffed at that. "Apaches have been fighting each other since the beginning of time."

"Thank God for small favors. If all the bands ever got together we'd have hell to pay, sure as shootin'."

The Apache hunter nodded agreement. The pulque

was beginning to have an effect on him, clouding his thoughts, thickening his tongue.

"Why did they replace George Crook with this man Miles?" he asked.

Horn shrugged. "I guess it was 'cause ol' Crook was thought to be too friendly with the Indians."

"Crook is why you've had peace with the Apaches all these years."

"That ain't the way the big augurs up in Washington see it. They look out west here and they see all the Indian problems have been resolved—except for the Apaches. The Lakota Sioux, the Comanche, the Nez Percé, all of 'em conquered. Then they look at the Apaches and they see more bloodshed comin'. And I think this time they're right. The Apaches are altogether different from the others. So here comes General Miles. He chased Chief Joseph and the Nez Percé all over the north country, so they figure there's nobody better to handle the Apache situation. Anyway, all you got to do is ride up to Camp Bowie with me—it's not more than two days from here— sign a piece of paper, and pick up your first month's wages. Forty dollars. Better'n you can make pushing cows, I can tell you. Then we'll just sit back and wait for hell to start a-poppin'."

"No, thanks."

Horn was taken aback. "You're turnin' down the job?"

"That's right."

"You never intended to sign on, did you? Then why'd you come all this way and waste my time?"

"Just curious to know what was going on."

Horn had the look of a man who knew he had just been taken advantage of. "So you're fightin' your own private war against the Apaches, and you don't want the United States Army buttin' in—is that it?" He nodded to himself. "Yeah, I've heard stories about you, Barlow. How you gave up a soldierin' career to take up with an Apache squaw, and how when she got killed by a broncho Apache, you vowed to kill every one of them you could find."

"Shut up, Horn." The Apache hunter felt the anger rising within him. He didn't want the memories dredged up. He drank to forget them, after all.

But Horn didn't heed the warning. "Mebbe that Apache buck killed her 'cause he thought she had no business warmin' the blankets of a White Eyes. Not that I fault you. I've had me one or two Injun gals, and they sure do turn into wildcats when the sun goes down. Thing is, nothin' lasts forever. You lose one, you get another. I wouldn't spend my whole life—"

The Apache hunter wasn't in the habit of issuing two warnings. He overturned the rickety table, shoving it sideways to get it out of the way as he lunged straight at Horn. But the army scout was quick. He grabbed the jug of pulque before it could slide off the table and tried to smash it into the Apache hunter's skull. The latter threw his arm up just in time to deflect the blow; the jug shattered against his shoulder, drenching him with pulque. Still, the impact was enough to throw him off balance. He lost his balance and fell. Horn was quick to seize the advantage, kicking him in the chest. The Apache hunter sprawled backward, the wind knocked out of him. Sucking air

into his anguished lungs, he saw that Horn had brandished a knife and was moving in; the six-shooter
was still at his hip, but apparently he didn't think he
would need it. The Apache hunter lashed out with a
kick of his own, knocking Horn's legs out from under
him. Horn fell clumsily. The Apache hunter managed
to get to his feet, grabbing the chair he had been
sitting in a few seconds before, and swinging it over
his head, brought it down on Horn. Or, at least,
where Horn *had* been. The army scout rolled out of
the way and scrambled to his feet. The chair smashed
into so much kindling on the cantina's puncheon
floor. Crouching with his back to the wall, Horn
groped for his pistol now. The Apache hunter had
nothing left in hand but one of the chair legs. That
was enough. He brought it down on Horn's gun arm,
then heard the bone crack a heartbeat before Horn
bellowed in pain. The pistol fell from numbed fingers. The Apache hunter swung the chair leg again,
this time at Horn's head, and connected squarely.
Horn went down like a poleaxed steer.

Still heaving for air, still befuddled by too much
pulque, the Apache hunter stood there a moment,
staring down at the unconscious man. Belatedly he
remembered the bartender and turned to see what
the Mexican was doing. He found himself face-to-
face with a short, stocky man with broad, coarse Indian features. He caught a glimpse of a blue army-
issue tunic, loincloth, Apache desert moccasins and
a flat-brimmed hat. He also caught a glimpse of the
pistol in the man's hand, an old Walker Colt, just as
it came down on his head.

His world went black.

He came to with something cool and wet against his face. Instinctively he reached up to feel it—and touched a warm, soft hand. His eyes opened, slowly focused on a face he remembered all too well. The years had been kind to her. She hadn't changed at all. She smiled at him, a trembling smile. She was relieved that he had regained consciousness, but nervous too, having anticipated this moment for some time, without knowing what to expect.

"How did I get here?" he asked, his voice a croaking travesty of its former self.

"Manuel. He followed you to the cantina. When the two men left, he went in and found you lying on the floor, and brought you here to me."

The Apache hunter remembered now—the short, stocky man with the Indian features and the army tunic, the big, heavy old Walker Colt crashing down on his head. He tried to sit up—and the pain lanced through his skull and down his spine, and he nearly blacked out. Her hands on his shoulders, Angevine pushed him gently down.

"You must rest," she said. "You are still bleeding."

He touched his head, and found that she had put a dressing on him.

"You will be safe here," she said.

He didn't tell her that he wasn't safe anywhere. He didn't know what to say to her. Sensing that he was growing increasingly uncomfortable in a silence of his own making. Angevine smiled.

"When we first met, you did not speak Spanish very well. But now you do."

"I've spent a lot of time here in Mexico."

She nodded. "You are the one they call the Apache hunter. I always thought it had to be you."

As usual, he was at a loss for words. How could he explain that even though he had spent so many years in Mexico, he'd not once come by to see her— even though she had often been on his mind? It made absolutely no sense to him, so there was no reason to think he could explain it so that it made sense to her.

He turned his head, studying his surroundings— the interior of a one-room adobe. There were a small fireplace and a small trestle table fashioned from cedar logs split down the middle. There was a plain curtain in one corner, partially drawn so that he could see a narrow bed beyond. He assumed the bed he was occupying belonged to Manuel.

"Your son," he said, seizing on a topic that would be easier for him to discuss. "He's all grown-up. He was just a boy when I—" He stopped suddenly, aware that he'd brought the conversation right back to the place he had wanted to avoid. "But you . . . you haven't changed," he said clumsily.

"I have changed in some ways. In other ways, no."

"I . . . I'm kind of surprised that you're still here. Thought maybe you might have moved on after . . . after what happened."

"This place is all I know. Where would I go?"

He detected an edge of despair—and maybe a trace of anger—in her voice. Now they had come to a place where she did not want to dwell. She had been sitting on the edge of the bed—he could feel the warmth of her body through the blanket beneath which he lay—but now she rose quickly. "You must rest," she said again. "We will talk later." And before he could say anything—like "thank you"—she had left the adobe, and he was alone again.

He dozed off—and woke to a commotion. The first thing he noticed was the wolf-dog, standing beside the bed, looking at him with its baleful yellow-gold eyes. Beyond, Manuel was trying to explain himself to Angevine.

"But, Mother, it is *his* dog. I saw them together in the zocalo."

"It is *not* a dog," she said, exasperated. "It is *el lobo*, and I do not want such a creature in my house. You must take him away at once."

"But, Mother, the people will try to kill it. They are afraid of it."

"*I* am afraid of it!" With Manuel slow to do her bidding, she turned on the wolf-dog herself. "You! You filthy beast—get out of my house!"

She moved toward the wolf-dog, and it turned its head to look at her, unafraid, and the Apache hunter saw its lips beginning to draw back from its massive fangs, preface to a warning growl. He sat up on one elbow, ignoring the shooting pain in his skull, fearful of what might happen if Angevine continued her advance.

"Stand still," he said. "Don't come any closer."

Angevine obeyed, stopping dead in her tracks.

"You," said the Apache hunter, speaking to the wolf-dog. "You better git."

The creature looked at him, and a low, hoarse whine issued from its throat.

"I said git!"

Head down, tail lowered, the wolf-dog slunk out of the adobe.

"Senor, the people will try to kill your dog!" exclaimed Manuel.

"A lot of people have tried that," said the Apache hunter, wearily sinking back down onto the bed. "But he's still kicking."

"Just like you."

Manuel was grown, thought the Apache hunter, but not enough so that he wasn't impressed by the fact that a dangerous man, a killer of other men, resided, at least temporarily, under his roof.

"Mano," said Angevine, "fetch some water from the well, please."

Once Manuel was gone Angevine turned and gave the Apache hunter a long look. "I have never seen such a thing," she said.

"You mean the dog."

"*El lobo.* But he cares about you, like a dog."

"We've traveled many miles together."

"He is your friend."

"The closest thing I have to one, I guess."

"Yet you sent him away."

"You wanted him out."

A smile touched the corners of her mouth, and then he thought he understood that long look. He'd just made a choice, a choice she approved of because she'd come out the winner. It was a small thing, putting out his old traveling companion for her sake, but it evidently meant a great deal to her. The Apache hunter remembered what he'd first learned in his time with Oulay—that if a man thought he understood a woman, he was only deluding himself.

Manuel came back in, and the Apache hunter's instincts began to tingle, because he knew immediately that something was wrong. Even if this adobe was right on the zocalo, Manuel had not had the time needed to draw water from the community well. Indeed, he no longer even had the water bucket in hand.

"There are two men outside," he told the Apache hunter. "They want to see you. They are the two men from the cantina, senor."

The Apache hunter had already taken note of his long gun, leaning against the wall within reach of the bed, and his gun belt, coiled like a rattlesnake on a three-legged stool near at hand.

"I better go out and see what they want."

"No," said Angevine. "You must not stand. I will send them away."

"I better go," he said firmly, and started to get up.

Realizing the futility of further argument, Angevine helped him. He still had his trousers and shirt on, but she'd pulled off his boots, and the Apache hunter glanced ruefully at them, there on the floor at the end of the bed. Putting them on would require more effort than he thought he could afford. On the other hand—a matter of simple pride—he didn't fancy going out to meet Horn and his compadre, and maybe fight them again, in his stocking feet. But there was no time; the last thing he wanted was trouble in Angevine's home, and if they grew impatient waiting outside, they might come in looking for him. He managed to sling the gun belt over his left shoulder, picked up the long gun and checked to make sure there was a cartridge in the breech.

"Don't worry," he told her. "They probably just want to parlay."

She went behind the curtain, but only for a few seconds, emerging with an old but clean double-barreled ten-gauge shotgun.

Something in the Apache hunter's expression made Manuel smile. "She is a good shot. Almost as good as me. I killed three rabbits in one day with that gun, and all of them—"

"Mano," she said quietly. "Don't brag."

The Apache hunter laid a hand on the young man's shoulder. "I know she can shoot."

He stepped outside, wincing at the bright daylight that stabbed at his eyes. Horn and his friend were still sitting their horses. The former had a bandage around his head, under that high-peaked Montana hat. He grinned when he saw the Apache hunter, but there wasn't anything friendly about it.

"I see you've made the acquaintance of Mickey Free," said Horn, with a lazy gesture in the other man's direction. "He probably didn't introduce himself. He don't talk much."

"Yeah, and you talk *too* much."

"Yep. I'll give you that. Mebbe I was out of line with all that talk about your squaw. But that's all water under the bridge now. I come to give you one more chance to join up with us."

"No, thanks."

"Mickey Free brings word that Geronimo and a bunch of Netdahe ambushed a cavalry detachment and jumped the reservation. Happened two days ago."

It took a moment for the Apache hunter to fully

digest the implications of this news. Like, apparently, just about everyone else, he'd found it hard to believe that Geronimo would be content to live out the rest of his days on San Carlos, minding his p's and q's. Still, years had passed since the last major Apache raid. And even with just a handful of Avowed Killers, even if he didn't stop until he reached the security of the Cima Silkq, Geronimo on the loose qualified as a major raid.

"Looks like the bronchos wiped out the whole patrol," continued Horn, " 'cept for one man. A lieutenant by the name of Summerhayes. Don't know him. Some feller sent out here by Washington. Supposed to be an expert on the Apaches." His tone was laden with skepticism.

Summerhayes! The Apache hunter could scarcely believe his ears. Another name out of a past he'd tried to put behind him.

"The answer's still no."

Horn shrugged. "Well, me and Mickey are ordered to head west along the border, see if we can cut their trail. Reckon they're already in Mexico by now. But you never know. See you in the mountains, Barlow."

"I hope not."

Horn grinned again, then sawed on the reins to turn his horse sharply and ride away. Mickey Free, inscrutable as stone, gave the Apache hunter one last look, and followed.

The Apache hunter watched them go until they were out of sight. He knew what he had to do. There were Netdahe on the loose. It was time to go hunting, to track them down and kill them. That had been his way for years now, and not once had he questioned it. This time, though, he found he had no enthusiasm for the job. He knew the reason for that. Turning, he saw her standing in the doorway of the adobe. The old shotgun was still in her hands, and she was watching him, and though he didn't really want to, he met her gaze, and saw that look in her eyes. He had just showed up in her life again—and now he was going to leave. And she wouldn't know if she was ever going to see him again.

Manuel was standing behind her and to one side. The Apache hunter shifted his gaze to the young man.

"Better get my horse," he said flatly.

"Yes, senor." Manuel's voice was full of disappointment.

"No," said Angevine firmly. "Wait. You can go in the morning. That will be soon enough, and will give you a little time to heal."

The Apache hunter didn't like the idea of lingering here. He had to go—there was no question about that—and it was difficult enough to see that look in her eyes just this once. But could he not give her this small concession? She wanted him to stay forever, but was asking for only one night.

He nodded. "Sure," he said. "Daybreak will be soon enough."

Chapter 6

Racing south on the horse of a dead yellow-leg soldier, Geronimo was fairly well pleased with the way things had gone.

He and the six Netdahe who followed him were all mounted, and each of them had an extra horse besides. That was one reason Geronimo had planned the ambush. He and his Avowed Killers could have easily slipped away from San Carlos under cover of night, eluding the cavalrymen who had been sent to arrest him. But they needed horses to reach the Cima Silkq. And the best available horses belonged to the soldiers.

Ordinarily, an Apache broncho would have spurned a cavalry mount. They were big and strong and had stamina, but they had one serious shortcoming. They were grain-fed. And there was no grain to be had on a run across Apacheria. Soon they would weaken. Geronimo even expected some of them to perish on the way. An Apache mustang knew how to survive on the sparse grasses one could find on the malpais. But the horses of the Chiricahua, just like their owners, had been weakened by long incarceration on San Carlos. They weren't worth taking.

Geronimo had learned many lessons in his years as a renegade. One of these was to take advantage of whatever was available. So he had instructed his Netdahe to avoid killing the cavalry horses, if at all possible. In the end, fourteen had been taken. It was fortunate that the yellow-legs trained their mounts to stand their ground in the din of battle. A horse's instinct was to flee such carnage—the crack of rifle and pistol, the shouts and screams of men fighting and dying, the stench of powder smoke, the smell of blood. Some of the cavalry horses had fallen in the melee, but Geronimo was sure that they had been slain by the yellow-legs themselves, who had been firing wildly at the fleeting figures of the Netdahe. Fourteen horses were a good haul. That meant each of the Avowed Killers had a second horse to switch to if the first faltered or died. The Netdahe had stripped the animals of blanket, saddles, even bridles—all unnecessary weight. They rode bareback, using only halters of twisted rope, which each had been instructed to carry.

It was good to be free again, thought Geronimo. For many years the warpath had been the only home he'd known. And the years spent among the Chiricahua had been torture for him. Even before the soldiers had come to take him away in chains, he had been plotting a breakout. But he had wanted to lead more than six Avowed Killers in his bid for freedom. He had begun the process of recruiting Chiricahua warriors, but he'd had to be careful, lest Juh found out. The last thing Geronimo wanted to do was antagonize his brother-in-law. And last night, as he summoned his Netdahe to his jacal to make preparations for the breakout, he hadn't dared to invite any of the Chiricahua malcontents he had been cultivating. He simply could not take the chance.

He could still hope, however, that one day they would join him. Geronimo had a keen sense of the flow of history, and a clear vision of his role in the destiny of his people. He was fairly certain that this would be the last time the Apache would fight the White Eyes. His hope that his breakout would escalate into full-fledged war. Once he reached the Sierra Madre, and had acquired some sturdy mountain mustangs to replace the cavalry mounts—the ones that survived this journey—he would begin to lead raids down out of the high country and against the ranches and villages of the Nakai-Ye. These would be easy pickings, and Geronimo was confident that such raids would be successful. The Mexican soldiers would not dare pursue him back into the Cima Silkq; Apache raiders had used those mountains as sanctuary for generations, and the Nakai-Ye soldiers had learned that to enter them was to sign their own death warrants. Eventually word would reach the Apaches who remained on the reservations north of the border that Geronimo and his Netdahe were carrying on the struggle against the traditional enemies of the Chi-hinne. Eventually, weary of living under the thumb of the White Eyes, many of them would break out and join Geronimo in the mountains. Geronimo envisioned the day when he was jefe of a large band of Apaches—Chiricahua and Coyotero, Mimbreno and Mescalero alike. From the Cima Silkq they might continue the war indefinitely, and perhaps, in time, they would be strong enough to ride back north of the border and strike again at the White Eyes.

This was one reason Geronimo was making haste to reach the Cima Silkq. It was customary for Apache raiders to strike at the first available target. The yellow-leg soldiers no doubt expected him to cut a swath of death and destruction through the Arizona Territory. Geronimo thought he might be able to elude capture or death for a few weeks if he followed this course. But he had bigger plans, and to realize them required a quick dash to the Cima Silkq, for there they would be out of the Americans' reach.

Not all of the Apaches at San Carlos would join him. He doubted Juh, for instance, would leave the reservation, because he would know that the malcontents would choose Geronimo as their jefe rather than him. And then there were the ones like Chato, who had all along argued that trying to live in peace with the Pinda Lickoyi was the only way that the Apache, as a people, could survive. Thoughts of Chato left a bad taste in Geronimo's mouth. The Netdahe leader simply could not fathom how an Apache could risk his own life to save that of a yellow-leg soldier. Such Apaches were traitors to their people, and in Geronimo's view did not deserve to live. The urge to kill Chato had been strong. Yet he had refrained. Geronimo always tried to think ahead, to plan for every eventuality. He tried never to burn bridges behind him. He had shown mercy toward Chato. He had spared the life of the American lieutenant. If his plans turned to dust, and he was recaptured, such mercy on his part might pay dividends. At the same time, by destroying the yellow-leg detachment, he had made a powerful statement that would resonate throughout the che-wa-kis of his people. The Pinda Lickoyi could still be beaten. Not driven out of Apacheria entirely—Geronimo was not so naive as to think that was possible—but at least made to pay a heavy price for their trespass.

In his younger days Geronimo *had* believed that the White Eyes could be driven from Apacheria forever. That all it would take to achieve this worthy goal would be for all Apaches to stand up and fight. But the various bands were unable to set aside their age-old differences long enough to join forces. Meanwhile, the White Eyes, who were nothing if not clever, had played one band against another. Geronimo despised most of all the Apaches who served as scouts for the yellow-legs. The new yellow-leg jefe, the man called Miles, had by all accounts disbanded the Apache scouts, and for this Geronimo was grateful. Had Miles been wise enough to retain his Apaches, they might have been able to prevent Geronimo and his Netdahe from crossing the border into Mexico. Their absence was a principal reason for Geronimo's confidence.

All in all, then, the Netdahe leader thought he had every right to be pleased with recent developments. He no longer languished on San Carlos. He had ruined the yellow-legs' plan to lock him up in some dank stone cell. He had presided over the destruction of an entire cavalry detachment. And he no longer wore Pinda Lickoyi iron on his wrists. The shackles had been shot off by Natoosay, one of his Netdahe faithful, who had used a pistol at point-blank range to destroy the locking mechanism. Best of all, it looked as though they would reach the border without problem. Though Geronimo was certain that the yellow-legs had begun the hunt for him, there was no sign of pursuit, and by tomorrow they would be safely in Mexico, where the American horse soldiers could not follow. There was only one problem, as far as Geronimo could see. Do-klini had been mortally wounded in the ambush, and Geronimo expected him to be dead before the sun rose again.

Do-klini had taken a yellow-leg bullet in the belly. His fellow Netdahe knew from experience that such a wound was almost always fatal. So far, Do-klini had managed to keep up with them. But they expected him to fall behind at some point during the day, and all were pretty certain that Geronimo would not slow down, much less stop, for the wounded man's sake. If he managed somehow to keep up, fine; if he didn't, he was on his own. Such was the way of the Netdahe, who had always been fugitives, and knew the rules of the game. Geronimo regretted the impending loss of Do-klini, who had been with him longer than any of the others, save Nah-tez. But such was the way of the world. Nothing lasted forever.

They rode south, pushing the cavalry mounts hard, throughout the door, slowing down only twice—on the occasions when, for the sake of the horses, Geronimo dismounted and began leading his mount. He did not need to order the others to do likewise; they followed his lead as a matter of course, and usually without question. Relieved of their riders' weight, the horses were given about a quarter of an hour each time to recuperate from the long run that had gone before. As a result, they lost none of the cavalry horses that first day.

When night fell, Geronimo pressed on, as an early moon provided enough light for them to negotiate the malpais. Only when the moon was about to set, and the night more than half over, did the Netdahe leader finally stop. The place he had chosen was a depression surrounded by brush and rock out-croppings. The Netdahe dismounted and sat or lay down on the hard ground, holding on to the halter ropes, ready at an instant's notice to leap back aboard their mounts and continue. They drank a little water from the army-issue canteens taken from the corpses of the soldiers they had slain nearly twenty-four hours earlier. Geronimo pulled the ragged brown se-rape that he had worn out of the Chiricahua encamp-ment close around him, for the desert night had grown cool, and his bones ached. He stretched out on the ground and was about to go to sleep when Uklenni approached him.

"Do-klini is no longer with us," said Uklenni.

Geronimo sat up. His black eyes were bright with anger. Uklenni was the youngest of his followers. He had been thirteen when he'd become Netdahe. Geronimo had thought then that Uklenni had prom-ise, even though he tended to be careless and wasn't very intelligent. Uklenni sounded worried, and in his voice, there was a plea. He wanted Geronimo to do something about Do-klini, and there was nothing that could be done. And even had there been, Uklenni was not behaving like a Netdahe. An Avowed Killer did not display sympathy or concern for his comrade.

To do so in this case was to dishonor Do-klini. A Netdahe relied only on himself in life, and expected to die alone, without benefit of the comfort one might derive from the presence of friends or family. Having lost the ones he loved—this, after all, was why he had become an avowed killer of the enemies of his people—a Netdahe needed no one either in life or death.

"Go up there," muttered Geronimo and nodded toward the highest of the nearby rock outcroppings. "Keep a lookout to the north."

Geronimo's tone of voice was one of chastisement. Uklenni turned quickly away and headed for the rocks.

"Keep an eye out for the yellow-legs," Geronimo called after him. "Not Do-klini."

Several of the other Netdahe chuckled. Shame-faced, Uklenni quickened his steps. It was Geronimo's intent to shame him; by stating the obvious, he was treating Uklenni like a child rather than a warrior.

A short while later, Do-klini rode into the camp. Geronimo was already asleep, but woke immediately and sat up. Even in the darkness of the now-moonless night, he could see that Do-klini had lost so much blood it stained the left side of the sorrel he rode. His himper was black with blood as well. Geronimo was surprised that a man could survive such prodigious blood loss. He and the other Netdahe watched as Do-klini slid off his horse, falling to the ground. The only sound he made was a muted grunt, even though the fall caused him immense agony piled on top of a day of endless suffering. For a moment he writhed in the dust. The others simply looked on. No one went to him to offer help. Eventually he managed to sit up. Geronimo gave him a curt nod before lying back down and returning to his slumbers.

Before daybreak the Netdahe leader was awake again. When he woke he was instantly and fully aware of his surroundings. Though he made almost no noise as he stood upright, the others heard him, and were up as well. Geronimo glanced across the camp to the place where Do-klini had come to rest a few hours before. To his surprise, the wounded man was still alive. Do-klini could not stand on his own; he had to climb the sorrel's foreleg, grabbing the mane to pull himself up the rest of the way. In this way he indicated to his Netdahe brethren that he was prepared to continue with them. But Geronimo had come to a decision with regard to Do-klini. He did not bother trying to explain it verbally. Instead, he plucked a single cartridge from the army-issue pouch slung over a shoulder and walked over to present it to Do-klini. The wounded man stared at the cartridge for a moment, coming to an understanding of what Geronimo expected of him. Then he took the cartridge and sat down, cross-legged, on the ground. Geronimo turned away and went to his horse. The other Netdahe followed suit; each man gave Do-klini a single cartridge before mounting up. Uklenni was the last to perform this ritual. Unlike those who had gone before, he lingered a moment before Do-klini, his face taut with pent-up emotion. Geronimo knew why Uklenni was so moved. Do-klini had been a mentor to him, and Uklenni was finding it difficult to treat him like any other Net-dahe. Do-klini realized Uklenni's dilemma and, after taking the single cartridge, made a curt motion with his head, indicating that Uklenni needed to mount up at once. Geronimo noticed that a trickle of blood was beginning to leak from the corner of Do-klini's mouth. Uklenni forlornly turned away.

Geronimo kicked his horse into motion and, lead-ing his spare, rode out of the depression, the others in tow. None of them looked back. They had paid Do-klini a final tribute with their cartridges. It was a Netdahe ritual. Though not in this case—the Netdahe had stripped the bodies of the yellow-legs they'd killed of all the ammunition they could carry—cartridges were usually in short supply, and by giv-ing one to a brother who was being left behind, they showed that, in spirit at least, they remained with him. Geronimo didn't know if those cartridges would be put to good use, or go to waste. That all depended on how long Do-klini would cling to life. The Net-dahe leader's hope was that he would live long enough for the horse soldiers to arrive, and that the dying man would be able to kill one or even a few of the yellow-legs before he perished. Geronimo hoped this not only because it might reduce the num-ber of the enemy, but also because it would afford Do-klini an opportunity to die the way a Netdahe should die—in battle.

They had traveled for more than an hour, and the morning sun was well clear of the eastern rim, when they heard distant gunfire. Checking their horses, they listened with bated breath. There was a single rifle shot, followed by another and then a flurry of pistol and rifle fire. Next came a moment of silence. Then a single pistol shot. Geronimo unslung a leather case he carried on a shoulder strap. Opening the case, he brandished a pair of fieldglasses. He had taken them, years ago, from the dead fingers of a federale officer. He brought them to his eyes and scanned the northern horizon. There it was—what he had been expecting to see since yesterday. A plume of dust. The horse soldiers had cut their trail and were in hot pursuit. They had killed Do-klini and now were pressing on.

Geronimo quickly put the fieldglasses away before kicking his horse into a gallop. To the south stretched a flat, arid plain covered with sagebrush, and then a line of hills, indigo blue in the distance. To the eye of someone unaccustomed to the desert, it was a vista indistinguishable from any other. But Geronimo knew this land as well as anyone, and had come this way on purpose. He knew that when he reached those hills he would be across the border. The horse soldiers were closing in. They had to hurry.

For several hours they rode hard, pushing the cavalry horses to the limits of their endurance—and, in a couple of cases, beyond. One of Natoosay's horses began to make wheezing noises and slowed down. Natoosay did not try to make it speed up; he knew what had happened, and that any such efforts would be futile. The horse was wind broke. He leaped from the back of that one to his second horse and let go the halter rope of the first. A short time later, bright red blood began to spew from the nostrils of Lucero's horse. The animal stumbled, and an instant later fell, but Lucero was already astride his second mount. He let go of the first one's halter rope and rode on without a backward look. The first horse thrashed on the ground as its lungs filled with blood, but Lucero would not waste either the time or the cartridge it would take to put the beast out of its misery. The horse was of no further use to him, and so he forgot about it.

It was not yet midday when Geronimo called a halt. They had reached the hills, and he knew for certain that they were now in Mexico. He slid off his horse and brandished the fieldglasses again. For a long time he stood there, as still as stone, watching the plume of dust that marked the progress of the yellow-leg column pursuing them. Finally he slowly lowered the fieldglasses, only to raise them to his eyes once more, like someone who has seen an apparition, and looks again in the same place, hoping that what he saw the first time is gone. When at last he turned back to his horse, and the other Netdahe saw his expression, they were surprised. Uklenni, for one, was sure he had never before seen an expression like that on Geronimo's face. For once, the Bedonkohe looked perplexed and worried. And seeing him thus worried Uklenni. The young Netdahe wanted to ask what was surely on everyone else's mind—what exactly had Geronimo seen with the long glass that so concerned him. But he refrained, as did all the rest. One did not ask Geronimo such questions.

And so they sat their horses and watched their leader go to his mount. Once astride the cavalry horse, he looked at them. But he explained nothing. Turning the horse's head to the south, he kicked it into a canter.

Nah-tez and Natoosay were peering north, their horses side by side. Uklenni guided his own mount closer to them.

"What is it?" he asked. "What is the matter?"

Nah-tez seemed not to hear. "They must be lost," he said, as though talking to himself. "They must not know where they are."

"They know," said Natoosay. "Those are American soldiers, Nah-tez, not Mexicans. They know where they are, and what they're doing."

Nah-tez merely grunted. He rode on after Geronimo and the others.

Natoosay glanced at Uklenni. "The yellow-legs," he said, "have crossed the border. Ugashe!" he said, kicking his horse into motion, and following the trail of his brethren.

Uklenni took one last look at the dust plume and went after him.

They rode all that day, and lost four more horses. Uklenni was whipcord strong and had plenty of stamina, but two days of hard riding were taking their toll on him. He was thirsty—the army-issue canteen he carried contained only a few drops of water now—and hungry too—all he had eaten in nearly three days was several handfuls of the paste made from flour and crushed nuts and berries that Geronimo had instructed them to bring along. Ordinarily he might have looked forward to the coming of night. Apaches did not usually travel at night, but once again, as Uklenni expected, Geronimo pressed on long after sundown, using the light of the early moon. When, finally, they stopped among the boulders that lay strewn across a steep slope at the base of a sandstone butte, Uklenni was too tired to worry about food or water any longer. He merely collapsed on the ground beside his horse, the halter rope in one hand and his rifle in the other, and immediately went to sleep.

Someone shook him awake. Uklenni wasn't sure if he'd slept for hours or only minutes, until he glanced up at the sky and saw by the positioning of the stars that about an hour had passed since they'd stopped here. It was Natoosay. "Geronimo wants to see you," said the latter. Uklenni was instantly on his feet. Natoosay took charge of his horse and the young Netdahe climbed up the slope through the boulders to the place where he had last seen Geronimo.

Nah-tez was there with the Bedonkohe. Both of them were sitting on their heels, waiting for him.

"Tomorrow morning," said Geronimo, "we will pass through a canyon. When we enter it, you, Nahtez, will take the halter rope of my horse and Lucero's. Uklenni, you will take the ropes of Natoosay's horse and of Santana's. There will be a great bend, and a ledge, where all of us except the two of you will step off our horses. You will take our horses and ride on through the canyon. You will continue south for the rest of the day. On the second day you will come to a river. You will turn east, riding in the shallows, until you come to a place where the cottonwoods grow thickly along both banks. You will see a long, slender rock reaching into the sky. There you will turn north, and return as quickly as you can to the canyon. We will be waiting for you there. Do you understand?"

Uklenni nodded.

"Good," said Geronimo brusquely. "You have a few more hours for sleep. Then we go."

Nah-tez rose and Uklenni accompanied him down through the boulders.

"Do you know why we are doing this?" asked Nah-tez.

"Because Geronimo has told us to."

Nah-tez grunted. "But do you know why?"

Uklenni shrugged. "At first, I thought he was planning to lay in wait for the yellow-legs with Natoosay, Santana, and Lucero. But that cannot be so, or he would not send us so far away."

"That's right. We will have eight horses, including the two that we ride. By the time we return to the canyon, six of those horses will be rested, for they will have carried no riders for three days. I expect we will leave the two horses we have ridden, for there are only six of us now, and we will all have fresh mounts."

"But the yellow-legs' horses will not be rested."

"It's simple. But then, the best plans usually are."

Uklenni was silent for a moment, now completely aware of the huge responsibility that had been placed upon him. Geronimo was entrusting him—and Nah-tez—with all of their horses. If anything happened, if they lost the horses, then *all* would be lost. It was very unlikely that Geronimo and the others would be able to elude capture for long if they were on foot. Why had Geronimo given this important task to him? Why not to Santana, or to any of the others, all of whom had more experience in all things Netdahe than he? As usual, Geronimo had not seen fit to explain his decision, and Uklenni knew that it would be useless to ask. He simply had to do what was required of him, and prove that Geronimo's confidence in his abilities was not misplaced.

He was, after all, Netdahe. Like most other Avowed Killers, he had started out on the path of vengeance. His father, a Mescalero Apache, had fallen victim to the White Eyes whiskey; his soul and mind had been poisoned by cheap snakehead liquor. Uklenni blamed the Pinda Lickoyi for this more than he blamed his father. That was bad enough, but then his mother was raped and murdered by white men. Uklenni's father had sought solace in the bottle. Uklenni had sought solace by shooting one of his mother's rapists through the head and using a knife to eviscerate the second. This, at the age of thirteen. The territory had placed a bounty on his head. Uklenni had always suspected that it was the distinction of having a wanted poster with his likeness on it that had persuaded the Netdahe to take him into the fold. Of course, it was not a very good likeness, and was ten years old, besides, when he arrived at San Carlos with Geronimo and set up residence there with an assumed name, and no one the wiser.

It was not Geronimo, but rather Do-klini who had befriended him. Do-klini, who had become like a brother to the young killer. Uklenni grieved for his brother, but found solace in knowing that Do-klini had died the way a Netdahe *should* die. He could only hope that when his time came he would be afforded a similar opportunity.

But that would have to come later. For now he had to stay alive, and avoid the yellow-legs at all costs. Geronimo depended on that.

Before daybreak they were off again. As Geronimo had said, they soon came to a canyon, and not far into it arrived at a sharp bend where a ledge at the base of a steep, rocky slope stood at about waist level. It was a simple matter for Geronimo, Natoosay, Lucero, and Santana to slip off their horses and onto the ledge in passing. Uklenni and Nah-tez continued on, leading the riderless horses of the others. Uklenni looked back once, to see Geronimo standing on the ledge, watching them go. The others were already climbing up the slope with the agility of mountain goats. Uklenni raised a hand in farewell. Geronimo did not respond.

Uklenni and Nah-tez rode all day, pushing hard and making good time. Though he looked back many times, Uklenni never saw a sign of pursuit. Not even a wisp of dust in the sky. But he had to assume that the soldiers had fallen for the ruse in the canyon, and were following their trail. Now that he'd had time to contemplate the situation, Uklenni appreciated the brilliance of the scheme devised by Geronimo. It would have been risky if the yellow-legs were still employing Apache scouts; some Apaches were so skilled in the art of tracking that they might surmise, by the depth of a hoof imprint in the sand, that a horse carried no rider. Uklenni doubted that any white man would notice.

Midmorning of the second day found them at the river. They turned east, and came eventually to the place where the cottonwoods grew thickly on both banks and a sandstone pinnacle rose majestically into the sky, just as Geronimo had described. They had kept to the shallows for several hours by this time, and Uklenni expected this tactic would slow the pursuit somewhat, as it forced the yellow-legs to proceed slowly along either bank of the river, searching for the place where their prey emerged, and not knowing how far they would have to go before they rediscovered the Netdahe sign, or in which direction it would go once it diverged from the river. As they headed north, beginning that leg of the journey that would take them back to the canyon where Geronimo and the rest of the Netdahe waited, Uklenni wondered what the horse soldiers would think when they *did* find the sign, and saw that it was going back toward the border.

They pushed on until well after sundown, and were up and on the move again before dawn. Uklenni felt better about things, now that he knew that in a half day's time they would arrive at the canyon and be reunited with their brethren. They had managed to keep well ahead of the pursuit. No mishap had befallen them. They still had all the horses in tow. Geronimo's plan had worked. He and Nah-tez had *made* it work. Uklenni was both relieved and proud.

He heard an odd, whistling sound just a heartbeat before the horse Nah-tez was riding tumbled head over heels, throwing its rider. Nah-tez was hurled twenty feet through the air. The riderless horses he had been towing scattered. In the back of his mind, Uklenni thought that they would not go far. Cavalry horses were not likely to stray, and this bunch, accustomed by now to one another's company, would be inclined to stay together.

Uklenni checked his own horse, threw his left leg

over the animal's neck, and slid to the ground. Holding the ropes to four horses, he approached the spot where Nah-tez and the horse he had been riding lay in the stunted sagebrush that covered the arid plain across which they had been traveling. Uklenni saw first that the horse had been shot through the chest. It was still alive, but barely. Uklenni was afraid that the same could not be said for Nah-tez. But as he drew near, he was relieved to see Nah-tez move. The older Netdahe tried to stand, but fell over on his side, clutching his leg. Looking closer, Uklenni saw that the leg was broken; the bone had torn through the flesh right above the desert moccasin. Nah-tez made no sound, but his face was contorted into a rictus of agony.

"Ugashe!" hissed Nah-tez, through clenched teeth. "Go! Ride!"

Uklenni was slow to respond. He was reluctant to leave Nah-tez in such dire straits. He didn't understand why the older Netdahe so urgently wanted him to leave. And then, a few seconds later, he *did* understand. He heard that whistling sound again. This time it passed right overhead, very loud in his ears, and he saw one of the loose horses leap into the air with that horrible scream horses are capable of making before falling to the ground, dead.

Someone was shooting at them.

No. Not at *them*. At the horses. Someone was killing the horses.

Who could it be? Uklenni had been shot at enough to sense that there was only one shooter. He realized now that the unseen assailant had a big-caliber long gun—a single shot. He could kill from a great distance, and there was no hope of getting close enough to kill *him*, not on this flat, sagebrush plain that offered no cover.

There was that sound again—the sound made by a big-caliber bullet waffling through the air. This one struck one of the horses Uklenni was holding—not a killing shot. The bullet hit the animal in the flank, knocking it down. It was all Uklenni could do to keep the others under control. In spite of his pain, Nah-tez was crawling through the sagebrush to his rifle, which had fallen only a short distance away. He began firing in the direction whence the long shots were coming; he didn't have a target—there was nothing to see—but he had to do something, had to fight back, even if the effort was wasted. As he fired he continued to shout at Uklenni to go, and Uklenni realized then that Nah-tez was right. It was up to him to save the horses that were left. There were five horses left, and if he hesitated very long, there would be none. The man with the long rifle could sit out there, safely beyond the range of their repeating rifles, and pick off the cavalry mounts one by one. And the raid would be over.

. Uklenni made up his mind. He leaped back aboard his own horse. He had the halter ropes of two of the other animals already in hand, and there were two others who stood loose. These he gathered up without difficulty. He heard the sound again and the blood seemed to freeze in his veins, and he fully expected to see one of the remaining horses go down. Instead, the bullet made a cracking sound as it whipped past Uklenni and sailed harmlessly on across the plain. The shooter was aiming at him, knowing that by killing Uklenni he eliminated the possibility that any of the horses would escape. But he'd missed. Uklenni decided that the only explanation for this was Ussen. The Apache god had seen fit to intervene. Taking one last look at Nah-tez, he kicked his horse into a gallop and rode away, four ponies in tow. Since the shooter was located somewhere to the west, he rode due east; every stride made by his horse increased the range and reduced the chances that he or one of the horses would be hit. Once more he heard the whistling sound of a big-caliber bullet, but this time it seemed far to his right. Nah-tez stopped shooting—Uklenni assumed he was saving his ammunition. The man with the long rifle might be foolish enough to move in closer, to see whether Nah-tez was still alive. Even if he didn't, the yellow-legs would be along eventually, and then Nah-tez would be afforded the opportunity, just as Do-klini had been, to die like a Netdahe.

His heart heavy, Uklenni rode on alone, and in a matter of hours reached the canyon. He had not yet reached the great bend where Geronimo and the others had dismounted without leaving sign when he saw Natoosay coming down a rocky slope to intercept him. Uklenni had never been so happy to see someone. But his relief was short-lived. Moments later he was faced with the task of explaining to a grim-faced Geronimo how it was that he had returned without Nah-tez and three horses.

Geronimo listened to the whole story without saying a word. When Uklenni was done, he nodded, and said, "At San Carlos I heard talk of a man who rides with Seiber. His name is Tom Horn. Horn killed Nah-tez and the horses."

Uklenni didn't dare correct Geronimo on the subject of Nah-tez, because whether Nah-tez was alive at this particular moment or not, he would *soon* be dead. This was as certain as tomorrow's sunrise. Uklenni had heard of Seiber, the yellow-leg's chief of scouts. Seiber was both hated and respected by the Netdahe. He was nearly as accomplished as an Apache when it came to tracking, and he had excelled as the jefe of the army's Apache scouts. He had treated them decently, and in return they had shown him unshakeable loyalty. But Uklenni did not know this man Tom Horn.

"They say Horn uses a buffalo gun," continued Geronimo. "That he kills from far away."

"He was alone," said Uklenni. "Why was he not with the yellow-legs? And how did he find us?"

"It doesn't matter," said the Netdahe leader. He looked at the horses, and then at his followers. Doklini dead, and now Nah-tez. That left Natoosay, Lucero, Santana, Uklenni, and himself. Five men, and five horses left. The Cima Silkq was still days away. Could they reach the mountains? Geronimo thought that they probably could. But as he studied the dusty, haggard faces of the other Netdahe and looked beyond the weariness, he detected something that worried him even more than the odds of reaching the sanctuary of the Sierra Madre. His followers were beginning to doubt him and his plan. They were starting to think it had been a mistake to make a run for the Cima Silkq. They wondered why he hadn't stayed north of the border, attacking Pinda Lickoyi targets—there were many, all ripe for the taking—even though it would mean capture or death. Because it seemed increasingly likely that they would be captured or killed between here and the mountains. The weariness, the hunger, the thirst—all that they suffered to ride with Geronimo—needed to be for *something*.

Geronimo's scheme with the horses had not worked, at least not in the way he had envisioned it. The yellow-legs had outsmarted him, somehow. At least one of them, the one named Tom Horn. An Apache would not follow a leader just because he was ordered to. The leader had to demonstrate that he was worth following and that he had power—power to make good things happen. And for a broncho Apache, good things meant enemies to kill, horses to steal, women to rape. Geronimo assumed that Tom Horn had become wise to his trickery, had come to the conclusion that most of the horses he and the yellow-legs guided were following, did not carry horses. Perhaps he had been unable to convince the officer in charge of the column, and so had struck out on his own, knowing that eventually Uklenni and Nah-tez would double back to pick up their brethren. It was an old Apache trick, used to tire out the horses of their pursuers. That wily old fox Seiber had taught his subordinate well. Seiber knew many Apache tricks from his own experience, and long association with the Apaches who had scouted for the army under his command had informed him of many more. Tom Horn had wanted to kill all the horses, knowing that in doing so he could probably end the raid. He had failed to accomplish that. But he had succeeded in undermining Geronimo's power—and Geronimo's hold over the Netdahe who followed him. There was only one way to get it back. In war, a leader had to know how to adapt to an ever-changing situation. Though he wanted to continue on toward the Cima Silkq, avoiding any and all contact with Pinda Lickoyi and Nakai-Ye, Geronimo recognized that he would have to do otherwise. He would have to conduct a raid.

There were two convenient targets. A Nakai-Ye village called Santo Domingo lay not far to the west. The inhabitants of that village would be easy to kill. Even such a small band as his would have no problem, and face little resistance. They could kill many Mexicans. But there would be no horses in Santo Domingo. At best they might find a few burros, a mule or two. The second potential target was a hacienda, a half day to the east. There would be many horses there. But also many vaqueros, with many rifles. That would be a difficult target, and he and his followers might well fail. On the other hand, he would acquire much more power by orchestrating a successful attack on such a place. The horses were an enticement because they might be able to steal enough of them to ride without stopping all the way to the Cima Silkq. As it was, with only one horse to a man, they would have to slow the pace substantially.

Geronimo made up his mind. There was no reason to explain things to the others—time enough for that later. He mounted his horse and led them out of the canyon. Reaching open country, he turned east.

That night, when they stopped, Geronimo took his

fieldglasses and left them, without explanation, going
on foot to reconnoiter the hacienda. He returned a
couple of hours later, woke them, and told them his
plan. It would have been better if they could have
afforded the luxury of scouting the hacienda all day,
so that the Netdahe could familiarize themselves
with the layout of the place, and so that they might
get a better idea of the number of inhabitants.
Rancherias in the northern provinces were usually
far removed from towns of any significance; they
therefore became little communities on their own,
providing those who lived there with all the ameni-
ties they could reasonably expect on the frontier. Vaqueros often lived and worked at the same rancheria
their entire life. They married, had families, and
when they grew old, their families—and the patron—
took care of them until they died. So there were
many women and children present, as well. Geronimo estimated that as many as one hundred Nakai-
Ye lived at the rancheria. They would have to settle
for that estimate, because he wanted to attack at
dawn. Though they had not seen telltale dust during
the previous day's travel, he suspected the yellow-
legs were still on their trail. The only question was,
how far back they were. To linger in the vicinity of
the hacienda for another day would be courting
disaster.

As best he could, Geronimo described the
rancheria to his Netdahe. Such places were built like
military outposts, with walls and gates and armed
sentries. This was a necessity on the northern frontier, because even though the Apache threat—the
greatest threat of all in the old days—was no longer

a major concern, there were still plenty of bandits roaming the hinterlands, some in gangs so large as to resemble armies. The main compound was completely encircled by an adobe wall that appeared to be as tall as a man, and several feet thick. There were thick-timbered gates on the north and south walls of this enclosure. The hacienda itself, a large two-story casa, was located on the east side, and on the west were a number of smaller adobe casas and barracks for the vaquero bachelors. Also contained within this enclosure were numerous other outbuildings—a smokehouse, storerooms, even a small chapel.

To the east of the main compound, behind the hacienda, was a second, smaller one. The perimeter wall of the second compound consisted of adobe in places and cedar posts, lashed together upright. In this enclosure was a barn and several corrals, as well as a large holding pen. It was in this pen, as the dawn light began to streak the eastern sky, that the Netdahe saw the rancheria's horse herd. This enclosure also had two gates, one on the north wall and one on the south.

"There must be a hundred of them," murmured Uklenni. He lay on his belly, wedged between Natoosay and Lucero, just behind the rim of a low ridge to the southwest of the rancheria. From this vantage point, approximately a quarter mile from the nearest compound wall, they had a fairly clear view of all that went on inside the two enclosures. At the end of the line of prone Netdahe, Geronimo used his fieldglasses to get a better look. He did not study the horses—he already knew where they were, thanks to his previous reconnaissance. In fact, he had slipped

right up to the walls of the second enclosure, to test
the sturdiness of those portions fashioned from cedar
posts. Instead, he spent what little time he had—his
intention was to put away the fieldglasses before the
sunrise, for fear that the lenses might catch the sunlight and flash a warning to the sentries that he knew
were posted at the four corners of the main
compound—studying the interior of the main compound. The rancheria was just awakening. Smoke
from cook fires rose from a dozen chimneys. People
were emerging from various buildings. A man
stepped out of a door on the upper level of the hacienda to stand upon an arched balcony that extended
the length of the grand structure. This, Geronimo surmised, was the patron, the ranchero, the man who
ruled all that he could survey from that high perch.
He was the man to whom all the others paid homage.
They gave their sweat and blood for him, and in
return he provided them with everything they
needed, including protection. As the morning light
stretched out across the flatlands that spread in all
directions from the rancheria, the Netdahe could see
cattle scattered in small bunches. There was no way
for Geronimo to know how many cattle carried the
ranchero's brand. But based on the number of buildings he could see in the compounds, and the size of
the horse herd, he estimated that the patron could
muster as many as forty vaqueros. Of all the Nakai-
Ye, Geronimo had respect for the vaquero more than
any other. These men were tough, hardy, smart. They
knew how to shoot, how to track, how to live out in
the malpais. They were of an independent nature and
sturdy stock. They lived hard, fought hard, and if

need be, died hard. Five Netdahe were no match for
forty vaqueros.

The sun was about to rise. Geronimo put the
fieldglasses back in their leather case and slid down
the back slope away from the rim. The other Netdahe
joined him there.

"In a little while," said Geronimo, "they will bring
the horse herd out through a gate. They always take
their horses behind the walls at night, and run them
out in the morning. There will be several guards with
the herd. They will not let the horses stray too far
from the hacienda. But it will be far enough. Lucero,
you and Natoosay will stampede the herd and, in the
confusion that follows, steal as many of the horses as
you can. To the east of us is a deep ravine. You will
drive them into this and ride south. The herd guards
may come after you. If so, the rest of us will be waiting for them. There will be a few horses still inside
the rancheria, so some of the vaqueros may also give
chase. They too will die."

Geronimo could tell by the expressions on the faces
of his men that they approved of the plan. It was
daring and dangerous—but characteristically bril-
liant. By stampeding the entire horse herd, they en-
sured themselves sufficient time to make good an
escape, since it would take the vaqueros some time
to round up their scattered ponies.

No more needed to be said. They crawled back
to the rim and watched the rancheria until, just as
Geronimo had described, the gate at the southern
end of the second enclosure was thrown open and
the vast horse herd was set loose. The Netdahe were
awed by the sheer size of the herd. Uklenni was cer-

tain that he had never seen so many horses together,
probably two hundred in all. He counted six herd
guards. It was going to be difficult for Natoosay and
Lucero to get close enough to such a heavily guarded
herd to stampede it. But they were eager to try. This
was the sort of challenge a Netdahe relished. At Geronimo's signal, the pair hurried down the back side
of the hill to the waiting horses, and rode away.

Geronimo and the others lingered a while longer
on the rim. The Netdahe leader wanted to make sure
he'd been right in supposing that the vaqueros
would hold the herd on the plains south of the
rancheria. In his judgment, this was the best grazing
ground, for there was sparse grass available on both
sides of a creek whose course was marked by wil-
lows and cottonwoods. His educated guess was right
on the mark. The herd guards pushed the horses
about a half mile south of the rancheria before letting
them stop. Many went immediately to the creek to
drink their fill. Then they began to graze, spreading
out on both sides of the run. The herd guards stayed
on the perimeter, always on the move, circling wide
and preventing any of the horses from straying too
far afield.

Uklenni was growing impatient when Geronimo at
long last left the rim and headed for the cavalry
mounts ground-hitched at the bottom of the hill. He
and Santana followed, and the three of them rode a
wide arc to the south and then to the east, keeping
to the contours of the land so that they were always
out of sight of the rancheria. In this way they came
eventually to the ravine that Geronimo had incorpo-

rated into his plan. This ravine, surmised Uklenni, had once been a branch of the creek near which the horse herd was grazing, and was located approximately five hundred yards due south. They could not see the herd from here, or even the trees that marked the course of the creek, as a low ridge stretched several hundred yards east to west between the creek and the ravine.

Reaching the rim of the ravine, Geronimo and his two Netdahe found a natural redoubt of rocks. Here they dismounted and sat on their heels to await developments. Uklenni wondered how Natoosay and Lucero would accomplish the task set for them. Geronimo had given them no specific instructions on how to get close enough to the well-guarded herd to spook it. But then, both Natoosay and Lucero were skilled horse thieves. Geronimo had told them what to do, and it was up to them to figure out how to do it. Uklenni occupied himself by imagining what he would do had Geronimo entrusted him with the job. Racing full-tilt on horseback would be a fatal mistake; the herd guards would shoot him right off his horse before he even got close to the herd. So the only way to approach was on foot—or, to be more precise, on one's belly, crawling—and practicing enthlay-sit-daou. Apaches practiced enthlay-sit-daou as children. Netdahe had mastered this art of invisibility, of blending so perfectly into one's environment that one could hide in plain sight. The art involved more than a complete understanding of how the human form related to its environment, and how the human eye could be fooled into not recognizing what it saw. It had to do, also, with a mastery of the mind. One had to believe one was invisible to one's enemy to achieve enthlay-sit-daou.

Using enthlay-sit-daou, Uklenni mused, he might be able to avoid being seen by the herd guards until he was close enough to go into action. But the art of invisibility did not work on horses. He would have to approach the wind downwind so the herd would not smell him and sound the alarm. Once in close, he would wait until one of the herd guards passed nearby; then he would leap upon the back of the vaquero's pony and kill the rider with one swift stroke of his knife. After throwing the corpse to the ground, he would vault into the saddle and proceed to stampede the herd, perhaps with gunfire. Hopefully, the other herd guards would be too far away to get a clean shot at him with their pistols, and Uklenni knew from experience that it was exceedingly difficult to hit a moving target from the back of a horse with a rifle. He would stay low, lying across the neck of the horse, as he cut as many of the other animals out of the running herd, steering them toward the ravine. If both Natoosay and Lucero adopted this strategy, working in unison, they might be able to take a good many of the horses.

The wait seemed interminable to Uklenni, but in fact only a few minutes after he and Geronimo and Santana settled down into the rocks, they heard gunfire to the north, in the direction of the creek and the horse herd. A few moments later, Uklenni felt the earth trembling slightly beneath him. He readied his weapons. A cloud of dust swirled up from the bottom of the ravine to his left, and then the horses began to thunder past below him. He could scarcely see Natoosay and Lucero, so thick was the dust cloud. It was all he could do to refrain from letting loose a whoop of exultation. Seconds later, the first vaquero came into view, in hot pursuit of Natoosay and Lucero. Another was coming a short distance behind. Geronimo rose suddenly, rifle to shoulder, and fired once, twice at the first vaquero. The latter somersaulted off the back of his horse and lay still in the ravine bottom. Santana began shooting at the second man, who was only a stone's throw away. His horse reared, and he fell backward, but he came up shooting with his short gun. Uklenni left the rocks and sprinted along the rim of the ravine, firing his rifle as he went. The vaquero turned to run, but one of Uklenni's bullets struck him in the thigh and knocked him down. Rolling over on his back, the vaquero fired twice at the broncho Apache looming over him on the rim. The first bullet missed completely; the second cut a deep gouge in the flesh of Uklenni's upper leg. Uklenni took careful aim and shot the vaquero through the heart.

Geronimo lingered only a moment, to make sure no more vaqueros were coming, then ran to his horse and rode along the rim of the ravine, followed by Santana and Uklenni. Three-quarters of a mile farther on, the ravine turned sharply south, and then began to taper off. Here Natoosay and Lucero had driven the stolen horses up onto the plain, continuing south. The cloud of dust kicked up by the hooves of the horses was a beacon for Geronimo and the others to follow. Uklenni glanced behind and saw no signs of further pursuit. This time he could not resist. Raising his rifle overhead, he uttered a cry of savage exultation. They had done it! They had killed Nakai-Ye and stolen their horses. This was, indeed, a raid to remember.

Chapter 7

The Apache hunter had an uneasy feeling as he rode up to Camp Bowie. Since giving up his commission and departing the United States Army, he had steered well clear of all American military outposts and personnel. The reason was simple enough: The specifics of his parting company with the army were such that some considered him a deserter. And he supposed that, technically, he was. He'd had to make a choice, between protecting the woman he loved and the people he had come to respect, and his loyalty to the army. One might have thought such a choice would rank among the most difficult of his life. But the Apache hunter remembered it as a very easy decision to make, because, in a way, it had been even more simple than picking love and respect or duty and loyalty. It had been about right and wrong. The United States Army—his army, the one he represented by wearing the uniform—had been about to do wrong, about to inflict a terrible injustice upon the peaceful Chiricahua Apaches. The Apache hunter's conscience wouldn't have allowed him to participate in that, even if Oulay hadn't been involved.

That was something else the sight of an army outpost did to him—it dredged up the painful memories of the Chiricahua maiden he had made his wife. The time he had spent with the beautiful Oulay, daughter of the Chiricahua jefe Cochise, had been all too brief. The interlude had been the only happy period in his adult life. Her love had infused his life with a special intensity; he'd felt as though he could achieve anything with her at his side. At the same time, though, it had been a time of excruciating anxiety, for they lived in violent times in a violent land and he had always worried that something would happen to her. And, of course, it did, and it was as though the very breath had been snatched out of his lungs. He had never really been able to catch his breath since.

There was a great deal of hustle and bustle in and around the outpost. Soldiers and civilians—afoot, on horseback, a few in wagons—were passing in and out of the main gate. As he insinuated himself into this current of humanity, the Apache hunter noticed several jacales standing out on the flats just outside the camp's perimeter. They were abandoned; there was not a single Apache to be seen, though it looked to his keen eye that they had been occupied until fairly recently. Their presence intrigued him.

Two sentries stood watch at the gate, and the Apache hunter expected to be challenged by them. Instead, they let him pass without remark. He supposed that anyone could enter Camp Bowie as long as he or she wasn't an Indian. Once inside, he guided his horse off to one side and sat in the saddle for a moment to survey the camp's interior. Camp Bowie hadn't existed while he'd held a commission, but all frontier posts were laid out in much the same man-

ner, so he knew immediately where to find the headquarters building, the stable and blacksmith, the
enlisted men's barracks and Officers' Row. He wondered where, though, in all of this he would find
Charles Summerhayes. Wondered even if his friend
of long ago was still alive.

The parade ground was a beehive of activity; men
were shouting, horses whinnying, a thick cloud of
dust hung in the hot air. Even if he'd not known that
Geronimo had jumped the reservation, the Apache
hunter would have understood the reason for all the
commotion. The garrison was preparing for a long
field campaign, and there were only two reasons he
could think of for a military campaign in this region.
Either war with Mexico had been declared or there
was an Apache problem. From experience he knew
that preparation for such a thing involved a thousand
and one details. He could feel the excitement in the
air. A soldier's life—especially the life of a soldier
assigned to the frontier—was usually a mixture of
pure boredom and drudgery. The prospect of action
electrified these men. The Apache hunter figured a
good many of them had never seen action against
hostile Indians. After all, years had passed since the
United States Army had fought Apaches. Men such
as these, who had no experience fighting Apaches,
had no idea what they were in for. Their excitement
would soon be replaced by fear. The Apache hunter
almost felt sorry for them.

He waylaid a trooper who was hurrying by. "I'm
looking for Lieutenant Summerhayes. Know where I
can find him?"

"Hospital, I expect. Him and Lieutenant Warrick

got ambushed by Geronimo's Apaches. Warrick and most of the boys with him got killed. Summerhayes got hit, but he'll live, from what I've heard, though he might wish he was dead by the time General Miles gets through with him."

"How come?"

The trooper stepped closer, looking left and right like a conspirator to make sure no one was within earshot—as though anyone could hear a softly spoken word in the din that pervaded the parade ground.

"Because that ol' Geronimo made a fool out of the lieutenant—that's why. Made Summerhayes believe he was going to surrender, and Summerhayes convinced Lieutenant Warrick of that, and the whole detachment let its guard down. Besides, there's always got to be a scapegoat, you know."

The Apache hunter nodded and straightened in his saddle. He'd found out what he wanted to know from the soldier, and didn't care to engage in a conversation about the mountains of deceit that overshadowed the bitter history of relations between white men and Apaches. He was aware that most whites who lived in Apacheria earnestly believed that Apaches were the most deceitful people on the face of the Earth. The Apache hunter didn't agree; in his experience there were very few people one could trust, and the color of their skin didn't enter into the equation. He assumed the trooper was one of those who rated Apaches as trustworthy as rattlers. But the man was right about one thing: The Army would need a scapegoat. It was bad enough that nearly an entire detachment had been wiped out. Worse still, from the perspective of the powers-that-be in Washington, the United States Army had egg on its face, having the legendary Geronimo in its grasp and then letting him slip away.

The trooper pointed out the hospital—an adobe, indistinguishable from the rest, at the end of Officers' Row. The Apache hunter dismounted and led his horse across the hardpack. The coyote dun was a mountain mustang, unaccustomed to so much commotion, and the Apache hunter knew all the little signs that betrayed the creature's agitated frame of mind. He was somewhat agitated himself; like the dun, he had spent years alone in the malpais. But he was relieved to note that no one seemed to be paying him any attention. He saw no familiar faces, and began to entertain the hope that there was no one here at Camp Bowie who knew him from his army years. Except Summerhayes, of course—and he wondered if his old messmate would even recognize him in his present incarnation.

The door to the hospital was open, and as he drew near he could hear voices in heated discussion issuing from within. Hitching the mountain mustang, he drew his long gun from its saddle boot, racked it on one shoulder, and went on in. A tall, broad-shouldered man wearing cavalry trousers and a wrinkled white coat was standing with his back to the doorway, speaking to another who was partially blocked from the Apache hunter's view.

". . . so you know I do not approve of this!" the man with his back to the door was saying. "That wound needs time to heal, Lieutenant. The slightest exertion could reopen it. Infection could set in."

"I'll take full responsibility," said the other man. It was a voice familiar to the Apache hunter. It echoed down through the years to him of brighter, simpler, more hopeful times.

"I'm post surgeon," said the first. "You're *my* responsibility."

"Listen, Doc. Hear all that racket outside? This whole garrison is about to go after Geronimo. And I'm going after him too. Nothing—nobody—is going to stop me."

"You might as well lay back down and heal up," said the Apache hunter. "There's no big hurry where catching Geronimo is concerned."

A startled Summerhayes looked past the army physician and his eyes widened as he saw and recognized the Apache hunter. He rushed forward, grabbing the latter's hand and shaking it. In the process he aggravated his wound. His face went completely white, and he gasped at the lancing pain. His left arm was in a sling to immobilize it, and the left side of his tunic around the shoulder was bulky thanks to the dressing underneath.

"Easy there, partner," said the Apache hunter, solicitiously.

"Great God in heaven," breathed Summerhayes. "It really *is* you. You really *are* alive."

The Apache hunter smiled ruefully. "I guess you can call it living. And yourself? I thought you'd be at least a colonel by now."

"Promotions are few and far between in a peacetime army."

The Apache hunter nodded. "May be why some officers can't seem to wait for a new war to break out."

"What happened to you?" asked the surgeon, frowning at the Apache hunter's face.

"You mean this." The Apache hunter touched his face, still very swollen along the cheekbone and around his right eye, and very tender to the touch at the jawline. "A pint-sized son of a bitch named Tom Horn, that's what."

"Seiber's man?"

"That's the one."

"I thought he was sent down into Mexico to *talk* to you about scouting for the army," said the surgeon.

"Like I said, he's a son of a bitch. So am I. Guess we just didn't hit it off."

"So you're here to help us," said Summerhayes, pleased.

"No."

The lieutenant's expression switched instantly from one of pleasure to dismay. "Why not?"

"Because I intend to track down and kill Geronimo and every Netdahe who rides with him," said the Apache hunter, and his voice was as cold and harsh as a mountain winter. "And if I go with the army I won't have the opportunity, since General Miles won't stand a chance in hell of catching up with the bronchos."

"I wouldn't sell the general short if I were you," advised the surgeon stiffly. He didn't like it when a civilian criticized the army. "Miles did the impossible up north a couple years back, catching Chief Joseph and the Nez Percé before they could escape across the border into Canada."

"That's fine. But this isn't the north country. And the Netdahe aren't Nez Percé."

"Just who are you that you know so much?"

The Apache hunter glanced at Summerhayes, then back at the surgeon. "I'm nobody," he said.

"Well, General Miles is somebody," replied the surgeon stiffly. "And you should have a care what you say about him around here." He turned his attention to Summerhayes, and the Apache hunter got the distinct impression that the Camp Bowie sawbones was no longer concerned about his patient, since the latter was exhibiting the bad judgment of being nobody's friend. "As for you, Lieutenant, if you insist on taking chances, I won't try to stop you. This is the United States Army, after all, and if a man signs up to serve his country, he should at least have the right to die for his country too."

"Thanks, Doc. That's very . . . heartwarming."

"Get out of here." Unamused, the surgeon turned dismissively away from both of them.

Summerhayes headed outside, and the Apache hunter accompanied him, sticking close and watching his friend carefully, since the lieutenant didn't seem all that steady on his feet. The brightness and heat of the midday sun struck him like a physical blow as he stepped out of the adobe. He stopped, involuntarily raised an arm to shield his eyes, and swayed slightly. The Apache hunter realized then just how weak his friend really was. The post surgeon had been right. He had no business being on his feet, and the idea that he could participate in a campaign against hostile Apaches, with all its rigors and dangers, seemed utterly ludicrous. In fact, the effort could kill him. His injury was too severe, too fresh. Still, the Apache hunter held his tongue. It was obvi-

ous that Charles Summerhayes wasn't going to listen
to anyone.

"I've got to speak to General Miles," he told the
Apache hunter as he gazed at the tumult in the parade ground. "By God I am not going to lay in a
sickbed while everybody else goes after Geronimo."

"Sure." The Apache hunter wondered if Summerhayes was aware of the scuttlebutt that he had
just been exposed to by the trooper at the gate. Or
had he had the time to figure out for himself that he
would be made to bear the brunt of the blame for
Geronimo's escape and the ambush of the detachment? The Apache hunter wondered too if he
shouldn't forewarn his friend, before the confrontation with Miles. But again he kept his own counsel.
All the warnings in the world wouldn't make a bit
of difference. Summerhayes was bound and determined to go after Geronimo; the Apache hunter had
a hunch he knew why, and he was surprised, pleas-
antly so. The Charles Summerhayes he'd known
many years ago, back when they had shared a barracks as new shavetails in an Apacheria outpost, his
friend had not been the type who'd stand up for
himself, or take a decisive course of action and stick
to it no mater what. He'd been a weak, timid young
man. No longer.

Summerhayes began to make his way through the
melee toward the headquarters building, and the
Apache hunter stuck close beside him, in case he faltered.

"I thought you were crazy," said Summerhayes,
"back when you, essentially, abandoned the army for
the sake of the Chiricahua. And for Oulay's sake, of
course." He paused, then shot a worried glance at

the Apache hunter, thinking that maybe he shouldn't have mentioned a name that could well still cause his old friend to suffer great anguish. "Now here I am faced with the same dilemma. What do I do if Miles won't let me go after Geronimo?"

"Then you have to make a choice."

Summerhayes nodded, looking grim. "One of those choices that comes along every now and then. The kind where you lose something no matter what you do." He smiled ruefully. "It's kind of strange, don't you think?"

"What?"

"You start out in life with all this promise. People say you have great opportunities ahead of you, that you can do this and accomplish that. But eventually you realize that life is just *losing*. You may find something you really want. But you'll lose it. Or someone you really love. But that won't last forever. You lose your youth, your dreams, your . . . potential. And the only real accomplishment is if you can keep from losing everything all at once." He glanced again at the Apache hunter, a worried look on his face. "This isn't self-pity. I know I used to wallow in that back in the old days."

"Yeah, a little," said the Apache hunter wryly.

They walked on for a moment in silence, dodging men and horses and wagons, trying not to choke on the dust.

"At least you're here. Still above snakes, as they say in these parts. I often wondered if you were still alive," Summerhayes said.

"Me too."

Summerhayes laughed. "I can't believe you accepted their offer."

"I didn't. I turned 'em down."

That stopped Summerhayes in his tracks. "Then . . . why are you here?"

"Came to see you."

Summerhayes thought that over for a minute. "I didn't know you were the sentimental kind."

"I didn't come to see how you were doing," replied the Apache hunter. "I came to find out exactly what happened with Geronimo. I figured you were the one I should talk to, since you're the only survivor of the ambush."

It wasn't entirely true—he had been interested in Summerhayes' welfare. But he would never admit it.

"Not the only one. There was Chato."

"Chato? He was there?"

"Yeah. But he wasn't with Geronimo and the Netdahe. He volunteered to ride along as far as Camp Bowie. He figured nothing would happen to the prisoner as long as he was around as witness."

"He and Geronimo are friends?"

"I wouldn't say that. In fact, I got the impression he doesn't like Geronimo very much. But he was worried about his own people. About what they might do if Geronimo was 'shot while trying to escape,' or some such thing."

The Apache hunter nodded.

"Chato saved my life," added Summerhayes. "If he hadn't been there, Geronimo would have finished me off."

He continued walking, and the Apache hunter fell

in alongside. "How many men are riding with Geronimo?"

"Maybe six or seven Netdahe is all, as far as I know."

"Mickey Free said there might be as many as twenty or thirty."

Summerhayes shook his head. "Only six or seven attacked the detachment. I know the army probably doesn't want to believe that so few Apaches could kill so many troopers. But they did."

"They're Netdahe," said the Apache hunter grimly, as though that alone explained everything. And it did. "And the cavalry horses. Did the Netdahe kill many of them?"

"A few. Not many." Summerhayes waited, expecting the next question posed by the Apache hunter to clarify why he'd asked the previous one. But the Apache hunter fell silent for a moment, deep in thought, and Summerhayes was too impatient to wait very long. "What does that tell you?"

"That Geronimo will probably not linger long on this side of the border. If he and his men took the extra horses, it means he plans to ride hard and long. He'll make for the Sierra Madre and if he runs some of his horses to death doing it he won't care, because now he's got replacements."

"So you don't think he'll conduct raids along the way?"

The Apache hunter shrugged. "You never know. The Apache is an opportunist. He won't go out of his way, but if someone's unlucky enough to be in his path . . ." He abruptly changed the subject. "What are *you* doing back here?"

"That's a long story," said Summerhayes ruefully.

"Let's just say I have General Crook to thank for it. He thought they needed an expert on Apaches down here, so I was selected. Imagine that: me, an Apache expert, so much so that Geronimo had no trouble pulling the wool over my eyes."

"So you're blaming yourself for what happened."

"Maybe a little. But I blame Geronimo more."

By this time they had reached the headquarters building. Summerhayes identified himself to the sentry posted at the door, and requested to see the officer of the day.

"Yes, sir, Lieutenant, I know who you are," replied the sentry, and there was, thought the Apache hunter, a decidedly unfriendly inflection, bordering on insolence, in his voice. If Summerhayes noticed this, he gave no sign. The sentry opened the door and called inside for the officer of the day, who appeared in the doorway just long enough to take one look at Summerhayes before disappearing inside. A few moments later, Summerhayes was being escorted into the presence of General Miles. And the Apache hunter was going in with him, thanks to the intervention of the lieutenant, who identified him as the new scout recruited by Al Seiber. It was a bald-faced lie, but Summerhayes was well beyond the point of worrying about such things. The Apache hunter was impressed; it took a fair amount of guts on Summerhayes' part to bring someone—particularly a civilian—before the military district's commanding general under false pretenses.

General Miles was, as usual, pacing the room like a caged cat when Summerhayes and the Apache hunter entered; he was dictating a report to one of his aides, the latter resplendent in his dress uniform. The general dismissed his aide and settled in behind the desk, clasping his hands on the desktop and looking with grim solemnity at Summerhayes.

"I'm glad to see you up and about, Lieutenant," he said, "though a little surprised, since the post surgeon informed me that your wounds were severe."

"Not as bad as all that, sir."

Miles fixed his piercing gaze on the Apache hunter. "And you're the one Seiber sent Horn down to get. Where is Horn, anyway?"

"He and Mickey Free are out to cut the Netdahe trail."

Miles nodded. "Think they'll succeed?"

"Probably. But it won't do you much good."

"And why is that?"

"Because as long as Geronimo is running, you won't be able to catch him."

Miles stared at him. "I'm about to send three full companies of soldiers after the fugitives. You're saying they will fail, even with the assistance of Al Seiber and his scouts."

"That's what I'm saying. And I noticed you're taking along a few field guns too. You might as well leave them here. Even if you caught up with the Apaches, they sure wouldn't stand still long enough for you to shoot at them with those things. Besides, where Geronimo will take you, you won't be able to haul those guns."

"I see," said Miles, his tone icy. He didn't like being second guessed, and here was this dusty, bearded desert rat telling him that his plan of campaign was doomed to failure.

The Apache hunter could have kept his criticisms under wraps. It was no skin off his back if the general's plans went awry. What did it matter to him, these days, if the United States Army spent the next six months rattling around Apacheria chasing ghosts? The problem was that he'd taken an instant dislike to Miles. Part of this was the result of his high regard for Miles' predecessor, General Crook. And part of this was experience; he knew that commanding officers who didn't understand Apaches or Apacheria tended to get a lot of people killed unnecessary. Not that he expected Miles to change his plans based merely on his say-so. Men like the general did not often or easily admit to mistakes.

"If you don't think we can catch Geronimo, sir, then why did you agree to join the campaign?" asked Miles.

"I didn't sign on, actually. Though I might have, if you'd kept the Apache scouts on the payroll."

"Apaches, scout or otherwise, can't be trusted." As he spoke, Miles gave Summerhayes a pointed glance. "Then, if you aren't going to help us, what *are* you doing here?"

"I'm here to get details from the lieutenant on what I'll be up against when I find Geronimo and his followers."

"When you find them." Miles settled back in his chair and glowered at the Apache hunter. "So you will be able to find them, but we won't."

"You can find him—in the Sierra Madre, in about a week or ten days. But you won't be able to catch him before he gets there."

"You will ride straight to the Sierra Madre, then."

"That's right."

"But you are not responsible for the lives of civilians in this territory, sir. I must do all within my power to apprehend Geronimo and his renegades before he does the sort of damage that Apaches are notorious for doing. The longer they remain at large, the more white men and children may be murdered, white women raped, property looted and burned."

"They won't be doing any of that right now," said the Apache hunter. "They're too busy running."

"Then giving chase *is* the right course of action. If it keeps them on the move, and doesn't give them time to create mayhem," retorted Miles.

"I never said you shouldn't chase them," said the Apache hunter, growing weary of the debate. "I just said you'd never catch them."

Miles turned his attention to Summerhayes. "Do you agree with this man, Lieutenant?"

Summerhayes didn't hesitate. "He knows more about the Apache than any other white man I know. So, yes, sir, on that topic I would accept anything he says."

It was not the response Miles wanted from a subordinate—that was obvious from the expression on the general's face. At this point, Summerhayes didn't care. He had already fallen from grace as far as Miles was concerned, and he wasn't going to lie—especially about a friend, or about something as serious as the present situation—in an attempt to fall back into it.

"Well," said Miles, with a degree of vicious satisfaction, "you will excuse me, Lieutenant, if I do not hold your opinions in very hard regard. After all, it was your opinion that Geronimo might surrender peaceably, and that if we attempted to take him by force that the Chiricahua would rise up against us, that has gotten us to where we are today. Don't you agree?"

"Yes, sir," said Summerhayes stiffly.

"In fact, we should have done it the way Major Bendix wanted it done. We should have gone in there and slapped iron on Geronimo and dragged him away—and to hell with what the Chiricahua thought. Then we wouldn't have this problem, would we, Lieutenant?"

"No, sir."

The Apache hunter rose to his friend's defense. "You'd have a bigger one, General," he said, "because the lieutenant was right about the Chiricahua. Juh is holding them back right now, but there is a lot of discontent in San Carlos, by all accounts. All they'd need is an excuse. And you would have given them one."

Miles spared the Apache hunter the merest glance. "I take it you are here to make a request," he told Summerhayes.

"Yes, sir. I request to be seconded to one of the companies, in order that I may participate in this campaign."

"Request denied," Miles snapped without hesitation. "You're not well enough and you're not needed. I want you to remain here at Camp Bowie until you are recovered enough to make the journey back to Washington."

Summerhayes had been expecting this response. "Then I request a furlough, sir. Since I have sustained a wound in the field, and since I am not needed in any capacity, I hope you will see fit to grant that request."

Miles grunted. "And if I grant this furlough, you will ride off into Mexico on some quixotic quest, I suppose. You'll try to capture Geronimo single-handedly, and in so doing make amends for your part in the disaster that befell Lieutenant Warrick and his command."

"I could never make amends for that, sir."

Miles was silent for a moment, studying the face of the officer who stood before him, whose face betrayed the tortured soul within. The Apache hunter, watching Miles, saw the general's expression soften.

"Then perhaps I have misjudged you, Lieutenant," said Miles. "Perhaps it's that you hope to make the guilt go away. At times in my career, especially during the War Between the States, I experienced that same guilt and remorse. I've wondered why I survived a battle when so many of my close comrades did not. Why you're still breathing and they aren't. Why you will see your loved ones again, and they never will. You'll only get yourself killed, Summerhayes, if you go after Geronimo in your present condition. I know the prospect doesn't worry you. You may feel now as though you would rather die."

"At least I wouldn't feel the guilt any longer, would I, sir?"

"As your commanding officer, I would be remiss in allowing you to do what you propose."

"Then grant my request as one soldier to another, sir."

Miles nodded. "Of course. You'll have your furlough papers in hand today."

"Thank you, sir."

"Good luck, Lieutenant. And may the Lord have mercy on your soul."

Once the door had closed on the general's office, Summerhayes sagged weakly against a wall. There wasn't a shred of color in his face. The Apache hunter figured that the relatively simple act of standing at attention for a few minutes had drained every iota of strength from his friend. Realizing that the officer of the day was watching, Summerhayes steeled himself, straightened, and walked out of the headquarters building under his own steam. He proceeded off the porch and to the edge of the parade ground, then stopped and grabbed the Apache hunter's arm.

"I'm not asking to ride with you, Joshua," he said. "I wouldn't impose on you to that extent. I just want you to know that." He paused, realizing fully the position in which he had put the Apache hunter. "I know, you're thinking you can't do that. That as a friend you couldn't let me go it alone. But I want you to."

"I'd let you go it alone," replied the Apache hunter, "except that you're probably going to reopen your wounds and bleed to death the first or second day. I might as well hang around long enough to give you a decent burial."

Summerhayes looked at his friend and understood that the Apache hunter, though appearing perfectly serious, was employing gallows humor.

"I'm not kidding, Joshua," he said, a mild rebuke in his tone.

"I'm only half kidding. You probably *won't* make

it to the Sierra Madre. But if you do, we can part company then. Because the last thing I need when I'm hunting Netdahe is to nursemaid a shavetail who's spent the last ten years behind a desk in Washington."

The words stung. "I can remember how to take care of myself," said Summerhayes.

"Good."

"So you think you can track down and kill Geronimo and a half dozen Netdahe all by yourself."

"Sure."

"And just how do you propose to accomplish that?"

"I'll just kill them one at a time."

Summerhayes was silent for a moment. "But . . . why? Is it still all about Oulay even after all these years? And how many of them have you killed?"

"I don't keep count."

"The one who killed her is probably dead by now. So when does it end?"

The Apache hunter walked, silent, with his head down, for a long moment. "When they're all dead," he said, at length. "Or I am."

They agreed to leave Camp Bowie at first light. This suited the Apache hunter, since it would give Summerhayes a few more hours to recuperate before hitting the trail. Besides, he was in no hurry—which set him apart from just about everyone else at the outpost. Summerhayes was in a hurry to get himself killed. The other soldiers were in a hurry to start chasing an Apache phantom across the malpais. General Nelson Miles was in a hurry to eradicate the stain on his career that marked the destruction of

Warrick's command; no matter how hard he tried
to lay the blame on Summerhayes, Miles was still,
ultimately, responsible for Geronimo's escape. The
general had a very high personal stake in the capture
of the Netdahe leader.

The Apache hunter declined an invitation from
Summerhayes to bunk in the camp. He wanted to
leave Camp Bowie as quickly as possible. It gave him
an odd, uncomfortable feeling being around so many
soldiers. The environment reminded him not just of
simpler, happier times, but also of his parents, especially his father. Timothy Barlow had been a career
army man. He had served under Andy Jackson in
the Seminole War. He had fought too in the Mexican
War. The army had been Timothy Barlow's life, and
like all fathers, he had wanted his son to follow in
his footsteps. The Apache hunter didn't want to think
about his father, though. Because the next thought
was always speculation about just how disappointed
Timothy Barlow would have been in his son, were
he still alive. Timothy Barlow had always conducted
himself with honor. And there was no honor in be-
coming a killer like the Apache hunter.

Summerhayes' question—*When does it end?*—
echoed in his mind as he left Camp Bowie that afternoon, having promised his friend that he would be
waiting for him at the gate at sunrise on the morrow.
And in conjunction with that echo was the echo of
another's voice, of Angevine asking him if she would
ever see him again. Doing what he was doing, especially after so many years had passed, did not make
much sense. This he was willing to admit. But he felt
compelled to continue doing it. What was the source

of this compulsion? Was it still, after all this time, about revenge? Was it still about Oulay? Something Nelson Miles had told Summerhayes stuck in his mind. *I've wondered why I survived a battle when so many of my close comrades did not. Why you're still breathing and they aren't.* Was it some deep-seated guilt that motivated him? Summerhayes had alluded to the fact that he'd killed many Apaches, and still he felt that compulsion. So he could not free himself no matter how many he killed. This revelation had come to him years ago. Now he began to think that the real reason for his compulsion was the desire to die. He would at last be free of the guilt.

And why not? Did he have anything to live for? The answer to that question was not a simple one. He had an opportunity for a new beginning; this he had discovered in Santo Domingo only days earlier. There was an offer no man could miss in Angevine's eyes, in her voice, and in her touch. So why did he act as though he didn't see that offer? What was he afraid of? It was a question he did not want to answer, so he tried to force her from his mind.

That night he camped a couple of miles from Camp Bowie, in a small clearing wedged in between an outcropping of sandstone slabs jutting out of the ground and some wind-twisted salt cedar. This was far enough away from the outpost that he didn't have to smell the stench of the place; it was the curse of a man who had lived too long in the wilderness that he lost all tolerance for the sounds and smells of civilization—far enough away too that he didn't need to worry about being stumbled upon by trigger-happy soldiers or civilian contractors. With Apaches on the loose, none of them were going to venture this far from the safety of the camp after dark. Even though, rationally, they had to know that the Netdahe would not be lingering around Camp Bowie, that Geronimo had to be hundreds of miles away by now. But such was the power of the Netdahe reputation—not to mention the reputation of Geronimo. No white man or Mexican who lived in Apacheria would sleep well tonight if they knew the legendary Bedonkohe was free.

That included the Apache hunter. Because there was always that slender chance that he was wrong about the renegades, that they could be right here, and not a hundred miles away. Geronimo was unpredictable. This was one of the reasons he had managed to elude his enemies for so long. And the problem with Apaches was that you probably wouldn't see them until they were in the process of killing you. So, almost as a matter of course, the Apache hunter took certain simple precautions before he went to sleep.

He woke an hour before dawn, his instincts alerting him immediately to danger. As silent as a ghost, he rose and moved through the thicket of salt cedar to a spot where he could see the small clearing where he had made his camp. His horse was still there on its picket. His blanket was there too, still draped over a pile of kindling and stones arranged to resemble, somewhat, the shape of a person asleep. And sitting nearby, with his back to the place where the Apache hunter was concealed, was a warrior. The latter sat on his heels, motionless. Puzzled, the Apache hunter slowly, quietly drew the pistol from his holster.

"Don't shoot," said the warrior, in English. He didn't move a muscle, didn't even turn his head. "I am not here to kill you or to die. I am Chato, Chiricahua Apache."

The Apache hunter couldn't be sure if the Indian was alone. But if this was a ruse to draw him out into the open, it would be very unlike an Apache. He stepped out of the cedar thicket, the pistol still in hand, still leveled at the warrior's head. One shot and the man would be dead. No broncho bent on mischief would sacrifice himself needlessly to draw out a single White Eyes. Apaches, who had always in their history been greatly outnumbered by enemies, understood the math; they were always careful to calculate the odds before any action. If they could not exchange one of their own for three or six or ten of the enemy, they usually avoided a fight. They weren't afraid to die. It wasn't cowardice, but rather pragmatism. They sold their lives dearly.

The Chiricahua slowly turned his head to look up at the Apache hunter. "I know you," he said. "We met once, a long time ago." He studied the other's face a moment before adding, "You do not remember. But I remember."

"What do you want?" asked the Apache hunter. His tone of voice was flat, giving nothing away. Neither did his expression. The pistol was still pointed at the Apache's skull.

Chato looked at the blanket-draped pile of stones and kindling, and there was amusement in his voice. "That fooled me—for a little while. Then I came closer."

"You haven't answered my question."

"I have come to kill Geronimo and his Netdahe."

"By yourself."

"Yes. Do you not hope to do the same? You are the hunter of the Netdahe. The one who kills the Avowed Killers. Is that not why you are here?"

"Pretty much," conceded the Apache hunter. He gave the surrounding darkness another careful scan, more confident than before that Chato had come alone. His horse did not seem alarmed, and in the past it had always served as a reliable sentry. Instead, the animal was placidly watching him and Chato.

"Thing is," continued the Apache hunter, "you must know that Geronimo is long gone from here. So what are you doing wasting your time hanging around the post?"

"I came to see what the soldiers do. For that will determine what Geronimo does."

"This General Miles is going after him. Already has one column on the hunt, and in a day or two he'll be leading the rest out of here. The way I see it, Geronimo is halfway to the Sierra Madre by now. Where else can he go. He'll settle in up in the mountains, and every now and then hit a Mexican village or army patrol. He could stay up there for years, unless Miles is right. The general thinks he's going to march his army up into the Cima Silkq and capture or kill the renegades."

"You are going with him?"

"No. Though I wouldn't mind seeing him hunt Apaches with those mountain howitzers he's planning to haul halfway across eternity."

Chato was silent a moment, staring off into the darkness. "Geronimo has betrayed the Chiricahua.

We took him in, and he repaid us with deceit. But that is his way." He glanced solemnly at the Apache hunter. "A rattlesnake is a rattlesnake, a scorpion a scorpion. They have their nature. Geronimo is the same. It was a mistake to give him a place among us. And now my people will pay for that mistake."

"Then why go after him?"

"Because for the Apache to live, Geronimo must die."

The Apache hunter thought that one over. "Does Juh know what you're planning to do?"

Chato nodded. "Of course. I told him."

"And he gave you his blessing?"

"I didn't ask him if I could go," replied Chato curtly. "I told him."

The Apache hunter considered his options. To join forces with Chato was not in *his* nature. He preferred to do his manhunting solo. But he already had one partner: Charles Summerhayes. At least, until Summerhayes succumbed to his wounds. And he was thinking that Chato would be an asset, rather than a liability. For one thing, he might be able to learn a great deal about the He who followed Geronimo. It always helped to know thine enemy.

"Lieutenant Summerhayes is coming with me," he told Chato. "You might as well too if you want."

Chato considered the offer. He didn't ask why the Apache hunter was dead-set on tracking down and killing the Netdahe. Like most others, he knew this man's story. He had already considered the advantages of accompanying this man. A lone Apache traveling through a countryside up in arms because a band of troublemakers had jumped San Carlos would have a lot to worry about long before he even caught up with Geronimo. Most White Eyes and most Nakai-Ye would shoot first and ask questions later. Once he reached the Cima Silkq, he could part company with the Apache hunter.

"I will ride with you," he said.

The Apache hunter only nodded. Saddling his horse, he told Chato to stay put; he would return to Camp Bowie and fetch Summerhayes. Chato agreed. This was as close as he dared get to the outpost. The soldiers would be inclined to shoot anyone who bore even a slight resemblance to an Indian.

Arriving at the post at daybreak, the Apache hunter found Summerhayes dressed, with a horse saddled and ready.

"Well, you lived through the night," the Apache hunter said wryly. "Congratulations. I was thinking maybe I should swing by the quartermaster's and pick up a shovel, since I'll probably have to dig your grave before nightfall."

"I'm going," said Summerhayes. So weak he could barely stand, he wasn't amused by his friend's gallows humor. "Like I said, you don't—"

"Yeah, I know. Let's get going."

He waited until they were out the Camp Bowie gate before informing Summerhayes that they had another traveling companion. Summerhayes was glad to hear it.

"I owe him my life," he told the Apache hunter. "Maybe I'll get the chance to repay that debt."

They found Chato at the night camp, and rode

south together. Less than a mile from the outpost
Chato made a sudden noise of surprise and brought
his rifle up.

"*El lobo!*" he breathed.

The Apache hunter looked—and knocked the barrel of Chato's rifle down before the Chiricahua could
get off a shot.

"I'd be obliged if you didn't shoot it," he said.
"That's a friend of mine."

The wolf-dog came loping closer, and fell in behind them. It was obviously pleased to see the
Apache hunter, but uncertain about the other two
humans. It circled this way and that, checking out
Chato and Summerhayes with all of its senses. It was
particularly interested in Chato, since he knew that
his man companion hunted Apaches—and this one
looked and smelled like an Apache.

"Don't worry," the Apache hunter told the others.
"He'll get used to you, after a while."

"I should hope so," said Summerhayes fervently.
The presence of the wolf-dog made him all the more
determined to remain conscious and in the saddle.

Chapter 8

Heading south out of Camp Bowie, the Apache hunter mulled over the irrefutable fact that this was, in all likelihood, the last great Apache raid. Even if Geronimo and any of his followers were taken alive, he doubted they would be returned to a reservation; the army wasn't naive enough to buy into any promises of good behavior, and certainly wouldn't want to afford their Apache nemesis the opportunity to jump the reservation again, whenever the urge struck him. No, a captured Geronimo would spend the rest of his time in shackles. The Bedonkohe probably realized this too. So the Apache hunter expected him to go down fighting. With Geronimo dead, the chances of another breakout were substantially reduced. The Apache spirit had been pretty effectively crushed beneath the heels of the White Eyes.

Once Geronimo and his Netdahe were dealt with, what would he be left with? Maybe there were a couple of renegades left in the Cima Silkq; he'd been working on that assumption for some time now, and had flushed out three in the past few years. Then again, maybe there wouldn't be any left. What would he do then? With no wild Apaches left to hunt, what would become of him? Since the murder of Oulay his life had had but a single purpose. Now he had to face the possibility that he would soon have *no* purpose in life. Could he finally set aside his vow of vengeance and discover a *new* purpose? He wasn't sure. But he had a hunch he knew where to find that new reason for living.

The Apache hunter believed in fate. He thought of it as the tool of a sometimes capricious, even cruel, God who often tested a person's faith beyond its limits. Or maybe Fate was just God's way of crafting a hell on earth for those who did not deserve his mercy. The Apache hunter had seen the hands of fate—or God—in the chain of events leading up to Oulay's death. He had cursed God for letting her be taken from him. He wasn't sure why he was being punished so severely. Did anyone, ever? God worked in mysterious ways, or so people said. He had been plunged into his own living hell, wandering alone in the wilderness, a man who lived solely for the purpose of bringing death to others, and achieving no solace from his actions. Yet he could not let go of it. He could not turn away from vengeance. Sometimes he'd thought this was because he did not want to live. Without Oulay, was there a reason to? Sometimes he thought it was because he blamed himself for her death. He should have stayed with her, protected her always, every day, every hour, every minute, from the many dangers of the world in which they'd lived.

But now, in his opinion, Fate had dealt him another card. Was it simply coincidence that the summons from Tom Horn had taken him back, after all

these years, to Santo Domingo? To Angevine? Was
God finally showing mercy? Now that he was on the
trail of the last of the Netdahe, was he being shown
the way to a new and infinitely better purpose? Or
was he being set up for an even deeper level of living
hell? Was God waiting for him to take a chance and
open his heart to her—only to have her snatched
away from him by some cruel twist of . . . fate? There
was the crux of the matter. Did he dare suffer again
what he had suffered all these years because of
Oulay? Or did he keep his heart a fortress of stone?
The latter course was certainly the safest. It was also
the loneliest. He'd resigned himself to living the rest
of his life alone. But that wasn't really living.

Should he risk living again? The question occupied
his thoughts during the day, kept him awake at
night. It was a distraction—and he could not afford
to have any distractions when he reached the Sierra
Madre. So he had decided to swing by Santo Domingo on the way. He wasn't sure what might be
accomplished by doing this, by seeing Angevine
again. He told himself that he simply wanted to
make sure she was okay. After all, Netdahe were on
the rampage. That was partially true, but then he had
all along doubted that an attack on a Nakai-Ye village was what Geronimo had in mind, at least for
now.

He was pretty sure about Geronimo's intentions.
He had hunted Apache warriors long enough to
know how their thought processes worked. The Bedonkohe hoped to set an example that would inspire
other Apaches—those still living on the reservations,
to take to the warpath. If he and his handful of fol-

lowers succeeded in eluding the United States Army, and if they conducted a series of successful raids, the Apaches at San Carlos would surely get wind of it. At first, it would be a few bored young bucks, raised on stories about Mangas Colorado and Vittorio and their heroic struggle against the Pinda Lickoyi. Then more would go, and still more. Some would be captured. Some would perish on the way to the Cima Silkq. Some, though, would make it. If he could hold out long enough, Geronimo might one day muster a sizable force of broncho Apaches. With a hundred warriors he could drench the northern provinces of Mexico in blood. No one—not Angevine, not Manuel, no one—would be safe.

So he had to stop Geronimo and his Netdahe. Was it fair to Angevine, then, to pay a call, only to leave on a job from which he might not return? No, it wasn't fair at all. The right thing to do was to avoid Santo Domingo altogether, at least until the Apache threat had been dealt with. He told himself this a hundred times. But it didn't do any good. He kept to a route that would take him back to . . . her.

It was fortunate for Summerhayes that the Apache hunter decided to make for Santo Domingo. He had traveled but a few miles from Camp Bowie before coming to the conclusion that he would never make it to the Sierra Madre. Every step taken by the horse beneath him sent shock waves of pain through his body, pain so severe and constant that it made him want to retch. Enduring such unrelenting torment sapped what little strength he had left in his body; midway through the first day, he was fading in and out of consciousness. He would have fallen from his horse had the Apache hunter not been there to catch him. From that time on, the Apache hunter rode stirrup to stirrup with Summerhayes, while Chato did likewise on the other side of the ailing lieutenant. They made an early camp that evening. Summerhayes was feeling too wretched to eat. He lay down and tried to sleep. Waking the next morning, he was racked with chills and fever, and could not even climb into the saddle.

"He is dying," said Chato. "There is nothing we can do for him."

The Chiricahua sat on his heels near the semiconscious lieutenant, looking as though he was prepared to maintain a death watch for as long as it took.

"I'm not going to just sit here and watch him die," said the Apache hunter. "Santo Domingo is a half day's ride away."

"He cannot ride half a day."

"Sure, it might kill him. But what difference does it make if he dies here or on the trail?"

Chato looked at the Apache hunter. "He is your friend."

"I've lost friends before," the other said brusquely. "Let's get him on his horse."

He broke out the rope he had used for years to lash corpses to a horse for transport down out of the mountains and to the Mexican army outpost at Dolorosa. He tied Summerhayes' feet together under his horse's barrel, then took the rope several times around the lieutenant's waist before tying it off to the saddlehorn. They rode as they had the previous afternoon, with Chato to one side of Summerhayes and the Apache hunter on the other. The latter was angry; there was nothing he could do to save his friend, and that feeling of helplessness was the source of his anger.

Summerhayes was still alive when they reached Santo Domingo. The Apache hunter considered this a bona fide miracle. There was another miracle in store for him: the feeling that surged through him when he saw Angevine again. She came running out of her adobe, and the smile on her lovely face was brighter than the noonday sun. She rushed up to his horse, and put a hand on his leg, gazing up at him as though there was nothing else in the world of any interest to her; she didn't seem to notice, for instance, that he was traveling with an Apache. Didn't even pay attention to the wolf-dog, which sat on its haunches nearby.

"You came back," she said, like it was the last thing she'd expected to happen.

There were things he wanted to say, but he couldn't get them off the tip of his tongue. "I, um, I have a friend here"—he gestured lamely at Summerhayes—"who's badly hurt. Can you help?"

She looked at Summerhayes just as the latter passed out and lurched sideways in his saddle, restrained by the rope so that he could not fall, but leaning so far to one side that it looked as though his spine would snap. She went quickly to him and tried to hold him up.

"Cut him loose!" she gasped. "Carry him! Hurry!"

The Apache hunter slashed the rope, and he and Chato gently transferred Summerhayes into the adobe, to the very bed the Apache hunter had occupied not too many days earlier. The wounded man was bleeding—his tunic was heavy and black with blood. Angevine cut away the tunic, and then the blood-soaked dressing underneath, to get to the wound.

"We must close this," she told the Apache hunter. She looked up at Chato, and for the first time seem to realize that she had an Apache in her house. It didn't faze her for long—she asked him, quite calmly, if he spoke Spanish.

"A little," said Chato.

"Build a fire, please." She turned to the Apache hunter. "Manuel is hunting. We'll need plenty of fresh water. Will you go to the well?"

He nodded. Chato headed for the fireplace. The Apache hunter grabbed the water bucket and went outside, taking the time to tether all the horses before heading for the zocalo, relieved that the wolf-dog was content to sit near the door in the shade cast by the adobe. He was hoping to get to the well and back without drawing attention to himself. Because sooner or later the villagers would discover that there was an Apache in their midst, and later was better. It was fortunate that Angevine's adobe was located at the edge of town; apparently no one had noticed them riding in, or else the alarm would already have been raised. His coming in with the wolf-dog on his previous visit had caused quite a stir, but that would have been as nothing compared to the tumult that Chato's presence would trigger.

The zocalo was empty. It was midday—siesta time. He carried a bucket filled to the brim back to the adobe and, at Angevine's direction, poured the water in a large wooden tub. Chato had a fire going. Angevine requested more water, and the Apache hunter obediently returned to the square for a second time. This time, though, he found the zocalo occupied. And not by *campesinos,* either. None other than Tom Horn, accompanied by a single soldier, a corporal, was just then riding into the square, making for the well. They spotted the Apache hunter as soon as he saw them, so there was nothing for him to do but continue on to the well. As the two riders dismounted, he dropped the well bucket down the shaft.

"Howdy, Barlow," drawled Horn. "So you're still here. Didn't you hear? There's a war on."

"A half dozen Apaches on the loose," said the Apache hunter, waiting for the well bucket to fill up. "Doesn't sound like much of a war to me."

"Well, it ain't like I blame you for hangin' around this godforsaken place. Reckon most men would want to put their boots under the bed of that purty little nurse of yours."

"You've still got a big mouth."

Horn grinned, touched the side of his head. "And still got a knot the size of Delaware on my skull, thanks to you. But I ain't one to harbor a grudge."

"I am."

Horn shrugged and gave the zocalo a long survey. "Your half dozen bronchos have raised all kinds of hell east of here. The Cordoba hacienda got hit. They killed four vaqueros and made off with about fifteen, twenty horses. The corporal here's got dispatches for General Miles, and I'm along for the ride."

The Apache hunter was surprised. Why had Geronimo hit a rancheria? It didn't make sense. "What

did he need horses for? He had plenty with him
when he crossed over the border."

"Well, not exactly. Major Bendix has been chasin'
'em hard. Some of their ponies gave out. I killed a
few others. They tried an ol' Apache trick, but it
didn't work. Geronimo and three others dropped off
in Gavilan Canyon. Two of the bronchos took their
horses and made tracks south. It was Mickey Free
who caught on. He told Bendix that most of the
horses didn't have riders. See, Geronimo aimed to
run us into the ground. His two bronchos would run
south a day or two, then circle back north and pick
him up. Most of his horses would be fresh. Bendix
wasn't all the way convinced, but he let me ride east
and Mickey west, just in case Mickey was right, and
the bronchos had doubled back. Well, I was the lucky
one. Ran right into them. Killed several of their
horses, wounded one of the bronchos. The other one
got away. The broncho I hit bled to death that night.
I moved in the next mornin' and found him stone-
cold dead. We killed another one a couple days earlier. That one must've been hit when the Netdahe
ambushed that detachment coming back to Bowie
from San Carlos. Anyway, he lasted longer than
most, then holed up in some rocks to die. We came
along before he did, and sent him on his way. So
that leaves Geronimo and four others, by my count."

The Apache hunter was cranking up the well
bucket. "That explains why they took the horses."
He figured there was more to it than that. Things
hadn't been going according to Geronimo's plan, and
the Netdahe had to have been discouraged. A successful raid on a difficult target like the rancheria

would boost their spirits—not to mention their faith in their leader.

"I figure that with the new horses, Geronimo's in the Sierra Madre by now," said Horn. "Bendix is plannin' to wait on General Miles at the Cordoba place. Rest and refit."

The Apache hunter filled his bucket with water. "Well, that's nice," he said, sounding completely uninterested.

His attitude made Horn curious. "I would've thought you'd be hot on the Netdahe trail. That *is* what you do, after all, isn't it?"

"You're right. Geronimo's in the mountains by now. So I'll know where to find him if I need to."

"Miles told a reporter from some big Eastern newspaper that he would not return to the United States without Geronimo, either dead or alive. Now I'll grant you that the general doesn't know a whole lot about fightin' Apaches. But on the other hand, I wouldn't bet against him when he's got his mind set on something. If you want to get the Netdahe yourself, you might want to hurry things along."

The Apache hunter nodded. "Thanks for the advice." Hefting the bucket filled with water, he turned away.

Arriving back at Angevine's, he found her heating the blade of a knife at the edge of the fire. When it was glowing hot, she ordered him and Chato to hold Summerhayes down. When they had a good hold on the unconscious patient, she laid the heated portion of the blade against the entry wound. Summerhayes came to with his body lurching up out of the bed, a guttural sound emerging from a wide-open mouth.

Then he sagged back down onto the bed, again out cold. They rolled him over so that Angevine could cauterize the exit wound. A few moments later they were assured that the bleeding had stopped. Chato and the Apache hunter moved out of the way and watched while she cleaned the dried blood from Summerhayes' upper torso before applying a new dressing. When she was finished, she stood back and breathed a weary sigh, brushing stray tendrils of raven black hair out of her eyes. These she turned on the Apache hunter, and this time he couldn't look away. They looked at each other for a long time, and the rest of the world seemed to him to fade away, and that was good; he realized that for years now his world had been one in which he did not *want* to live.

The spell was broken by Manuel's arrival. He was carrying the shotgun over one shoulder, a couple of rabbits slung over the other, and a pleased smile on his face. The smile got bigger when he saw the Apache hunter. Then he spotted Chato, sitting motionless, out of the way in a corner, and he gave a start.

"Don't worry," said the Apache hunter. "He's one of the good ones."

Manuel looked dubious. The Apache hunter couldn't blame him. As far as Mexico's *campesinos* were concerned, there *were* no good Apaches.

Angevine reached for the rabbits, intending to clean and cook them, but the Apache hunter took them instead. "Let me," he said, gently. "You're tired out." She protested, but he insisted, assuring her that he could make a pretty fair rabbit stew. He proceeded to prove it. By the time they had finished eating, it was dark. Chato ventured outside, to sit with his back to the adobe and smoke his pipe. The Apache hunter joined him.

"Geronimo hit a hacienda east of here," he told the Chiricahua. "Killed some men, stole some horses. General Miles will be bringing his army there. I'm of a mind to ride over and see what the haciendero intends to do."

"He will send his men after the horses," said Chato. "But he will not catch the Netdahe."

The Apache hunter nodded. "Maybe so."

Chato glanced at him, and then out across the malpais, which was softened by the final glow of day; distant buttes were shaded pink and gray, and a deepening indigo filled the low places on the desert plains.

"This is not a bad place to be," he observed. "I would want to stay here if a woman looked at me the way that one looks at you."

"Seems like nobody knows how to mind their own business," lamented the Apache hunter.

"Go to the hacienda. Before daybreak, I will continue on to the Cima Silkq alone."

"There's no hurry. You're right. The haciendero's men won't catch up with Geronimo. And neither will Miles and his soldiers. The Netdahe will be there in the mountains for a while. Summerhayes will be down for a few days at least. I'm not going to leave him behind, because once he's on his feet again, he'll be riding south again, and he won't make it by himself."

He didn't like the sound of it. Because he was just making excuses, stalling. And Chato knew that.

"It is true," said Chato. "It is also true that if I stay here there will be trouble."

The Apache hunter was thinking that Chato would be no match for five Netdahe. He was a great warrior, but that wouldn't be enough. Of course, he wasn't about to say as much. Chato had certainly computed the odds already. But there were things the Chiricahua felt compelled to do. The Apache hunter knew what that was like.

Angevine offered them her floor to sleep on, but Chato refused and spread his blanket outside the adobe. The Apache hunter decided to do the same. He wasn't quite ready to spend a night under the same roof as Angevine. He slept well and woke early, to find Chato preparing to leave. The wolf-dog had already left, and the Apache hunter was wondering if he would ever see the beast again. Maybe it had sensed that something had happened to the man it had traveled with all these years—that a change had come over the man, and that the man's heart was no longer on the wild and lonesome trail, but rather here in this little adobe on the edge of a border town. The wolf-dog would never be domesticated—it could not live in such a place. The Apache hunter experienced a keen sense of loss. *Nothing lasts forever,* he told himself. *You, of all people, should know this.*

Chato mounted up, and the Apache hunter stepped forward to extend a hand.

*　　　*　　　*

Coming in from high ground to the west, the Apache hunter was provided a panoramic view of the Cordoba rancheria, its two large compounds in the middle of a vast plain of green and brown, cut through by the darker green ribbons of trees lining creekbeds. Located south of the larger compound was the U.S. Army bivouac, with its rows of white tents. The Apache hunter's route to the main gate of the larger compound took him directly past this encampment, so he wasn't surprised when a pair of cavalrymen on sentry duty stopped him and asked him his business.

"I'm here to see the patron," said the Apache hunter.

"Major Bendix says no one comes or goes without him knowing about it," said one of the troopers. "What's your name, mister?"

"Smith. Or Jones. Take your pick." Who he was and what he was doing at the rancheria was none of their business, and he didn't feel like cooperating.

"We got us a joker on our hands," one of the sentries told the other.

"You better come with us," said the other. He didn't quite aim his carbine at the Apache hunter, but almost; it was clear he wouldn't mind using it if the Apache hunter resisted.

The latter had no intention of resisting. He glanced toward the gate to the main compound, where several vaqueros were gathered in the scant shade cast by the high adobe wall. They were standing around smoking cheroots and cigarillos and looking very carefree, but the Apache hunter was pretty sure they were, in truth, paying close attention to his confrontation with the two bluecoated sentries, and they were close enough to hear every word.

"Sure," he told the cavalryman.

While his comrade stayed in place at the side of the wagon trace leading to the main gate, the trooper escorted the Apache hunter into the cavalry encampment. *Looks like the thrill of the chase is gone*, mused Barlow as he studied the expressions and body language of the bivouacked soldiers. They looked worn down. There was none of the excitement among these men that he had seen in their comrades at Camp Bowie several days earlier. He was sure it had been there at the outset, as they rode out in pursuit of the legendary Geronimo, dreaming of glory. And now all they had to show for it were saddle sores. They'd seen action, but not the kind they had expected; the Apache hunter was pretty certain that the wounded Netdahe left behind by Geronimo had bushwhacked a few of the soldiers before they'd flushed him out of his hiding place and killed him. That was the way of fighting Apaches—no banners flying, no gallant charges. The Apaches did not fight like gentlemen. They fought to win.

He was taken to the center of the camp, where a tarpaulin had been stretched between four poles to cover a couple of field tables—all this in front of an officer's tent. The Apache hunter saw Major Bendix under the tarpaulin with several subordinates, one of whom turned out to be the officer of the day, for it was to this lieutenant that the sentry reported. While this was going on, Bendix looked up from the maps spread out on one of the field tables. When he recognized the Apache hunter, he came forward.

"What's going on here?" he asked.

The officer of the day responded, explaining that the Apache hunter had been on his way to see Don Miguel Cordoba when he was stopped.

Bendix walked up to where the Apache hunter was patiently sitting his horse. "Tom Horn says you weren't interested in helping us catch Geronimo. So what are you doing here? You a friend of Don Miguel's?"

"Nope. Just thought I'd introduce myself."

Bendix gave him a cold stare. "I'll ask you again: What are you doing here?"

"I'm here to find out how many vaqueros this Don Miguel has sent after Geronimo. I guess I'm going to have to go into the Cima Silkq to kill Geronimo and put an end to this, and right now it's looking like those mountains are going to become the most populated part of Mexico pretty soon, which will make what I have to do all the harder."

"I see," said Bendix, his voice edged with sarcasm. "So Don Miguel's riders and the United States Army will go fumbling around in the Sierra Madre and interfere with your manhunt. Is that it? Strikes me that you have a very low opinion of this army, sir, considering that you once tried to make a career of it. I'll have you know that I intend to catch that devil Geronimo if it's the last thing I do."

The Apache hunter nodded. "And that's the problem, Major. If you capture Geronimo and take him back, one day this will happen all over again. Maybe he'll be wrongly accused of a crime. Or maybe he'll just want some attention. No. Geronimo has to die, because if he doesn't, and there's another raid, people I care about will be put in danger."

"Believe me, I would have no problem killing that son of a bitch," said Bendix. "But if he surrenders—as he is likely to do when we have him cornered—I am honor bound as an officer to accept that surrender."

"Right, but I'm not an officer, and I'm not honor bound to do anything."

"You will shoot him down in cold blood?"

"You bet," said the Apache hunter.

A vaquero arrived, in the style that vaqueros always exhibited—by riding full-tilt until reaching his destination, then checking his pony so sharply that the animal's front legs locked and its back legs slid out from under it, spewing dirt and rock.

"Don Miguel sends his regards to the captain," said the rider.

"Major," said Bendix, through his teeth. "I am a major."

The vaquero shrugged. "Don Miguel, he wishes to know why his guests are being waylaid outside his gate."

Bendix grunted. "Waylaid. I wasn't aware that Don Miguel had invited this man to his door."

"Don Miguel is a generous and friendly gentleman, senor. His door is open to everyone—except the Apache. He told me to tell you that he does not need the Yankee army to guard the gates to his home."

The Apache hunter didn't miss the use of the term "Yankee"—or the inflection of contempt it was dressed up in.

Bendix heard this too, and he didn't like it, not one bit. He had to struggle mightily to contain his anger. He was a soldier, not a diplomat, but in this time and in this place he had to be the latter rather than the former.

"My apologies to Don Miguel," he said stiffly. He gestured dismissively at the Apache hunter. "You're free to go, of course."

The Apache hunter turned his horse away. So did the vaquero, his smile at Bendix just as insincere as the major's apology.

Bendix called after the vaquero, "I'm sure Don Miguel knows that his 'guest' is the one they call the Apache hunter."

The vaquero did not respond to Bendix—did not even seem to hear the major's remark. But the sidelong look he threw in Barlow's direction was filled with curiosity—and wariness.

At the south gate of the main compound, the Apache hunter's vaquero escort called out to his companeros, who were lounging around in the shade of the wall. The heavy-timbered doors of the gate were already open a few feet, but the Apache hunter felt certain that if anyone tried to pass through them without permission the vaqueros would use their pistols. Now two of them moved to open the doors of the gate wider. Once inside, the Apache hunter noticed first how empty and quiet the compound seemed to be. He estimated that probably one hundred fifty people, maybe more, called this place home. But few people were visible, and most of these were men, all armed to the teeth. Such, he mused, was the after-effect of an Apache raid. The dread would linger on long after the threat was gone.

As they neared the big hacienda, a man emerged through a mahogany door. He was big and barrel-chested, yet carried himself with an easy grace. He was clad in a dark green chaqueta and black chino trousers. Here was a man of substance, as the pearl-handled revolver on his hip and the scrolled silver on his belt buckle testified. His black hair was streaked with gray, as were the well-trimmed goatee and mustache on his sharp-featured face. The Apache hunter did not need an introduction to know that this was Don Miguel, the patron of Rancho Cordoba.

Don Miguel took one look at the Apache hunter and made a curt gesture. "I do not know this man," he told the vaquero. "He is just a drifter. Give him food, and his horse water. Then send him on his way."

"But . . . patron . . ." The vaquero did not lightly disregard orders from his boss.

"Yes?" Don Miguel was impatient, half-turned to go back inside his hacienda.

"They told me that this is the Apache hunter."

Don Miguel's dark eyes narrowed with a quick and keen interest as he gave Barlow a second, longer look. "Is this true?" he asked.

"*Es verdad*," replied the Apache hunter.

Don Miguel thought it over for a moment. "Come. You are welcome in my home." With that, he went inside. The Apache hunter glanced at the vaquero, not sure what to do next. The vaquero nodded at the door, indicating that he should follow Don Miguel.

Dismounting, the Apache hunter drew his long gun from its saddle boot. This was habit—he did it without conscious thought. Belatedly, he wondered how the vaquero would respond to his entering the patron's casa so heavily armed. But the vaquero apparently thought nothing of it. Taking the reins of the Apache hunter's horse, he rode off in the direction of the second compound, and the Apache hunter, with one last look around, went inside.

As soon as his bootheels echoed off the polished wooden floor of the big house's main hall, Don Miguel called from a room to his right. The Apache hunter passed through a broad arch and found himself in a spacious room filled with fine furnishings. Mahogany, teak, walnut, velvet, silk, damask, crystal, gold, and silver—his senses were briefly overwhelmed by the rich elegance of it all. He was surprised to find such a place here on the malpais.

"My late wife, God rest her soul, had a taste for expensive things," said Don Miguel. He stood at a sideboard and was pouring from a decanter into a glass. He paused in what he was doing to cast a quick, almost reluctant, look around the room, and the Apache hunter thought he detected a profound grief in the man's eyes and voice. "I have no use for such things." He continued pouring, and his voice was gruff now, the grief again well-disguised. But the Apache hunter knew now that it was bravado, and he felt a kinship with Don Miguel, for he had experienced this very kind of loss. "But I keep them here, to honor her. She loved this house." He offered the filled glass to his guest. "Whiskey?"

The Apache hunter experienced that familiar craving.

This time, though, he managed to resist it. In this place and at this time, there wasn't room for the old demons he tried to fight with liquor—Don Miguel's own demons filled up the room and the moment.

"It's ironic," mused the haciendero, "that I never seemed to have time to spend with her while she was alive. I was too busy building this place, and then holding on to it against Apaches and rebels and bandits. Now that she is gone, I have too much time on my hands, and I sit here for hours and think about her." He fell silent for a moment, lost in the past. Then he looked, somewhat ashamed of this show of weakness, at his guest. "Forgive me. It is because I know your story that I speak of such things. Even Don Miguel Cordoba needs someone to talk to." He smiled a self-deprecating smile. "And who better than you to understand?"

"I'm sorry for your loss. I don't know if this will help, but I recently learned something."

"What is this lesson you have learned, senor?"

"That you have to let go of the past."

Don Miguel sipped his whiskey. "Good advice. But the past sometimes will not let go of you. Is that not why you still hunt the Netdahe?"

"No, that's not why. Not anymore."

Don Miguel was perplexed. "Then why are you here, senor, if you are not on the trail of that devil, Geronimo?"

"Oh, I'm still hunting *him* because I have to kill him. But I'll be killing him for an entirely different reason than I have killed all the Netdahe that came before."

Don Miguel finished his whiskey and proceeded

to pour himself another. The Apache hunter felt sorry for him. The liquor would eventually dull the pain, might even let him forget, for a little while. But he would always remember, even if he learned to let go of the pain.

"Whatever your reasons, I am glad you are on his trail," said the haciendero. "For I fear the American soldiers out there are not capable of stopping the Apache threat. They should not even be here in Mexico. The government was wrong to accept that treaty. Forgive me for saying so, but your government is arrogant. Many Mexicans vehemently opposed allowing American soldiers on our soil, but our government gave in to coercion from Washington. They said it would be in our best interests to let the Yankee soldier chase the broncho Apache across the border. The implication being that our own soldiers were not up to the task, which may be true. Nonetheless, it rankles. Mexico was invaded by your soldiers once before, and down here, memories are long."

"Yes. My father was in that war."

"As was mine. But I digress. If my vaqueros fail to catch and kill the Netdahe, I derive satisfaction from knowing that *you* will not fail."

"The Apaches kill your wife?"

"No. She died of consumption. Twelve long years ago."

"Then why do you hate the Apache so?"

"Why?" Don Miguel was incredulous. "Why? Because, senor, they are a plague upon my land, upon Mexico."

"This used to be *their* land."

"Don't waste your time trying that argument on me.

To the strongest go the spoils. Before the Apache, the land belonged to someone else. The Apache took it from them. Now we have taken it from the Apache. This is the way of things. At least most of the Apache understand that their time is over. Only the Netdahe fight on."

"Your people created the Netdahe."

Don Miguel's eyes flashed with anger. "*Sí*, I have heard all of the old excuses for Geronimo and the rest. That they were peace-loving Indians minding their own business until my people massacred their loved ones."

"Not an excuse. It happened—more than once."

"Of course it happened! How else were the *campesinos* to protect themselves? They did not have horses and rifles—they could not fight the Apache face-to-face. Though I will say, in their defense, that the one thing they *did* have was the courage. Just not the means. And so they lured their enemy into a trap, promising peace and friendship. Is that without honor? Yes, probably. But survival trumps honor every time, senor."

It occurred to the Apache hunter that Don Miguel had just given voice to the justifications used by Apaches for the guerrilla tactics they had employed so effectively for so long. Outnumbered and outgunned by their enemies, the Apaches were forced to resort to hit-and-run operations, to ambush and deception. If they had not, they would have been destroyed long ago. People said the Apaches were without honor. But for an Apache, there was no honor in dying a useless death.

So that meant there was no right side in this

generations-old fight, mused the Apache hunter. No right or wrong, good or evil. Nothing so clear cut. Except for one thing—who would be the winners, and who the losers. It seemed inevitable that the United States would vanquish the Apache nation. It was just a matter of time. But on an individual basis, the divide was less clear. He had lost, and he had won. A person would have to tally up the balance sheet at the end of his days and figure out whether he'd been a winner or not.

"I assume," said Don Miguel, "that you will go directly from here to the Sierra Madre. If there is anything you lack—food, ammunition, anything—all you need do is ask. And if you need men to ride with you, men who are skilled at tracking and shooting, I can provide you with ten, fifty, a hundred."

"No offense, but your men would just get in my way. Speaking of which—how many have you sent after your horses?"

"Twenty. Led by my segundo, Ochoa." Don Miguel smiled slyly. "But you know, senor, that they are not really after my horses. I realize I will never see those horses again. Geronimo will ride some to death to reach the mountains. Those that survive will be turned loose to run wild, or killed by the bronchos. No, Ochoa and his men go for the same reason that you are going. And if you aren't quick about it, amigo, they will do your job for you."

"I'll take that chance. A friend of mine was wounded by the Netdahe. He's healing up—or dying, I'm not sure which, just yet—over in Santo Domingo."

"And after Geronimo is gone, and there are no more Netdahe—then what will you do?"

The Apache hunter shook his head. "I don't know. Try to start living again, maybe."

"Do you know anything about cattle?"

"I ran a few head up north. For a while."

"Even if you didn't, it wouldn't matter. You are always welcome here. I could use a man such as yourself, senor. Because even when the Apaches are gone forever, there will be a new threat."

"I'll consider it."

It was too late to return to Santo Domingo that day, so he stayed the night at the Rancho Cordoba and started out at daybreak. Arriving at Angevine's, he was relieved to find Summerhayes conscious. The fever was gone and he was on the mend. The Apache hunter told him about the Apache raid on the Cordoba hacienda. Told him too that Chato had gone on alone.

"Why didn't you go with him?" asked Summerhayes.

Barlow glanced at Angevine. "I'm in no hurry."

Summerhayes saw something in the way they looked at each other—something that told him all he needed to know.

"Well," he said wryly, "I'm glad you're not sticking around here just for me. Give me a couple of days and I'll be up and around."

"No, you will not," said Angevine, showing a flash of temper that surprised both men. "You won't get out of that bed until I tell you to."

"Yes, ma'am," said Summerhayes hastily.

She walked away, shaking her head. "I don't understand why you men are in such a hurry to die."

That night, after supper, the Apache hunter went

outside and sat with his back to the adobe, out of the lamplight coming through the open door. When Angevine came out to join him a few moments later, he started to rise—he'd been on the trail for a lot of years, but he hadn't completely forgotten his manners. She put a hand on his shoulder to stop him, and sat down next to him, wrapping her arms around her legs and drawing her knees up under her chin.

"You are going into the mountains soon," she said. "Going after the Apaches."

"Yes." He wasn't going to lie to her. He couldn't. "But I'll be back this way."

She looked at him, her gaze very earnest and sad. "My husband said that—before he left me for all those years."

He didn't know how to respond.

Angevine sighed. "You should go now. Tomorrow. Before your friend grows stronger. Leave him here. He is too weak to make the journey. If he loses more blood, he will die."

"You're right. I'll go at first light."

She stood up, and he wanted to take her hand, to keep her beside him, to tell her how he felt. Instead, he just sat there. She looked down at him a moment, then said, "I will be waiting," and, bending down, brushed his cheek with her full, soft lips. Then she was gone, hurrying inside.

He woke the next morning to find his horse saddled and waiting. Summerhayes was still sleeping.

Chapter 9

As the days passed, Kiannatah came to appreciate the Mexican girl more and more.

It wasn't just the sex. Kiannatah had been celibate for a very long time, and when he covered her the first time, he did so roughly. She did not struggle, and though she cried out softly when he took her, she did not weep after. Instead, she touched his shoulder softly, a gentle caress, and told him that he did not have to do it "that way." From then on, every night, she was his willing partner. They made love by the light of a small fire built at the back of the cave he called home, and he always marveled at the rich brown glow of her skin, at her tight, smooth body, the long thick black hair that hung almost to a waist that he could completely encircle with both of his hands.

From the first day he let her come and go at will. He wasn't sure, at first, whether she would stay of her own volition. But even if she tried to run, where would she go? He would catch her before she could escape the mountains, and there was no place she could hide in the Cima Silkq that he would not find her. Not once did she give any indication that she wanted to flee; she seemed quite content to stay with him, despite the primitive accommodations. She cooked for him, fetched water for him, on occasion killed small game for their dinner, and even destroyed two of the many rattlesnakes that infested the steep, rocky slopes around the cave. She made a loincloth from the skin of a mountain deer, and took to wearing this rather than her dress, explaining to Kiannatah that she preferred to save the dress for some special occasion, and implying that she understood—and found acceptable—the likelihood that she would spend the rest of her life in these mountains without the opportunity to acquire more clothing of that sort. She did not seem at all ashamed of her nakedness—and why should she? In fact, it seemed to him that she adapted so quickly and so well to the kind of life that lay in store for her that she became as one with the primitive environment in which he dwelled, and it looked perfectly natural for her to go around only in the loincloth. The sun burned her long, slender legs, her boyish hips, her small, rounded breasts; it streaked her raven black hair with copperish highlights; it made her, in Kiannatah's opinion, a beautiful creature.

Even though she never complained, Kiannatah decided it would be worth the risk to leave the safety of the cave, high up on that remote, snake-infested mountain, and build a jacal in a better location, where the game would be more plentiful, and where one did not have to endure an exhausting climb to fetch a little water, just to make life a little easier for her. One morning he gathered up his weapons, leaving her only with a knife, and told her that he might

be gone for more than a day. He did not explain
where he was going or why. A broncho Apache did
not customarily explain himself to a woman. She did
not want him to leave. It wasn't that she feared being
left alone, but rather that she was worried something
might happen to him. She begged him to take her
along. He curtly refused. When she insisted, Kiannatah grew angry. His anger stemmed from the sudden
realization that he did not want to leave her any
more than she wanted him to go. He instantly recognized this feeling as a weakness. His instinct was to
strike back, and he raised a hand, intending to hit
her. She did not cringe, but rather raised her chin at
a defiant angle and looked him squarely in the eye.
There was no fear in her gaze, only forgiveness for
the transgression he was about to commit. It was then
that Kiannatah had an epiphany—he needed this
woman child, wanted her to be with him until the
end of his days. There was a magic about her. It
came naturally; she did not wield it. This magic had
captured him completely, had opened his heart,
which he had thought was closed to such feelings
forever. Lowering his hand, he told her to stay close
to the cave, and assured her that he would be back
soon. She said nothing more, merely followed him
out onto the ledge and watched him go down the
slope. Near the bottom he looked up and saw her
there, standing like a slender bronze statue in the
hot, bright sunlight, the wind catching her hair and
throwing it out to one side like a banner unfurling.

He found the place he had once occupied, years
ago. Back then he had taken another Mexican woman
as his captive. He had kept her for a while, but she

was not like the woman child waiting for him at the cave. She had no magic, and he had not cared for her—evidenced by the fact that he had killed her when she became a liability and a burden. The place was in a sad state of disrepair, and Kiannatah decided that it would not do.

Later that same day he found an old adobe—once the abode of a Nakai-Ye prospector, probably, now a burned-out shell. By this time, Kiannatah was leaning toward building a new jacal in a place of his own choosing. He knew of several likely spots that were remote, set deep in the mountains, filled with game and endowed with a good supply of year-round water. In such a place he and the woman child might be able to live for a long time without interference from the outside world. Not forever—Kiannatah did not believe in forever. But he could dare hope for a year or two. And a year or two was like forever to a man like him, a man who had never had reason to plan beyond the morrow.

He made another decision that day—to continue killing the Nakai-Ye whenever the opportunity presented itself. Perhaps he would even begin to actively track them down and kill them. He could find them easily enough, now that the mines had been re-opened. He would strike fear in the hearts of all Mexicans, and make them think twice about coming into the Cima Silkq. If he sat back and did nothing, more and more of them would come, thinking that the mountains were, finally, safe, and the chances of their stumbling across him and the woman child would steadily increase.

Late in the day he was on his way back to the cave

when he crossed some recent sign. Horses—five of them, all shod. Nakai-Ye, then. They were not, however, anywhere near the most common routes used by those who came to and from the mines. Out of curiosity, and because they were fairly close to his hideout, Kiannatah followed the sign for a while. A little farther on, he saw that the horses had been stopped, and several of the riders had dismounted. He knelt down and closely studied the human sign. The hair on the nape of his neck stood on end. These were not Nakai-Ye, after all. These were Apache riders. On stolen horses, no doubt, since Apache ponies were unshod. And if the horses were stolen, then these were renegades. Where had they come from? Kiannatah was fairly certain that there had not been—until now—five other broncho Apaches in the Cima Silkq. So they had come from elsewhere, seeking sanctuary here.

They had come from the reservations north of the border. That was the only answer that made sense.

Kiannatah sat there on his haunches for a spell, considering the implications of this startling discovery. Any way he looked at it, it was bad news for him. He wasn't willing to share the Cima Silkq with other renegades, because these five would only bring trouble with them. They would establish a base somewhere in the high country and proceed to raid the rancherias and villages on the desert plains all around. This would trigger a hue and a cry across the land. Five broncho Apaches could cause a lot of damage. They might even wreak such havoc that the Nakai-Ye soldiers might have to venture once more into the mountains in an attempt to flush them out.

Not that he believed the Mexican Army would be successful, but the Nakai-Ye could inadvertently stumble upon him and the woman child. Then there was the Apache hunter to think about. He would surely step up his efforts to scour the mountains for Apaches. That too increased the danger for the woman child.

Kiannatah was not concerned for his own welfare. But the woman child's safety was of paramount importance to him. She was Nakai-Ye, but she might be taken for an Apache. Even if this were not so—even if her true identity were discovered, she would most likely be killed. A woman who had taken up with an Apache, voluntarily or not, was not going to be accepted back into the fold by her own kind. They would have no use for her. She would be damaged goods, and put down, like a rabid dog.

With growing resentment at the intrusion of the five renegades, Kiannatah continued trailing them. When night fell he saw their campfire. They thought themselves safe in the mountains, and they had undoubtedly been on the run for many days; they thought the fire was an acceptable risk, under the circumstances. Kiannatah crept closer, silent, invisible. He worked on the assumption that there would be a sentry. They might not have posted one, but if he erred it would be on the side of caution.

Eventually he arrived at a spot where he could look down into the camp and see the Apaches. Wedged in between big rocks, screened by a few wind-twisted salt cedars, Kiannatah crouched there, staring at one of the five men who sat around the

fire. He was more than fifty yards away, but the firelight clearly illuminated the features of the renegades. Kiannatah didn't know four of them, but there
was no doubt in his mind as to the identity of the
fifth.

Goyathlay. Geronimo—the man who had been as
a father to him. His mentor. Now his enemy.

This meant the other four were Netdahe.

I should kill them all right now, he thought. It would
not be easy, but Kiannatah was supremely confident,
even when it meant taking on five Avowed Killers,
even when that number included Geronimo, the
leader of the Netdahe, the Bedonkohe prophet, the
legendary raider. The one many Apaches thought
possessed special powers. Kiannatah had once revered Geronimo, had been one of his most devout
followers. He had firmly believed that Geronimo
could foretell the future, could commune with Ussen,
could even control, to an extent, the elements. In
those days he would have followed Geronimo anywhere. Would have given his life, gladly, for the Ben-
donkohe. But not anymore. Not since that day when
Geronimo had turned against him. It was then that
Kiannatah had realized the truth. Geronimo was no
different from any other Apache leader. No different
from Cochise or Juh. He would fight the enemies of
the Chi-hinne only when it was to his advantage,
and when things got too hot he would abandon the
way of the Netdahe. Kiannatah had never abandoned
the way. He killed who he wanted to kill, took what
he wanted to take. When he had wanted to take
Oulay, daughter of Cochise, Geronimo had balked,

for fear of antagonizing the Chiricahua chieftain. Kiannatah feared no one, not even the mighty Cochise. Thus he had become a liability to Geronimo.

I am still the only true Netdahe, thought Kiannatah. He'd assumed that Geronimo, like all the other Apaches who'd lost the will to fight, had gone to live on the reservation. That was something a true Netdahe would *never* do. The man he had once revered was now, for Kiannatah, the object of his contempt. Those who rode with him were, by association, worthy only of contempt, as well. It would certainly not be difficult for the one true Netdahe to destroy such men. To do so would avert all of the potential problems their presence here might cause. He could kill them, and leave their corpses where they lay, and the scavengers would come and tear the bodies apart, scattering the bones they left, and no one would ever know what had become of the great Geronimo and the four who rode with him. There would be no raids, no Nakai-Ye intrusions into the Cima Silkq, and the Apache hunter would, hopefully, someday soon conclude that there was no one left for him to hunt, and go away. There were plenty of reasons to kill the five, and Kiannatah could think of no good reason to let them live.

Kiannatah waited, motionless in the rocks and cedar, unseen—unseeable—the most dangerous predator in the mountains, more dangerous than the bear, the cougar, the wolf. The five Apaches huddled around their fire, warming themselves against the chill of the Sierra Madre night, unaware that the instrument of their deaths lurked so near at hand. Eventually the fire died down, and one by one the

Apaches stretched out on the hard ground to sleep. Geronimo was the last to do this. He sat there for a long time, gazing into the fire. Kiannatah did not look directly at him. Even an old man like Geronimo had instincts. Finally the Bedonkohe lay down. The last flame flickered out, leaving only a bed of glowing embers. Infinitely patient, Kiannatah still waited. The stars in the heavens moved. Night breeze moved the branches of the salt cedars. Occasionally one of the stolen horses, on a picket on the opposite side of the camp, moved. But Kiannatah never did. He was as motionless as the stone beside him.

An hour later he made his move, gliding confidently through the camp, coming within a few feet of several of the sleeping Netdahe on his way to Geronimo. They were, of necessity, light sleepers. But even if they had been awake, they would not have heard his passage. Reaching Geronimo, he stood there a moment, looking down at the Bedonkohe. He touched the pistol at his side; he could put a bullet in Geronimo's brain, and probably kill the other four before they could get to their feet and fire off a shot at him. But hubris got in his way. He wanted Geronimo to know the identity of his executioner. So, leaving the pistol in its flap holster, he drew his knife from its sheath and sat on his haunches so that he could lay the blade across Geronimo's throat.

The caress of cold steel against his Adam's apple woke Geronimo instantly. His eyes snapped open. But he didn't move. He was immediately aware of the nature of the threat, and when he looked up at Kiannatah, he became aware of its source. Those eyes, black as obsidian, widened with surprise as he recognized his assassin. He opened his mouth to speak, or perhaps to call out an alarm to the sleeping Netdahe—Kiannatah wasn't sure which. Kiannatah put a finger to his lips. Then, on the spur of the moment, he decided to wake the others himself. They would see their leader die, and be powerless to prevent it. Picking up a small stone, he threw it at the nearest sleeping form. This was Uklenni. The young Netdahe woke and sat bolt upright, reaching for the rifle that lay on the ground beside him. When he saw Kiannatah, just a few feet away, and saw the knife at Geronimo's throat, he froze, the tips of his fingers just brushing the rifle. Slowly he pulled his hand away from the weapon. Kiannatah nodded at the others. Uklenni understood what he wanted. In a quiet voice that carried no alarm, he spoke their names. In seconds all four of the Netdahe were awake and fully aware of the situation in which they found themselves. Kiannatah did not have to issue a warning; it was plain that he would slay Geronimo if they moved against him. They looked to their leader for guidance—if he had given any indication that he wanted them to kill the intruder, regardless of what that might mean for him, they would have done so. But Geronimo made no move, uttered no sound. He simply watched Kiannatah and, after the initial moment of surprise, revealed nothing by his expression.

Natoosay was the first to speak. "I know you," he said. "You are Kiannatah. We rode together against the Pinda Lickoyi."

"I remember," said Kiannatah. "Pay attention, Natoosay. You will see that Goyathlay has no magic that can protect him from a knife in the throat. He is without power."

"If you kill him," warned Natoosay, "you will kill any hope for the Chi-hinne."

"There is no hope for our people. And this man is *not* the savior of the Chi-hinne, even though he talks like he is. Do you think he fights for his people? No. He fights only for himself."

"Like Kiannatah," said Natoosay.

Kiannatah smiled. Indeed, he did remember Natoosay—a quick thinker as adept with words as he was with rifle or bow. "The difference is, I do not claim to be the savior of my people."

"You must not kill him!" exclaimed Uklenni. "The others will not come if they know Geronimo is dead."

"The others?"

"Geronimo says they will come when they hear that we are free in the Cima Silkq, attacking our enemies at will."

Kiannatah smirked. "Boy, you were taken too soon from your mother's breast. That will never happen. The spirit of the Apaches who live now on the reservations is dead. You cannot reawaken it. Do you know why Geronimo is really here? Because he was being forgotten. Now others can die so that his name will live on. But when it comes time for him to die, he will surrender."

Uklenni trembled with rage. Kiannatah had implied that he was a fool, no wiser in the ways of things than a child. Yet he could not act, because the knife still lay across Geronimo's throat.

"Why do you do this?" asked a surly Santana. "You are Netdahe. We are Netdahe. Join us, and we will fight our enemies together."

"No," said Kiannatah curtly. "I have never stopped fighting my enemies. I do not need you. These mountains are my home now. You do not belong here."

"If you kill Geronimo," said Uklenni, "you will have to kill us all."

"So be it."

He looked down at Geronimo and Geronimo, looking up at him, saw his own death reflected in Kiannatah's eyes.

"Wait!" said Natoosay. "You say these mountains are your home. Let him live, and we will leave the Cima Silkq."

"You have no honor," said Kiannatah scornfully. "You would say anything to save this worthless life, and none of it is true."

"We are all Netdahe. *That* much is true."

I am the only true Netdahe left standing, thought Kiannatah.

"He does not deserve to die in this way," insisted Natoosay. "Let him at least die like an Apache warrior. If you want to kill us, fight us like a man, like a Netdahe."

Kiannatah would not have responded to promises or pleas. But he responded to the challenge in Natoosay's words. Did they think he would not be able to kill them all unless he snuck into their camp like a thief in the night?

Abruptly he stood up, and now the pistol had materialized in his other hand. It was pointed at Geronimo's head. "You have until the sun sets again to leave these mountains," he told them. "If you are here on the following day, I will kill you. Then I will take Geronimo's head back to the reservations, and show the people who used to be Chi-hinne that this is the fate of those who come here."

Then he spat, not only to demonstrate his utter contempt for them, but also to infuriate them, because he was more than willing to finish it here and now, if they provoked a fight.

For his part, Natoosay was not surprised that Kiannatah was acting in this manner. As he had mentioned, they had ridden together under Geronimo many years before. Even in those days, Natoosay had considered Kiannatah to be the perfect Netdahe. He was an accomplished killer, and relished the slaying of his enemies. He was endowed with remarkable skill and strength and stamina. He was intelligent and cunning. But Natoosay had never fully trusted him. Kiannatah was one to stay apart from the others. And he sometimes challenged Geronimo's decisions, acting as though he *knew* better than the Bedonkohe. Natoosay had not been surprised when Kiannatah fell out of favor with Geronimo. Nor was he surprised to find Kiannatah still alive and looking as strong and dangerous as ever. Natoosay did not relish having to fight this man.

"These mountains belong to all Apache," said Uklenni. "What gives you the right to decide who can stay and who must go?"

"You have one day," said Kiannatah, and turned away.

"Kiannatah."

It was Geronimo. He was rising from the ground, and took a moment to brush himself off before lifting his head to look at the man who had just spared his life.

"You are no longer Netdahe," said Geronimo coldly, "or you would have killed me."

"If I see you again, I will."

He vanished into the darkness. The Netdahe reached for their weapons, and made as though to go after him, but Geronimo stopped them with a gesture. As usual, he did not explain himself. And, as usual, they obeyed, albeit reluctantly. Geronimo lay back down where he was, and seemed to the others to go back to sleep. Santana and Lucero followed suit. But Uklenni did not think he could sleep after what had happened. He looked at Natoosay, who was sitting cross-legged, with his rifle across his lap, studying the darkness.

"Natoosay," whispered the young Netdahe, "do you think we will leave the mountains?"

"No. There is no place for us to go."

"You know this Kiannatah—will he really try to kill us all?"

"I know him," said Natoosay gravely. "He is the best of the Netdahe. Also the worst. And yes, he will try."

Back among the rocks and the salt cedars, Kiannatah listened to these words. He had lingered just to be sure that none of the men in the camp would try to follow him. Convinced that they would not, he moved away.

He traveled through the night and was near the

cave at daybreak. He was anxious to see the woman child again—to make sure she was all right. But he took the precaution of doubling back on his trail, just to make sure that Geronimo was not following him. Only when he was sure of this did he proceed on to his hideout.

She was there, waiting for him, safe and sound, and happy to see him. It took her only a moment, though, to realize that something was wrong. She asked him what had happened, but he said nothing. With a shrug she picked up the two canteens they used to bring water up from the nearby spring. He spoke then, curtly telling her not to go. She obediently put the canteens down and sat cross-legged facing him—and there she sat, just watching him. Annoyed, he tried to ignore her. Later, he lay down and pretended to sleep. An hour later, when he sat up, she was still there, still watching him. At that point he gave in.

"There are Apache out there," he said, nodding toward the cave entrance. "Geronimo and four others."

He detected a glimmer of fear in her eyes when she heard Geronimo's name. Like all Nakai-Ye, she knew Goyathlay.

"You are right to be afraid," he said. "If they find you, they will kill you."

"But they are your own people."

"I have no people anymore. I am an outcast."

"So am I. But at least we have each other. What else do we need? We can leave these mountains. We can find another place."

"There is nowhere to go. This was the last place."

"Well, we can't stay here. You won't even let me leave this cave."

Kiannatah brooded in silence for a while. Now it was brought back to him why he had chosen to live alone for most of his life. Why he had not dared take a wife, nor indulged in dreams of having a family. Because having people you cared about was a liability. He had learned that lesson at a very tender age— that day he had seen his family slaughtered in Dolorosa. Having the woman child to watch over, to worry about, put limits on his options. But he could not simply leave her to her own devices. He had become accustomed to her company and did not want to be without it. And why shouldn't he indulge himself? He was Kiannatah, after all. Last of the Netdahe.

"No," he said, making a decision, "we will stay here. It is Geronimo who must go. Until he does. You will not leave this cave except at night."

"So now I am a prisoner here," she said.

He refused to dignify her comment with a response, and she went to the other side of the cave to sulk. Sometimes, he thought, the child in her held sway. That evening, he went to her, hoping to awaken the woman concealed within the child, but when he placed a hand on her shoulder, she petulantly pushed it away. Then she looked up at him, her eyes veiled by her long hair, and he was at a loss to tell what she might be thinking. Without a word he returned to the other side of the cave, lay down on his blanket, and went to sleep.

When he woke, the sun had not yet risen. It was

his intention to slip quietly out of the cave without waking the woman child. There was no point in waking her just to reissue his warning about leaving the cave during the day. She knew his wishes, and he could only hope that she would comply. If she didn't, it was likely that no harm would come to her; Kiannatah was fairly certain that Geronimo and his Netdahe posed the only real threat to him and the woman child, at least for the time being. And in a day or two, that threat would be eliminated.

But just as he was leaving the cave, she rose quickly and went to him and touched his arm. Shreds of gray predawn light were beginning to leak through the cave entrance, so he could just barely see her lovely, angular face. She was gazing at him very earnestly, studying his face.

"I just want to look at you one last time," she said softly.

A chill ran down Kiannatah's spine. Other women might have used such a remark as a devious attempt to dissuade him from leaving. But he knew that wasn't the case with the woman child. She spoke quite calmly, as though resigned to some terrible but inevitable fate, and with such conviction that he could not doubt that she sincerely believed this would be their last moment spent together. He recalled the occasion of their first meeting, when things she had said caused him to believe that she had the gift of foresight.

"I will return," he said confidently.

"I know," she replied. "But I will not be here."

Kiannatah frowned. What did she mean? "You must stay in this cave during the day. Go out, if you must, only at night. I will not be gone long. And when I return, the danger will have passed."

She looked around the cave—in the way, he thought, that someone looks at their surroundings knowing it is for the last time. Then she sighed. "You must forsake vengeance, Kiannatah," she said, in such a soft whisper that he could scarcely hear her, even though she stood so close to him that he could feel the heat from her body.

"It is what kept me alive," he told her, by way of an explanation. That in itself was proof of the change she had wrought in him, for he was Netdahe, and did not have to explain himself to anyone.

"I know. But you must let go of it. Or it will kill you next."

He shook his head, wanting to hear none of this, wanting to believe that it was nonsense, the imaginings of a female mind, yet fearing that there was more, much more, to it than that.

"I must go," he said gruffly and crawled out through the crevice into the growing light.

Halfway down the slope, he paused to look up at the ledge where the cave was located. "She was nowhere to be seen. As he continued on his way, he tried to shake the feeling that he would never see her again.

Chapter 10

Returning to the place where he had last seen Geronimo and the Netdahe, Kiannatah very nearly stumbled right into the camp of the yellow-legs.

It was still early—the sun had risen, but here in the mountains night-shadow still clung to the low places. The only thing that saved the Netdahe was a whiff of wood smoke. He dropped instantly to the ground and remained quite still for a long time, straining all his senses to detect any danger that might be lurking nearby. Finally he heard it—the telltale trickle of small stones down a slope, dislodged by a carelessly placed foot. He peered in the direction of the sound, and saw the soldier moving out from his place of concealment in some rocks on a slope to the left, about a hundred yards away, heading downhill, in the direction whence the wood smoke had come. Kiannatah saw the blue cavalry uniform. He could scarcely believe his eyes. The last thing he had expected to see in the Cima Silkq were yellow-leg soldiers! This was the country of the Nakai-Ye. So what were the American horse soldiers doing here?

The light was slowly improving, and now he saw the rising smoke from the cavalrymen's cook fires, heard the distant sounds of a camp rousing from its slumbers. The man who had left the slope had been a night sentry. That he had left his post without waiting for a replacement told Kiannatah that the yellow-legs were about to break camp. Taking a chance, assuming that, if there were other night sentries that they too had gone down to the camp, Kiannatah moved, crawling through the rocks and brasada until he found himself on a rim from which he could look down into a hollow and see the White Eyes. The cavalrymen had built their fires and brewed some coffee; they were in the process of saddling up to move out. Kiannatah counted thirty-two of them. Their jefe was a tall, lanky man wearing an insignia that Kiannatah did not know. The Netdahe assumed he was an officer of high rank. He was also, decided the Netdahe, a fool. But then, most of the yellow-leg officers were. Assuming that he was after Geronimo, why was he allowing fires that produced smoke that might be seen by his prey?

Of particular interest to Kiannatah was the absence of Apache scouts. There was only one man not in a cavalry uniform. He was a short, wiry man dressed like a cowboy—a red checkered shirt, a yellow bandanna, a high-peaked hat. He was sitting on his horse, rolling a cigarette, apparently waiting for the soldiers to form up. Kiannatah noticed the long rifle in its deerskin saddle scabbard. A buffalo gun. The cowboy was probably a marksman of considerable skill. He would be one to watch out for.

Kiannatah had left his hideout to find Geronimo and the Netdahe and kill them. He was confident that they were still in the Cima Silkq. He was less

confident that he would succeed. They were no
longer true Netdahe, but there were five of them,
and he was a pragmatist. Five Apaches would not
be easy to kill. In addition to being pragmatic, Kiannatah had learned to adapt to a changing situation.
His life had been such that situations were usually
fluid; plans often went awry or became unworkable,
and quick decisions had to be made. The presence of
the yellow-legs was a case in point, and Kiannatah
spent a moment trying to calculate the ways they
might affect his task.

Down below, the man in the cowboy garb spoke
to the yellow-leg jefe, and then rode out. He was
followed a few moments later by the horse soldiers.
They traveled in single file, with the last six men
towing heavily laden pack animals. Considering the
amount of supplies they carried, Kiannatah figured
that the yellow-legs intended to remain in the mountains for quite some time, if that proved to be necessary in order to complete their mission. It was bad
enough, thought Kiannatah, that Geronimo and his
renegades were in the Cima Silkq. Now he had
thirty-odd cavalrymen to worry about.

It was then that Kiannatah came up with a plan
Even if he succeeded in finding and killing Geronimo
and his followers, the soldiers would remain in the
Cima Silkq, searching for men they did not know
were dead. This presented Kiannatah with an addi-
tional problem. Somehow, the yellow-legs had to be
made aware that their prey was no longer on the
loose. Only then would they leave the mountains.
Kiannatah reasoned that the ideal way to do this was
to arrange it so that the yellow-legs did the killing

themselves. That would make it easier for him, since all he would have to do was lead the horse soldiers to Geronimo.

The scheme pricked his conscience. If he did this, he asked himself, would he be any different from the Apaches who had scouted for the yellow-legs in the past, the very Apaches upon whom he had heaped scorn? Kiannatah tried to find a difference, but could not. There was none. There was no justification for one Apache betraying another to the enemies of the Chi-hinne. The various Apache bands had often warred against one another down through the generations, but even this could not excuse the behavior of, say, a White Mountain Apache who helped the yellow-legs capture or kill a Mescalero or Chiricahua. Certainly, then, Kiannatah's personal feud with Geronimo was no excuse, either.

This realization, though, did not deter Kiannatah. His one and only priority was to get both Geronimo and the yellow-legs out of the Cima Silkq, in order to make the woman child safe. Nothing else mattered—including his honor. Objectively he could see just how great were the changes she had wrought in him, and that some of these changes were not for the better. But his heart ruled his head now, forcing him into actions that he would never before have contemplated.

To decide was to act. Seeing the general direction that the soldiers were taking, Kiannatah left his vantage point and went in search of Geronimo. To avoid discovery by the Bedonkohe and his followers would be difficult; now he had to remain unseen by the yellow-legs as well—at least until it suited him to be otherwise. He wasn't too worried about the horse soldiers themselves. Many years had passed since the Apache wars, and Kiannatah doubted that very many of the yellow-legs had the experience unique to—and necessary for—tracking and fighting Apaches. The cowboy with the buffalo gun, though, was another matter. It was best to assume that he was skilled at reading sign.

Kiannatah returned to the place where he had last found Geronimo. As he had suspected, the renegades were no longer there, and they had left no sign to indicate where they had gone. But he expected that Geronimo would instinctively move higher and deeper into the mountains. All he had to do was find them. Of course, the renegades would be watching for him; they would have taken his warning seriously.

Many were the hiding places in the Cima Silkq, and Kiannatah expected the search to take several days, and was prepared to stay on the hunt for as long as it took. All the while he had to keep an eye out for the yellow-legs with their cowboy scout. He saw them only once, and then from a great distance; nonetheless, with the cowboy scout's buffalo gun foremost on his mind, he was quick to disappear.

On the third day he had some luck. Climbing through some rocks, he startled a pair of turkey vultures, which rose up to his right, so close that the sudden explosion of flapping wings startled him. He crouched, muttering a curse under his breath; his first thought was that he might have given away his position to a lookout, if one happened to be posted nearby. Belatedly, he thought to check the crevice in the rocks whence the buzzards had taken flight. There he found a few traces of blood, a few bone shards, and some tufts of hair, which he identified as rabbit. Checking the ground for twenty paces in every direction, he found what he'd hoped to find— a fragment of a moccasin print in dirt that had settled into a depression into the rock. A carelessly placed Apache foot had left that print, of this Kiannatah was certain. He could extrapolate from the evidence that one of Geronimo's Netdahes had been hunting for food, had spotted a rabbit, killed it, and eaten it on the spot, leaving only the bones and hide and offal for the scavengers. Kiannatah knew how it was to forage for food while on the run. You took what you could find, and often did not have the time or means to build a fire and cook your food. The rabbit had not been sufficient game to take back to the others. The hunter had probably used a stone or spear or maybe a bow and arrow to make the kill; he would not expend a precious rifle or pistol cartridge. Finding food was a primary concern for the renegades now. Eventually Geronimo might allow them to kill one or more of the stolen cavalry horses. But not yet—not while a situation might arise in which they might need to make a fast getaway.

Kiannatah did not expect to be able to track the hunter back to his camp and companions. The hunter would not be that careless. But he did expect to find Geronimo somewhere nearby, for the hunter would not stray too far afield. He knew these mountains as well as any man, and reviewed in his mind the most likely places within a few hours' walk in any direction. There were several that provided good cover and year-round water, if you knew where to look for it. He thought it likely that Geronimo would have chosen one of those sites, and that he would be able to locate his prey before too much longer.

He was right.

They were camped in a hollow at the base of a sheer slope, where water from a creek trickled down into a pool that turned the grass beneath a canopy of green lush cottonwoods. Such an oasis was not unusual in the Sierra Madre—one simply had to be lucky to stumble upon them, because they tended to be found in the most remote areas. The rim of the cliff, accessible by a very steep game trail, gave a lookout an excellent vantage point from which to scan the surrounding countryside. The shortcoming of this vantage point was that if an enemy reached the trees unseen by the lookout, he could use them for concealment. Kiannatah knew of the place, and knew to check the rim of the cliff for a lookout. He saw the sentry before he actually spotted the camp. He slipped in behind and above the lookout and did not have to get in close, for all he needed to do was identify the man. When he was sure that it was Na-toosay, he left the area immediately.

He had located Geronimo—now he needed to lead the yellow-legs to him.

It wasn't difficult to find the horse soldiers—their movements were about as obvious to someone with Kiannatah's heightened senses as a stampeding herd of bison. But he had to be careful of the cowboy scout. The buffalo gun's bullet could put a hole in him the size of a man's fist. The second problem was how to leave a trail that would convince the yellow-legs' scout that it was genuine. The trail could not be obvious, or it would raise suspicion. The yellow-legs would be wary, ever mindful that ambush was a favorite Apache tactic. And, of course, he had to leave the sign where the cowboy scout would be likely to find it; he could not count on any of the horse soldiers to be skilled enough in tracking to spot it.

He kept an eye on the yellow-leg detachment the rest of the day, knowing that the safest way to locate the cowboy scout was to wait for him to return to the column. This he did, shortly before sundown. The soldiers had already made camp. Kiannatah took note of the direction whence the scout came. He had to work under the assumption that when he set out the following morning, it would be in the same general direction. And so, that night, by the light of an early moon, Kiannatah made his trail, being sure to leave sign across the routes most likely to be taken by the scout. He made certain that his trail pointed north, in the general direction of Geronimo's hideout. When he was done, and satisfied with his work, he found a high rock outcropping at the base of a steep slope, from which vantage point he could see back along his trail. There he waited for the dawn, sleeping fitfully. He was anxious to return to the cave—to make certain that no harm had befallen the woman child. Her parting words continued to haunt him. But there was no help for it—he had to rid the Cima Silkq of both Geronimo and the yellow-legs.

Early the next morning he spotted the cowboy scout, and felt a surge of elation as he realized that the man was following the course of his trail. Not precisely, but close enough. Holding to such intermittent sign was no easy matter. You had to be patient, trust your instincts, and rely often on educated guesswork. If a trail disappeared, as Kiannatah's frequently did, you had to determine the most likely course taken by the man you were following; with luck, you would find another track along the way; if not, you would have to quarter to the left and then, if necessary, to the right, hoping to pick up the trail again. The cowboy scout's instincts were well-honed. He veered off the trail a couple of times, but was soon right on it again. As he drew closer, Kiannatah left the rock outcropping and began moving deeper into the mountains. Always he took the path of least resistance. Geronimo and his Netdahe would be careful, but not too careful; they would assume that they were relatively safe within the Sierra Madre. They would chance staying down in the flats and canyons, where the going was easier. The cowboy scout would expect this to be so.

All that day Kiannatah remained ahead of the scout, expecting the latter to stay hot on the trail. He would not go back to bring the yellow-legs; he wouldn't need to. He would be leaving a plain enough trail that even the horse soldiers could follow it. Kiannatah had to be sure to keep out of sight—the scout would be scanning the countryside ahead, hoping to catch a glimpse of the Apache he was following; he could tell that the sign he followed was fresh. Kiannatah wasn't sure if the scout would shoot if he caught sight of his prey. Logically, he would simply want to follow, hoping to be led to the others. But one could never be sure about the White Eyes. The hesh-ke—the killing craze—could rise up strongly within them, especially where Apaches were concerned.

By midafternoon Kiannatah knew that he was drawing very near Geronimo's hideout. Access to the spot was gained by following a serpentine canyon to the place where it split into three parts, and taking the center part a half mile. Kiannatah proceeded into the center part before finding a place where he could scale the steep flanks of the canyon. He worked under the assumption that, once in the canyon, the cowboy scout would follow it to its conclusion. If he did, he would find Geronimo's encampment.

Kiannatah climbed quickly, making the difficult ascent with the agility of a mountain goat, so he was concealed in the rimrock by the time the scout entered the central fork of the canyon. He moved along the rimrock, careful not to be seen by the man below, and shadowing the scout as he proceeded. The scout stopped several times, looking for fresh sign and finding none. Occasionally he scanned the canyon walls and the rimrock high above, always thinking of an ambush. But he had plenty of nerve, and kept on, going slower, more cautiously, now. Would he be foolish enough to ride out into plain sight of the Netdahe lookout on the cliff above Geronimo's camp? Kiannatah hoped not. He had no idea how long it would take the yellow-legs to arrive, and he hated to think that the scout might spook Geronimo so that the Netdahe were long gone by the time the horse soldiers showed up. He was pleased, then, to see the scout jump down off his horse prior to reaching a bend in the canyon. If he had blundered on

round the bend, he would have been in full view of
the Netdahe sentry. Instead, the scout took his long
gun and, ground-hitching his horse, climbed up the
canyon wall opposite Kiannatah, to some boulders
stacked precariously against one another approximately a hundred fifty feet above the canyon floor.

Once the scout disappeared into the rocks, Kiannatah faded back away from the rimrock. He had seen
enough to be confident that the scout would not give
himself away to Geronimo. All he could hope for
now was that the horse soldiers themselves would
move quietly through the canyon. It was still possible
that Geronimo could escape, if given enough warning. Bearing this in mind, Kiannatah had resolved to
remain close by—close enough to hear gunfire from
the camp if the yellow-legs managed to catch Geronimo and his renegades there. Close enough, as well,
to catch up quickly with Geronimo if the latter managed to elude the horse soldiers. While hoping that
his scheme would work, Kiannatah knew that there
were many variables over which he had no control.
The one thing he *could* be certain of, however, was
that Geronimo and his followers were dead by nightfall. This was the ultimate goal, and while he would
have preferred the yellow-legs to do the deed, he
was ready and willing to take on the task himself.

At dawn that day, Natoosay had awakened to find
Geronimo sitting cross-legged on a slab of rock beside the spring-fed pool. The Bedonkohe seemed en-
tranced; he sat with his forearms resting on his inner
thighs, palms turned upward; his head had fallen
forward, chin resting on his chest. Santana and Lu-

cero were still sleeping, and Uklenni was up on the rim of the cliff. It had been Natoosay's intent to relieve the youngest Netdahe. Now, though, he forgot about Uklenni; all his attention was focused on his jefe. Natoosay was alarmed at first, for it didn't appear as though Geronimo was even breathing. But as he approached, the Bedonkohe raised his head, opening his eyes to gaze impassively at him.

"Forgive me, jefe," said Natoosay. "I did not mean to disturb you."

Geronimo simply shook his head. "You have followed me for many years, and you have never disturbed me. I will miss you above all the rest."

Natoosay was perplexed. "What do you mean, jefe? I will ride with you until the end."

"Yes. I know."

"You have had a vision?"

"No. Just a bad dream. Now go. Relieve Uklenni. He had slept long enough."

As he moved away, Natoosay was even more confused by Geronimo's last comment. It was uncommon for the jefe to joke. He was not known for his sense of humor. Yet his comment about Uklenni sleeping while on watch was said in such a way that Natoosay knew Geronimo was joking.

It was a strenuous climb to the top of the cliff that overlooked their camp. The game trail was narrow, steep, and treacherous. It was also the only way out for the occupants of the camp if access through the canyon was denied them. And if they escaped up the trail and over the rim of the cliff, they would have to leave their horses behind. Cavalry mounts or not, those were the only horses presently available to them, and until better ones were found as replacements, Natoosay thought much care should go into keeping them. But Geronimo was thinking of Kiannatah, and Kiannatah only. He did not think they had anything to fear from the Nakai-Ye soldiers. Nor did he think the American soldiers would follow them into the Cima Silkq. Natoosay was inclined to agree with that assessment, but felt that Geronimo was wrong not to be concerned about the vaqueros from the hacienda they'd hit some days earlier. The jefe didn't doubt that the haciendero had sent his vaqueros in pursuit. But he was certain that they would not risk entering the Cima Silkq, either. In short, Geronimo was putting his faith—and betting his life— on the reputation of these mountains as a place of almost certain death for a Nakai-Ye. That had once been so. Times had changed, however. The enemies of the Chi-hinne had grown much bolder, now that The People were so weakened. That the yellow-leg soldiers could cross the border with apparent impunity was evidence that things were not the same as they had once been. Natoosay thought it would be wiser to work on the assumption that the old rules no longer applied.

Geronimo, though, was thinking only of Kiannatah. He fully expected Kiannatah to carry out his threat. And here there were only two approaches to the camp—down the canyon in plain sight, or over the rimrock and down the cliff. And so they waited. Natoosay didn't mind the waiting. Like the others, he wanted to get this business with Kiannatah resolved before they moved on to something else.

Uklenni wasn't sleeping—Natoosay hadn't expected him to be. Taking charge of the Mexican fieldglasses that Geronimo was insisting the lookout use, Natoosay sent the young Netdahe back down to the camp with the suggestion that he sleep. Uklenni looked like he could use some rest. Natoosay imagined that his nerves were frayed after spending the night on watch for a man like Kiannatah. With Uklenni gone, Natoosay settled down in a spot from which he could clearly see the canyon and, at the same time, had an unobstructed view in all other directions as well. While most of his attention was focused on the canyon, every now and then he would look around him. Foremost on his mind was the certainty that Kiannatah would come soon. Could they prevail over the lone Netdahe? Natoosay wasn't sure. And, apparently, Geronimo wasn't sure, either. How else to explain his strange comment?

The early-morning hours passed uneventfully. At the base of the cliff, Geronimo and the three other Netdahe remained in camp. Only occasionally could Natoosay see them through a break in the cottonwood canopy. But he kept his eye on the canyon for the most part, sometimes using the long glass to get a better look, not that he expected Kiannatah to ride down the canyon and into the camp, in plain view. With Kiannatah, you never knew what to expect.

The last thing Natoosay expected to see was the dusty column of yellow-legs coming around a bend in the canyon—and heading straight for the Netdahe camp.

He couldn't believe his eyes, and he froze, if only for a few seconds. And seconds mattered, if Geronimo and the others were going to have time to ascend the trail to the rim of the cliff, and escape. Recovering from his surprise, Natoosay moved closer to the rim. In the urgency of the moment he forgot about his own safety, and left the cover of some rocks. He made the call of the owl—the agreed-upon alert— thinking while doing so that it was a very appropriate choice, since, in the Apache view, the owl was associated in several ways with death. Crouching there on the rim, cupping his hands around his mouth, Natoosay made the call—and then died.

He did not feel pain. He was alive and then—in the next instant—he was dead. He did not hear the thunder of the buffalo gun bouncing off the canyon walls. He did not see the telltale puff of powder smoke among the boulders on the canyon wall about eight hundred yards away. He was unaware of toppling forward off the rim and plunging down through the cottonwood branches, snapping his spine on a large limb, and then flopping like a rag doll on the rocks around the spring-fed pool.

Tom Horn moved as soon as he fired the shot, knowing that the .50 caliber Sharps Leadslinger threw out a lot of smoke. He reloaded on the move— a valuable habit that he'd picked up a long time ago. There was no doubt in his mind that he had killed the Apache on the low cliff at the end of the box canyon. He'd been expecting one of the Netdahe to show himself on that high ground sooner or later, because an hour earlier, as the morning light reached down under that stand of cottonwoods, he had caught a glimpse of several Apaches. They didn't offer him a good shot, and besides, he hadn't wanted to give his presence away until the soldiers arrived. But Major Bendix and his troopers were here now, and fortuitously, an Apache had stepped right out into the open. Tom Horn felt deep satisfaction with the result. Killing a man from such a distance gave him a sense of power he could not acquire in any other way. Who else but the Lord Almighty could do what he had just done—to kill so quickly and surely, from so far away, with but the twitch of a finger?

Down below, the horse soldiers were beginning their charge, while the Apaches over under the trees started shooting at them. Tom Horn found a likely spot to settle in and began to look for an opportunity to reach out and kill someone else. He had no desire to go down there and join in the hell-for-leather charge. He wasn't looking for glory. He wasn't out to prove himself on the field of battle. Honor was just a five-letter word, same as whore, and just about as valuable to him.

Given the circumstances, the four Netdahe Apaches gave a good accounting of themselves. As soon as they heard Tom Horn's shot, they grabbed their weapons and fanned out under the trees, and as the yellow-legs came charging forward they took careful aim and picked off one after another of the horse soldiers. But still the cavalrymen kept coming, and Uklenni experienced a twinge of despair that they could not be turned away at least long enough for the jefe to escape up the cliff trail. The first soldiers to reach the trees were well to his right, where Santana and Lucero were located; Uklenni saw the latter leave his place of concealment and, leaping like a panther, carry one of the Yellow-legs out of the saddle. As soon as they hit the ground Lucero struck, a savage stroke of the knife. Uklenni could not see the soldier Lucero straddled, but he did see a great geyser of blood as Lucereo's blade opened the man's throat. The blood didn't bother Lucero; bathed in it, he rose and turned—and was hurled violently backward as several bullets struck him in the chest. Two more cavalrymen came through the trees on their horses. One of them paused long enough to fire down into Lucero's body at point-blank range. Not more than a stone's throw away, Santana died almost in the same instant. Flanked by several troopers, he darted through the trees in the direction of Uklenni and Geronimo. Several soldiers tried to bring him down, but he was too fleet of foot. One yellow-leg got directly in his path. Without missing a stride, Santana brought his rifle up and fired a split second before the yellow-leg could. Santana leaped for the just-emptied saddle. Grabbing the reins, he turned the horse and, with rifle held high overhead, shouted defiance at his enemies. The cavalrymen closed on him from several directions. They shot him down. But, like all Netdahe, Santana was hard to kill. Though mortally wounded and unable to stand, he was still moving. A cavalryman dismounted and used the butt of his carbine to smash Santana's skull. He struck many more times than was necessary, taking delight in the act.

Seeing all of this, Uklenni was both saddened and enraged. He was not afraid, however—even though he knew that this was his day to die. Now, at last, he had his chance to prove his worth as a Netdahe. He raised his rifle, intent on killing the nearest yellow-leg, well aware that in firing a shot he would reveal his location to the enemy. As luck would have it, the direction of the horse soldiers' charge had taken them into the cottonwoods well to Uklenni's left. They were milling about under the trees now, searching for more Apaches—they had killed several and knew there were probably more. Because of this, Uklenni might have managed to escape. Yet fleeing never crossed his mind. He drew a bead on the soldier who had so viciously finished off Santana, and was on the verge of squeezing the trigger when Geronimo grabbed his arm, his grip like iron.

"We will kill no more White Eyes today," said the Bedonkohe.

Uklenni did not at first understand. Surely Geronimo was not intending to flee the battle. It was one thing for a Netdahe to attack his enemy, striking hard and quickly before melting away into the malpais. But when attacked, a Netdahe stood his ground and made the attackers pay dearly in blood for his life.

"We can kill many of them before we die," he insisted.

"No," said Geronimo sternly. He began to affix a white cloth to the end of his rifle's barrel.

Uklenni found himself wondering where the white cloth had come from, and how long Geronimo had been carrying it with him. "What are you doing?" asked the young Netdahe.

"You will kill more of our enemies," said Geronimo. "But not today."

Uklenni came then to the full realization of what

it was that Geronimo intended. It shocked him so that he gasped for breath. "No!" he cried out. "We will die here, with the others."

"You are young and foolish," chided Geronimo. "There is no honor in death."

"Kiannatah was right. You have no power." His tone was scornful—a tone he had never before adopted with Geronimo. But then, he now saw the Bedonkohe in an entirely different light. A true light. Dismayed beyond more words, he realized that he had been living an illusion. And the reality was one which he did not want to endure. Making a decision, he began to rise, intent on firing that shot anyway, hoping now that it would bring the yellow-legs so that they would kill him quickly, and end the anguish in his soul.

Before he could fire—before he could even rise— Geronimo struck him across the base of the neck with the stock of his rifle. Uklenni sprawled on his face, unconscious.

Standing, Geronimo stepped out from the trees that had concealed him, the rifle held up so that the white cloth could be clearly seen by the yellow-legs. Several horse soldiers saw him and gave a shout almost simultaneously, and in a matter of seconds, a dozen cavalrymen were closing in on the Bedonkohe.

"I am Geronimo," he called out, in English. "I fight no more. Do not shoot."

They didn't shoot. The call went out for Major Bendix, who arrived on the scene in short order. He recognized Geronimo and nodded, deeply satisfied.

"Well, I'll be damned," he said. "We got you, didn't we?"

Geronimo's broad, creased face was impassive. His rifle had already been taken from him, so he stood with hands behind his head, surrounded by the yellow-legs, several of whom had their carbines trained on him. He knew that he was not yet completely out of danger—one wrong move and a nervous trigger finger might twitch.

"You are a great warrior," he told Bendix. "The first to capture Geronimo."

"Don't patronize me, you son of a bitch. Where's Sergeant Birch?"

"He's dead, sir," said one of the cavalrymen.

"Then find him horse, damn it. He had the shackles." Bendix turned back to Geronimo. "You and your bronchos killed some good men today But you won't be killed—unless you try to escape."

"I will not try to escape. You have my word."

Bendix snorted, "The word of an Apache. Now there's something that's worthwhile."

The sarcasm in his tone brought forth laughter from some of his men. A stern glance from him quickly silenced it.

"You're lucky," Bendix told Geronimo. "Lucky that it was the United States Army that tracked you down because there are others out there who wouldn't bring you back alive. You've made some powerful enemies. I guess that means you're important. Important enough, anyway, that General Miles wants you alive."

Geronimo nodded gravely. His features, a stony mask, did not betray the elation he felt. The yellow-leg officer was right. He *was* important. Looking around him at the circle of horse soldiers, Geronimo decided that the cost in lives had been worth it. The raid had been worth it, because once again, he was the center of attention.

Kiannatah was elated too when he heard the distant gunfire. He had witnessed the passing of the yellow-leg column down canyon, and from that point on, he had waited with eager anticipation. For the first time, impatience almost got the better of him. Then the shooting started, and he permitted himself a modicum of self-satisfaction. His scheme was working. With any luck, the horse soldiers would kill Geronimo and his followers, and then leave the Cima Silkq. The shooting was fierce, but short-lived. Kiannatah waited still. He waited for hours, until, at long last, the yellow-legs came back up the canyon. Well-hidden on the rim, Kiannatah noted with deep satisfaction the bodies of Apache bronchos strapped in a dead man's ride across the backs of horses towed by several of the cavalrymen. Then he frowned. There were only three bodies. He searched the column from beginning to end. There was the cowboy scout, riding near the head of the column. And there were more than a half dozen dead yellow-legs, also strapped across horses. Then he saw Geronimo and Uklenni. They rode, side by side, at the middle of the column. They were shackled, and the men riding behind them had carbines aimed at their spines.

He was keenly disappointed. Geronimo was still alive. He had been captured—or perhaps he had surrendered. Contempt for the man he had once idolized surged through Kiannatah so powerful that it turned his stomach. His first impulse was to use his rifle and kill the Bedonkohe. Geronimo alive was a liability. He might escape again, might seek refuge in the Cima Silkq again, bringing danger once more to the woman child. Or he might tell the White Eyes that one last Netdahe—the *last true* Netdahe—still roamed free in the Sierra Madre.

But what could be done about it? Kiannatah considered his options, and found none of them to be acceptable. If he killed Geronimo—he could probably hit his mark from here with his long gun—that would simply alert the yellow-legs to his presence. They would launch a manhunt and comb the Cima Silkq for him. He could follow the cavalry column until it left the mountains, and then try to reach Geronimo, but he doubted that such an effort would be successful. With Geronimo in custody, the soldiers would be more vigilant than usual. He decided he had no choice but to let things stand.

The yellow-legs were leaving the Cima Silkq, and so was Geronimo—to that extent, his plan had worked. But the elation faded quickly as Kiannatah turned away from the rimrock and headed home. He could expect that either Geronimo or the horse soldiers—or both—would return one day to the mountains. The woman child would not be safe from them forever. Kiannatah chided himself for ever even entertaining the notion that he could make her future—not to mention his own—secure. *You should know by now,* he told himself, *that nothing lasts forever.*

Though she did not like the idea of remaining in the cave during the long daylight hours, the woman child was determined to obey Kiannatah. Fate, however, intervened. On the third day of his absence, a seven-foot rattlesnake fell from the rocky slope above the cave's entrance onto the ledge. Aroused, it slithered through the crevice. The woman child saw it, grabbed a knife, and tried to get close enough to cut its head off. But the rattler coiled and began to sound its warning, and the woman child wisely backed away. For a breathless moment, she stood there, knife clutched in hand, in a standoff with one of the biggest snakes she had ever seen, its fangs dripping with lethal poison. Then the snake uncoiled and fled, sliding away across the floor of the cave and into the shadows at the very back.

The woman child had no wood available—a result of Kiannatah's insistence that she remain inside the cave during his absences. She had a flint, so she could make spark, but she had nothing to burn. Without fire there was very little light illumination inside the cave—only the ribbon of sunlight coming in through the crevice. Her flesh crawled at the thought of spending even a moment longer in the cave with the rattlesnake. Yet Kiannatah had ordered her to remain inside. For several minutes she wrestled with the dilemma. In the end, she could not master her fear, and fled to the outside.

Ochoa, segundo of the Rancho Cordoba, was in a bad mood. He had led twenty of Don Miguel's best vaqueros halfway across Mexico and into the Sierra Madre—and for what? There was no hope of recovering the stolen horses because there was little chance of catching up with the Apaches who had stolen them. In fact, Ochoa doubted that he and the men who rode with him would see a single Apache unless the Indians decided to spring an ambush, which, he thought, was a distinct possibility. Ochoa was older than most of the vaqueros—and, he hoped, wiser. He had worked all of his adult life for Don Miguel, and now he was the rancho foreman. He had fought the Apaches many times. Had hunted them and, on a couple of occasions, been hunted by them. Rarely did one see an Apache unless he wanted to be seen. So, as far as Ochoa was concerned, this was a fruitless, not to mention, dangerous exercise. Still, he knew Don Miguel well enough to know that it was entirely too soon to return to the rancho empty-handed. He had to keep looking a while longer yet before the haciendero would be satisfied that they had done all they could. And during that time, it was his responsibility to keep the vaqueros alive. He had to do everything in his power to avoid leading them into an Apache ambush. They expected him, with his years of Apache-fighting skill, to do that much.

They had lost the trail of the Apaches almost as soon as they'd entered the Sierra Madre. As they got deeper into the mountains, Ochoa became more worried. Now, as they rode down a narrow defile, with a cliff rising up on one side and a gulley filled with brush on the other, Ochoa drew the Henry repeating rifle from its saddle scabbard. This was perfect ground for an Apache bushwhacking, he thought. Then again, there were a thousand such places in the Sierra Madre. He did not like these mountains. They were haunted by too many ghosts. There had been so much death and suffering here that the trees seemed twisted and tormented, and the wind carried in it

the whispers and pleas of lost souls. Ochoa did not
intend to become one of those lost souls. So he levered a round into the Henry's breech and kept an
eye on the rimrock.

When he saw the Apache, he caught a glimpse of
only long black hair and a loincloth. It was all he
needed to see. He shouted a warning to his companeros and at the same time brought the repeater to
his shoulder and fired a shot. The figure dropped out
of sight. The other vaqueros had brandished their
weapons, and a couple of them sent a round or two
at the place where the Apache had been, while others
warily looked elsewhere, expecting to see more
bronchos. But no more appeared. Neither did the one
on the cliff above them.

They looked to Ochoa for guidance. He was fairly
certain that he'd hit his mark. But Apaches were no-
toriously difficult to kill. He didn't relish what had
to be done. Dismounting, he called out five names.
He told the others to stay put and keep an eye out,
and began to climb the steep slope. The five whose
names he had called didn't need to be told to follow.
Ochoa immediately began to feel his age. The climb
took too much out of him. Halfway up he had to
stop to catch his breath. The younger vaqueros went
right past him, clambering up the slope with the agility of mountain goats. "*Cuidado, amigos!*" he warned.
They didn't seem to hear, and Ochoa reached down
deep and found enough strength to continue the ascent. Still, he was the last to arrive at the ledge, and
after hauling himself up over the rim, he had to sit
there a moment to recuperate. The others were standing in a circle, looking down at the Apache. It was

then that the Rancho Cordoba foreman realized that
the "Apache" was a woman. Just a girl really. She
lay on her back, arms akimbo, staring sightlessly up
at the blazing noonday sun. His bullet had caught
her in the chest, right between her small, pear-shaped
breasts. Ochoa anxiously scanned the slope above
them, thinking it unlikely that she would have
been alone.

Fascinated, one of the young vaqueros hunkered
down and threw aside the loincloth. "Jefe," he called
to Ochoa, "it's too bad you had to kill her so
quickly." He reached out to put his hand between
her legs.

Ochoa powered to his feet. A few long strides
brought him close enough to launch a kick that sent
the vaquero sprawling. The latter recovered quickly,
and Ochoa saw the anger darkening his eyes. Like
all of his kind, the young vaquero was a prideful
man, and there was only so much he would tolerate,
even from his own segundo. His hand moved to the
pistol holstered at his side. But then he saw the way
Ochoa was holding his Henry repeater—holding it
in a way that made plain his willingness to use the
weapon. Ochoa had lived long enough to read a man;
he saw the anger replaced by reason, and knew that
the danger was over.

"Don't touch her," said the Rancho Cordoba
segundo.

He had already noticed the crevice, had already
come to the conclusion that there was a cave beyond.
Now he moved in that direction. The vaqueros
watched him crawl through the crevice. They
watched, and waited, not knowing what to expect,

and prepared for anything, until Ochoa reappeared a few minutes later.

"She lived in there," he said. "Maybe alone. Maybe not. It's hard to say."

"What do we do with her, jefe?" asked one of the vaqueros.

The question exasperated Ochoa. The answer was obvious. There were no options. He wasn't going to leave her lying there, easy pickings for the mountains' scavengers.

"Cover her with stones," he told them.

They asked no more questions. The tone of his voice made it clear that to do so would be to risk taking the brunt of his wrath.

Ochoa watched them work. He knew that later, when he wasn't present, the vaqueros would speculate as to the reason for his short temper. But he didn't bother with an explanation. The truth was that he didn't like that he had killed a woman. Not even a woman, really. Just a girl. It didn't matter that she had been Apache. Or so he assumed; she might have been of another tribe, or perhaps a half-breed. Or she might even have been a Mexican, though Ochoa could not imagine why a Mexican girl would choose to live like a wild animal in the Sierra Madre. None of that mattered anyway. Not any longer. She was dead, and he had killed her, and he would have to carry the burden of that act on his conscience until he went to his own grave. Worst of all, it was for nothing—they were here because Don Miguel wanted to avenge himself upon the Apache bronchos who'd stolen his horses and killed his men. Ochoa knew, though, that revenge would change nothing.

The horses would still be gone, the men still dead. And now this girl was dead too, and there was one more ghost to haunt the sierra forever.

When the body lay beneath a pile of stones sufficient to deter the most determined scavenger, Ochoa sent the vaqueros back down to the horses. He lingered a moment, just long enough to murmur a short prayer as he stood near the rock pile. At the conclusion of the prayer, he asked for forgiveness for himself. And then he went back down the steep slope to the waiting vaqueros, and led the way out of the Sierra Madre.

That same day, Kiannatah arrived at his hideout.

He sensed, even before he reached the ledge, that something terrible had happened. He had seen the sign left by the vaqueros. The sign did not educate him as to their identity, but the horses were shod, and since he had seen the yellow-legs in the Cima Silkq already, it was entirely likely that these too were horse soldiers. Another detachment—like the other, on the hunt for the Netdahe. Instead, they had found his sanctuary. The woman child too? Kiannatah feared the worst when he saw that the riders had stopped directly below the ledge. *I just want to look at you one last time.*

Scrambling up to the ledge, Kiannatah could scarcely catch his breath. This was not because of the exertion of the climb, but rather because of the fear that clutched his heart. A numbing fear the likes of which he had never experienced. Seeing the pile of rocks, he rushed to it and began to push the stones aside. He worked feverishly, clawing at the rock, unmindful of the sharp edges that cut his hands and forearms. No pain could match the agony of his soul. And when he found her body, a guttural sound rose up from his throat, half-cry of anguish, half-shout of fury, so loud that it echoed off the impassive stony faces of the mountains that loomed all round, mountains that had seen too much suffering and death ever to be moved by it. Leaning over her, Kiannatah gently brushed her hair away from her face. His tears fell upon her cheeks and left marks in the rock dust that covered her. He tried to curl up next to her, thinking how much better it would be if he too lay lifeless under the stones, no longer subject to the one long misery that was life.

For a long time he lay there, and when, at last, he rose, it was reluctantly. He did not want to leave her side. But the only way to be with her was to die. And he would not, *could* not, die lying here beside her body. There was only one way to accomplish that. He would kill his enemy. Not all of them—not even those who had slain the woman child. There were too many. And besides, it was Geronimo who was to blame for everything that happened. It was Geronimo who was his greatest enemy.

Kiannatah covered the woman child with the stones. When he was done he sat cross-legged beside the pile and used his knife to gash himself. He cut his cheeks, his arms, his thighs, but felt no pain. He cut himself so much that when he left the ledge he was bathed in his own blood, and he left a trail of blood to mark his passing.

He arrived within a matter of hours at the trail upon which he had first seen the woman child—the trail used so often now by the Nakai-Ye as they passed to and from the mines He read the sign and concluded that the most recent travelers were heading east, out of the mountains, and were but a few hours away. At a steady, ground-eating lope, he continued in that direction.

That night he reached their camp. There were four of them, but that didn't matter to Kiannatah. They were gathered round their cook fire when he entered the camp. The vision of a blood-caked Apache appearing suddenly out of the night shadow paralyzed the four Mexicans with fear. Only when Kiannatah fired his rifle from the hip and one of the Mexicans flopped backward, struck right between the eyes, did the others move. Two scrambled for their weapons. The third tried to run. Kiannatah was on the move, a whirlwind of death as he closed with the Nakai-Ye, killing a second one with another bullet fired from the rifle, throwing himself to the ground and rolling as the third Mexican got off a single wild shot, and coming up in a crouch to drive the blade of his knife into the shooter's belly. Twisting the blade just so, he ripped the man from sternum to crotch. The pistol dropped from the man's fingers as he clutched at his midsection, trying vainly to keep his intestines from falling out onto the ground. Kiannatah did not wait to see him die, moving past him and hurling the knife at the fourth Mexican, who had fled in the direction of the horses picketed nearby. He threw it with such force that the blade was buried to the hilt in the other man's back. He sprawled forward and, bleating in fear, tried to crawl. Kiannatah pounced upon him, retrieving his knife and driving it with all his might through the man's right ear and into his brain.

Kiannatah picked one of the six horses—four that had carried saddles, and two packhorses—strung out on the picket line. Cutting the others free, he vaulted onto the chosen one and disappeared into the night. He had not noticed the canvas bags near the fire, the ones marked with the name of a mining company, one of which had been kicked over in the brief and deadly scuffle, spilling some of the raw gold nuggets it had contained.

The Apache hunter was less than a day away from the Sierra Madre when he met Major Bendix and his horse soldiers.

They weren't hard to find—their progress across the sagebrush flats was marked by a cloud of dust. He changed his course to intercept them, and as he drew closer, the column came to a halt. Tom Horn rode out to meet him.

"You're a day late and a dollar short, amigo," said the scout. "We've got Geronimo and another of the renegades. Killed two more. Looks like it's all over."

The Apache hunter was gazing past Horn, looking at the pair of Apaches astride horses in the middle of the column, and noticing the shackles on their wrists.

Major Bendex rode over to join them. "Horn, ride ahead, find us a good camp. We'll be stopping for the night in a few hours."

Horn nodded and lingered long enough to flash one last crooked grin at the Apache hunter. "Looks like you can mosey on back to your lady friend in Santo Domingo."

"And it looks like you'll have to find somebody besides Apaches to kill with your long shooter," replied the Apache hunter.

"Won't be a problem," predicted Horn, as he turned his horse away. "Plenty of people out here that still need killin'."

Bendix watched the scout ride away for a moment before turning his attention back to the Apache hunter. "You didn't get your wish. Geronimo surrendered. I'm taking him back to General Miles, alive. You're not going to try to change that, are you?"

The Apache hunter had already noticed that some of the cavalrymen had their carbines in hand. They weren't pointing them at him, but then they didn't need to for him to get the message. He was sure Bendix had warned them to be ready for trouble.

"Even if I wanted to, I couldn't," he allowed. "But as long as he's alive, this could happen all over again."

"Oh, I doubt that," said Bendix smugly. "In his last dispatch, General Miles informed me that a decision has been made in Washington regarding the Apache situation. They will be transported to Florida. That includes Geronimo."

"To Florida."

Bendix nodded. "I think it's safe to say we've seen the last of the Apache troubles out here."

"You're even taking the ones who have caused no trouble."

"They're Apaches," said Bendix, as though that explained it, as though that justified everything.

The Apache hunter had grown up in Georgia, and while he had never had cause to visit Florida, he knew enough about the place to know that there could not be a region more different from Apacheria. Florida would be a completely alien world for the Apaches, and he didn't think they would long survive there. But then, that was probably the reason for sending them there.

"You might as well line them all up against a wall and shoot them," he told Bendix, disgusted.

"This way we save on ammunition."

The Apache hunter made no reply. There was nothing more to be said. The United States government had at long last found a way to dispose of the Apache problem.

"We'll be moving out," said the major. "I'd invite you to ride with us, Barlow, but, frankly, I don't trust you."

"You shouldn't."

Bendix turned his horse away and returned to the head of the column. The Apache hunter sat his coyote dun and watched the horse soldiers, two by two, passing by. At the tail end of the column came the slain troopers, lashed down across their mounts. The army and the newspapers would hail them as fallen heroes, men who had gallantly made the ultimate sacrifice to make the frontier safe for civilization. They were the men who had tamed the Wild West. But the Apache hunter was skeptical. He didn't see very much that was "civilized" by the way his own kind had conquered this land. There certainly wasn't anything civilized about hauling a desert people off to some swamp in Florida, to slowly waste away. Effective—he would give them that—but certainly not civilized.

He was swinging his mountain mustang around to a north heading—a heading that would take him back to Santo Domingo—when he saw a geyser of dust kicked up not ten feet to his left. This was followed a heartbeat later by a deep, undulating sound like a peal of thunder growing steadily louder. He knew immediately that he had been fired at from a long distance, the shot going wide. Looking south, he saw a lone rider, galloping toward him at top speed. Even at this distance—nearly five hundred yards—he could see that the horseman was Apache. Who he was and where he had come from did not enter into the Apache hunter's thinking. His reaction was automatic, requiring no conscious thought. Spinning the coyote dun back around, he drew his rifle from its saddle boot and kicked the horse into a leaping gallop.

He'd forgotten all about the horse soldiers. Behind him now, they too spun around, and some of the cavalrymen began to bring their carbines to bear on the lone attacker. But Major Bendix bellowed an order for them to stand down. For one thing, their target was too far away, and the major was not one to brook wasting ammunition. For another, he thought it was more likely that they would hit the Apache hunter than the Apache, and while he didn't like Barlow, he didn't see any reason to kill him, especially by shooting him in the back.

Riding hell for leather straight at the broncho, the Apache hunter put the reins between his teeth and used both hands to bring his rifle to shoulder. The Apache was shooting at him; he couldn't hear the long gun's report over the thunder of hooves, but he saw

the telltale puff of powder smoke. He got off a shot,
to no effect. The Apache fired a third time, and he
responded in kind. The distance between them had
closed to a few hundred yards, and he knew that
eventually one or the other of them would hit his
mark. Considering how difficult it was to hit a moving target from the back of a running horse, it would
be more blind luck than anything.

Bendix and his troopers watched in fascination as
the two adversaries closed. It was, thought the major,
like something out of an epic poem by Tennyson, or
a novel by Walter Scott—like two knights jousting.
There was something about it both majestic and
tragic, something illustrative of both the best and
worst in man.

Kiannatah's fifth shot struck the Apache hunter's
horse. He let out a guttural cry of savage triumph as
he saw the coyote dun go down, the corpse plowing
into the dirt, its rider hurled more than twenty feet
forward. In a matter of seconds, he was there, looking at the Apache hunter, who lay sprawled, face-
down, motionless. He expected that the fall had
killed the White Eyes, but he wanted to be sure.
Leaping from the back of his horse, he drew his
knife. The crackling sound of carbines fired in a ragged volley reached him, distracting him; he turned
to look at the distant yellow-legs, saw the drift of
powdersmoke, and heard the angry whine of bullets.

"You fools!" he screamed, still in the grips of the
hesh-ke—the killing craze—a primal scream that bent
his body into a crouch and twisted his face into a
rictus of hate. "You are too far away! I am Kiannatah,
last of the Netdahe, and I will come to you!"

He turned back to finish his work with the fallen White Eyes.

Now, though, the Apache hunter was on his back. He had rolled over while Kiannatah's attention was diverted by the yellow-legs' shooting, and he had a pistol aimed at the Netdahe's chest. Their eyes met, and as he pulled the trigger, the Apache hunter saw no fear in the man he was about to kill. No fear, but rather, oddly enough, a grim satisfaction.

The bullet, striking at point-blank range, lifted Kiannatah off his feet and threw him backward. He was dead before he hit the ground.

Sitting up slowly, the Apache hunter saw a rider thundering past the troopers, coming straight for him. It was Tom Horn, riding to the sound of gunfire. He executed a running dismount, Leadslinger in hand, and looked down at Kiannatah's body with disappointment plain on his face.

"Looks like you finally got yourself one," he said.

"Yeah," said Barlow wearily. "The last one."

Epilog

Charles Summerhayes took his time checking out of Tucson's Palace Hotel. One thing he'd learned from traveling to the Arizona Territory from Washington was that frontier railroads were notorious for running late—even worse than Eastern lines, which was saying something. Besides, he could tell from the activity on the street that the Apache prisoners had arrived at the station, where they would be loaded onto two special trains for shipment to Florida. The noise down below had started at dawn, waking him from a deep, exhausted slumber. It seemed like everyone in town was turning out for the show. It was, after all, the biggest event ever to hit Tucson. The Apache threat was finally over for good, and this would be their last chance to see the infamous savages who had terrorized the territory for so many years. The biggest draw of all, of course, would be Geronimo.

Figuring that the special trains would make the railroad's scheduled runs even later than usual, Summerhayes dallied. And there was another reason he tarried; he just wasn't sure if he wanted to see the Apaches being herded like cattle into the railcars.

He remembered the effect seeing the handful of starving Apaches at the entrance to Camp Bowie had had on him a few weeks earlier: a once proud people reduced to beggars, in that case. He thought that, somehow, today's spectacle would be even worse. And so he lingered in his room until the walls began to close in, after which he went across the street to the restaurant for a late breakfast. There he dawdled over several cups of coffee until it was nearly noon, at which point he went next door to the White Elephant Saloon and had a good stiff shot of whiskey. Holding up the long, curved mahogany bar for a half hour, he eavesdropped on the conversations of others. The saloon was doing a brisk business—every table was occupied, and the bar was packed with men lined up virtually cheek by jowl. Naturally, every conversation was about the Apaches. About the terrible things they had done over the years. About how wonderful it was to finally be rid of him. About how the great General Nelson Miles had vanquished that murderous devil Geronimo. It seemed like everyone present had personal knowledge of some Apache atrocity or another, or else they had actually tangled with the barbarous miscreants themselves. They were murdering rapists and child killers, and if they couldn't burn in hell, then the next best thing was for them to rot in the swamps of Florida. Summerhayes didn't hear a single voice raised in defense of the Apaches. No one said anything about how they had simply been trying to defend their homeland from invaders. If anyone in the saloon thought that way, they weren't foolish enough to say anything along those lines. Neither was Summerhayes. When, prompted by Summerhayes' uniform, someone came up and asked him if he had been with Nelson Miles in the recent campaign against Geronimo, and offered to buy him a drink of the best whiskey in the house if he had been, the lieutenant, declining the offer, took his leave.

He stood for a while in the shade of the boardwalk fronting the saloon, at loose ends, watching the steady flow of civilians moving in the direction of the train station. Then a great shout rose up from the end of the street. A cowboy on a paint horse came galloping down the street, waving his hat overhead and shouting out that the Apaches had arrived. The air was charged with excitement. Some people started running, afraid they might miss their chance to get a glimpse of the two-legged devils. An elderly man in a brown tweed suit came up to Summerhayes and grabbed the lieutenant's hand in both of his, pumping it vigorously. "Thank you, Lieutenant, thank you!" he exclaimed." Thank you and all your comrades for ridding us of this awful plague. The territory will be able to prosper now. We will all be able to sleep better in our beds at night, knowing that those murdering bastards are far away from here. This is a great day—a great day indeed! The only way it could be better is if you soldier boys had lined all of them up and shot them."

"That would have been more merciful," murmured Summerhayes.

The old man didn't seem to comprehend. He let go of Summerhayes' hand and went hobbling as quickly as he was able up the street.

Curiosity—of the morbid variety, he supposed—

got the better of him, and Summerhayes started up the street too. A tremendous crowd had congregated around the station. The special trains—six stock cars and one Pullman attached to a locomotive, with a caboose bringing up the rear—the Pullman being for the military escort, and the stock cars being for the Indians—were already present. Black smoke was billowing from the smokestacks. The train was fired up and ready to roll as soon as its cargo had been transported to the stock cars from the wagons that had just pulled in. Summerhayes stayed back at the rear of the crowd, finding a vantage point on the boardwalk in front of a general store. Three children stood near him, two boys and a girl. Summerhayes took them to range in age from ten to thirteen years. The older boy was standing atop a cracker barrel to peer over the heads of the crowd, hoping to catch a glimpse of the Apaches. The younger boy wanted to get atop the barrel and see too, but there was only room for one of them at a time. The girl was leaning against the clapboard wall of the store, next to a plate-glass window, apparently bored by the entire scene.

"Hey, let me have a chance!" protested the younger boy.

"You ain't missin' nothin'," said the older boy. "Geronimo ain't been loaded onto the trains yet. I'll see him when he is."

"You don't know what Geronimo looks like," sneered the younger.

"I know he's seven foot tall," retorted the older. "Uglier than the devil himself. They say a look from

Geronimo has kilt more'n one person. Scared 'em to death."

"Oh, please," said the girl.

"What do you know?" asked the older boy hotly. "Given the chance, Geronimo would murder your whole family. Then mebbe one of his bucks would take you for his bride."

"Take me for a bride? I'm only eleven years old, stupid."

"That wouldn't matter to no Apache buck," insisted the older. "Why, you'd be carryin' some half-breed mongrel child by the time you was my age."

"You better shut up, John Henry," she warned. "You don't know half of what you think you know, and the other half is wrong."

The younger boy laughed, and the older one scowled down at him from atop the cracker barrel.

"You wouldn't be laughin' if an Apache buck got a hold of you," declared the older. "He'd slice every inch of your skin off your bones. You'd be screamin' your head off till he cut your tongue out."

The younger boy, who had a vivid imagination, turned white.

Summerhayes, listening to this exchange with a mixture of fascination and disgust, wasn't aware of the officer angling across the street toward him until the latter called his name. Summerhayes identified him immediately as one of the lieutenants he had first seen in the company of General Miles and Major Bendix on the day of his arrival at Camp Bowie.

"Going back to Washington, then," said the lieutenant.

"That's right"—Summerhayes decided to finish his sentence for him—"where I belong."

The lieutenant grinned. "You're a lucky man."

"How is that?"

"At least you'll be in the War Department, where things are always happening. Not much is going to be happening out here anymore. The Apaches were the last of the hostiles." He sighed. "A posting out here will be the same as being consigned to limbo."

"Well, I may not be in the War Department," muttered Summerhayes. He could only imagine the consequences to him of the report General Miles would have written about Geronimo's breakout, and his role in that debacle. He could have added that he expected an assignment in some unsavory place. The one thing he could be sure of—and thankful for— was that they would not send him to Florida as part of the force that would have to keep an eye on the Apaches. No, his reputation as an "expert" on Apaches was pretty well repudiated. Not that he minded. And he certainly would have hated duty in Florida. He did not want to watch the Apaches wither and die in a place so far—and so different— from their homeland.

"At least now we can get on with things out here," said the lieutenant, trying to look on the bright side of things. "We'll have bigger towns springing up. More commerce. More ranches and more farms. We'll make the desert bloom. Eventually this territory will become a state. And all will be better for it." He glanced at Summerhayes with a rueful smile. "That sounds pretty boring, doesn't it?"

"Don't worry. There'll be another war coming along eventually."

"We can only hope. Well, good fortune, Summerhayes." The lieutenant extended his hand.

Summerhayes took it. "Good luck to you."

The lieutenant moved into the crowd. Summerhayes turned to find that the three children with whom he had shared the boardwalk had disappeared. He was turning away when a shout welled up from dozens of voices at once. "There he is!" "It's him!" "It's Geronimo!" Summerhayes couldn't help himself—he turned back, peering over the milling crowd, through the haze of dust they'd kicked up. All he could see was the tops of the stock cars of one of the special trains. He couldn't see the Apache prisoners, or the wagons that had brought them. There would be Geronimo, and Juh, and all the rest of the Chiricahua Apache who had formerly resided at San Carlos. He had heard that even some of the Apaches who had served as scouts for the United States Army would be transported, as well. A special hell was reserved for them; they were perceived as traitors to their own kind by many of their brethren, and now even the white masters they had served were turning against them.

Summerhayes felt particularly bad about Chato's fate. The man had, after all, saved his life—and now there was nothing he could do to prevent Chato from being sent to Florida, not that Chato would want to stay behind. No, he would want to share the suffering of exile with his people.

And what of Geronimo? How would he fare in

Florida? Summerhayes suspected that it would be much the same as before for the Netdahe leader. Some Apaches would revere him as the man who was the last to succumb to the superior power of the Pinda Lickoyi, the one who had resisted longer than all the others. Others, though, would blame him for the fate that was now befalling the Chi-hinne. Summerhayes was of like mind with the latter group. This wasn't the first time that an entire tribe had been relocated. The "Civilized Tribes"—the Cherokee, the Creek, the Chickasaw, the Choctaw—had been moved from their homelands in the southeast to the Indian Territory of Oklahoma. But that had been because white men wanted the land those tribes occupied. Such was not the case with the Apaches. No one wanted that desolate stretch of malpais called San Carlos. No, this relocation was purely punitive in nature. There were plenty of tribes living now on reservations across the Great Plains, and Washington had no intentions of moving any of them to the Florida swamps. If men like Chato and Cochise—leaders who preached peace—had prevailed, the Apaches might have been able to hold on to a little of their land. Instead, the actions of a few like Geronimo had cost all of the Chi-hinne dearly.

Going back to the saloon, Summerhayes found the place nearly deserted, in sharp contrast to conditions during his first visit. Everyone, apparently, was at the train station. He stood at the bar and nursed a glass of whiskey until he heard the shrill warning of steam whistles. He was relieved to hear the sound. The circus was over. The parade of exiles was finished now. The Apaches had been crowded into the stock cars for their long journey to the east. Summerhayes tried not to dwell on the odds that any of them would ever see their homeland again. Such was the way of things, he told himself. And did it really matter? Did it matter where you were if you weren't free?

The saloon slowly began to fill up. Everyone seemed to be in high spirits. A great day for the Arizona Territory! Summerhayes couldn't tolerate the good cheer, so he left the place, hoping he would never see the Arizona Territory again. He understood the irony of this; after all, he'd been so eager just a few weeks before to see this country again. But it hadn't been what he'd expected. It wasn't the same. Maybe, he mused, that was always the way, when you tried to go back to something.

He walked over to the train station. The crowd of spectators had dispersed, now that the special trains had pulled out. Even the wagons that had transported the Indians, and the column of cavalrymen who had escorted those wagons here from San Carlos, were no where to be seen. The only people present were the telegrapher in his office at one corner of the depot, the station master, and an old Oriental man who was sweeping trash and debris from the station platform. Summerhayes sat down on one of the benches backed up to the depot wall on the platform, slid his single valise under the bench, and waited.

The station master approached him a few minutes later. "You waiting for the eastbound, Lieutenant?"

"Yes, I am."

"She was held up at Yuma for a few hours, on

account of the Apache trains," explained the station master. He consulted his stemwinder. "Scheduled here at eleven o'clock, but I figure it could be two o'clock in the afternoon before it arrives."

"That's all right. I'll just wait here."

The station master shrugged. "Suit yourself." He couldn't help but notice the sling under Summerhayes' uniform coat. "Served with General Miles, did you? I must say, where those Apaches are concerned, that Nelson Miles was sure the solution."

"No," said Summerhayes flatly. "I didn't have the privilege. I'm from the War Department."

"The War Department?" The station master scowled. "No offense, but I never thought that officers who rode desks back in Washington knew the first thing about what it's like out here where Indians are concerned. They're just part of the problem."

Summerhayes smiled ruefully, "I've discovered that you're quite right."

The station master was surprised by Summerhayes' acquiescence—and immediately relented. "Well, like I said, nothing personal. If you want some coffee, I've got some on the stove inside."

"I'm fine. But thanks."

The station master nodded, then entered the depot. The old Oriental had quietly vanished. Summerhayes was glad to be alone. He sat there, staring out across the track to the north, across the brown-and-yellow malpais at the jagged blue lines of mountains. Up there was Camp Bowie, and San Carlos. Up there, also, were the empty Chiricahua jacales. And the graves of the brave soldiers killed during the Netdahe ambush. It was all very depressing, and he tried to find the silver lining. One good thing had come of all this. Barlow had found a reason to live—and now, with Angevine, he was going to start living again. Summerhayes was happy for his friend. He had seen Barlow's soul die, when he'd heard the terrible news about Oulay. He had never seen the life go out of someone's eyes like that. Now, though, the life had returned, thanks to Angevine. Summerhayes had no idea what would become of Barlow—what he would do, whether he would remain the rest of his life in that sleepy little border town of Santo Domingo, whether they would ever meet again. And that, thought the lieutenant, was probably just as well. He wanted to remember Barlow the way he had seen him, standing there in that modest little adobe, looking at Angevine, with her looking back at him, and that unbreakable connection between them a tangible thing. Summerhayes believed that true love came only once into a person's life, if it came at all. But it had come twice into Joshua Barlow's life. And that was the one good thing.

It was very quiet now around the depot. Summerhayes heard the clicking of a telegraph key. He glanced westward, along the ribbon of steel, hoping to see a plume of black smoke that would mark the coming of the eastbound train. Suddenly, he felt the desire to leave Apacheria forever. He heard the telegrapher call out to the station master; there was a sharp edge of urgency in his voice. A moment later the station master burst out onto the platform. All the color had drained from his face as he rushed up to Summerhayes.

"Good God, Lieutenant! You won't believe what's happened!"

"Look," said Summerhayes, "I just—" He didn't want to hear it. He just wanted to go home.

"No! Listen!" The station master grabbed him by the sleeve. "When the Apache trains arrived in Lordsburg they did a head count. One of the Indians is missing. They say it's Massai. Somehow he must have jumped off the train without being seen."

Massai. Summerhayes searched his memory. No, he couldn't recall—

"Now it will start all over!" exclaimed the station master. "Oh, Lord!"

He ran to the end of the platform and disappeared down the street. Summerhayes started to laugh. Before long the entire town of Tucson would be in an uproar. There was an Apache on the loose. Soon every soldier in the district would be on the move. General Nelson Miles would take this personally and mobilize every resource available to him. Assuming that Massai would head for the Cima Silkq, Miles would use the Hot Trails Treaty to dispatch columns across the border.

Summerhayes stood up and walked to the end of the platform. Yes, there it was—that plume of smoke he'd been waiting for. The eastbound train would arrive shortly. He turned his gaze to the malpais. The distant blue mountains seemed to be dancing in midair, as heat blurred the desert flats. There were, after all, a few things that never changed. The desert could not be conquered, any more than the Apache spirit. And that suited Charles Summerhayes just fine.

The Pre-Civil War Series by
Jason Manning

WAR LOVERS
0-451-21173-1
Retired war hero Colonel Timothy Barlow
returns as right-hand man to President Jackson
when there's
trouble brewing on the border—trouble called
the Mexican-American War.

APACHE STORM
0-451-21374-2
With Southern secession from the Union in the
East, the doomed Apaches in the West are
determined to die fighting. But Lt. Joshua
Barlow is willing to defy the entire U.S. Army
to fight the Apaches on his own terms.

s666

No other series has this much historical action!
THE TRAILSMAN

#264:	SNAKE RIVER RUINS	0-451-20999-0
#265:	DAKOTA DEATH RATTLE	0-451-21000-X
#266:	SIX-GUN SCHOLAR	0-451-21001-8
#267:	CALIFORNIA CASUALTIES	0-451-21069-4
#268:	NEW MEXICO NYMPH	0-451-21137-5
#269:	DEVIL'S DEN	0-451-21154-5
#270:	COLORADO CORPSE	0-451-21177-4
#271:	ST. LOUIS SINNERS	0-451-21190-1
#272:	NEVADA NEMESIS	0-451-21256-8
#273:	MONTANA MASSACRE	0-451-21256-8
#274:	NEBRASKA NIGHTMARE	0-451-21273-8
#275:	OZARKS ONSLAUGHT	0-451-21290-8
#276:	SKELETON CANYON	0-451-21338-6
#277:	HELL'S BELLES	0-451-21356-4
#278:	MOUNTAIN MANHUNT	0-451-21373-4
#279:	DEATH VALLEY VENGEANCE	0-451-21385-8
#280:	TEXAS TART	0-451-21433-1
#281:	NEW MEXICO NIGHTMARE	0-451-21453-6
#282:	KANSAS WEAPON WOLVES	0-451-21475-7
#283:	COLORADO CLAIM JUMPERS	0-451-21501-X
#284:	DAKOTA PRAIRIE PIRATES	0-451-21561-3
#285:	SALT LAKE SLAUGHTER	0-451-21590-7
#286:	TEXAS TERROR TRAIL	0-451-21620-2
#287:	CALIFORNIA CAMEL CORPS	0-451-21638-5
#288:	GILA RIVER DRY-GULCHERS	0-451-21684-9
#289:	RENEGADE RAIDERS	0-451-21704-7
#290:	MOUNTAIN MAVERICKS	0-451-21720-9

Available wherever books are sold or at
penguin.com

S310